SAGE

THE READER

CLARK VIEHWEG

Black Rose Writing | Texas

ISBN: 978-1-68433-517-6
PUBLISHED BY BLACK ROSE WRITING
www.blackrosewriting.com

Printed in the United States of America
Suggested Retail Price (SRP) $18.95

Sage is printed in Garamond

*As a planet-friendly publisher, Black Rose Writing does its best to eliminate unnecessary waste to reduce paper usage and energy costs, while never compromising the reading experience. As a result, the final word count vs. page count may not meet common expectations.

For Kim
My Love Eternal

SAGE

THE READER

He Lives, he wakes, ---' tis death is dead, not he.
Shelley, Adonais

I wonder men dare trust themselves with men.
Shakespeare, Titus Andronicus

CHAPTER ONE
DYING

I didn't know I was about to die. Looking back at the moment, it is still difficult to believe that this experience of living, of being so full of life can end so abruptly. It is impossible for me to describe the state of non -being which is where my life became stuck.

I died in a rainbow mountain of diamonds. A brilliant yellow winter sun hung in a sapphire blue sky. The still mountain fresh air seemed crystal clear with a hint of refreshing pine. The world appeared blanketed with blinding white snow lending a quality of pureness to the event. Standing on a mountain top you could see forever. Quiet up there. Oh, so very quiet. I could hear my heartbeat – until it stopped. I had just celebrated being eight years old.

It would be ten long years, more than my entire lifetime at the time I died, before I lived a second time.

Snow had been falling day and night for the previous three days in South Lake Tahoe, leaving five feet of snow covering the town and seven to ten feet on the Sierra Mountain ski slopes. I watched the snow falling with my dad and mom. Big fat snowflakes floating down in a never-ending white curtain blocking the view from our windows. Stranded in our rental house, my parents had a severe case of cabin-fever, partly in an effort to keep me entertained. Both parents were active people busy with multiple projects and activities. Me, well I was a precocious boy of eight bored easily and interested in knowing everything.

The day after the storm ended was a Currier and Ives picture-postcard scene of snow blanketed pine trees and partly buried houses under a beautiful blue sky and bright sunshine. It took dad and me nearly three hours to clear a path to the garage and clear our driveway out to the highway. After letting mom know it was time to play, we loaded our skies in the SUV and took off for the slopes.

It was almost noon when we finally reached the ski resort. By the time we got to the lodge, the snow cats had groomed a few slopes and the ski lifts were flying people up the mountain. Posted avalanche warnings by the ski patrol were all over the mountains, pointing out safe routes with clearly marked danger signs where the risks of triggering an avalanche were considered high.

By mid-afternoon, the deep snow had all three of us tired and ready to call it a day. Our last ride on the ski lift had just dropped us off at the top of the mountain. From the mountain top, there are several trails one can take back to the bottom. Gun-barrel, the center trail is a scary slope that only expert skiers are expected to attempt. This slope runs directly from the top of the mountain to the bottom close to the lodge and ski lifts. My dad and mom thought they were ready to finish off our day with a grand exhibition. Dad was six feet five inches of muscle and bone. A contractor and housing developer, he had honed his body to that of an NFL linebacker. His black hair and blue eyes set him apart as one of the handsomest men in town. Mom was a trim five foot three with the body of a high school cheerleader and movie star looks. My parents had been skiing for many years and put me on skies at the age of four. They were not concerned about themselves skiing the wicked slope, but spent a few minutes arguing whether I should attempt such a steep run. Both parents wanted to complete their day on the daring trail and if I took a longer route back to the lodge, one of them would have to go with me. After watching me ski all day, they decided that I was prepared to tackle the monster, as everybody called the dangerous drop. Standing there that day at the top of the gun-barrel, drinking in the beauty surrounding us, was one of the most surreal events it is possible to have in this life. With no breeze and the lift noise far away, the silence seemed almost deafening.

The bright sunlight was at just the right angle to make the steep slope appear to be covered with brilliant diamonds. Intermixed with this sea of sparkling lights were bright flashes of red, blue, green and violet as sunlight laced the prisms of ice crystals with miniature rainbows. Sky-blue lake Tahoe way off down in the distance added depth to the dreamlike picture. The beauty of the scene was literally breath-taking. The steep dare-devil slope down the mountain added a tremendous rush of adrenalin making the coming event even more exciting. This was the last memory of that day I would ever recall.

My dad took off first with mom right behind leaving me to follow in their trails. I'm not sure what happened. Perhaps the sun had melted the top layer of snow resulting in a thin sheet of ice making the slope faster than normal. Maybe the heavy skiing in deep snow had tired my dad more than he realized. Or maybe the slope was beyond my parents' abilities. What I later learned is that my father was going too fast and lost control leaving the course plowing into a steep snow bank triggering an avalanche. My mom who was directly behind also got caught in the main deluge of snow. I was just far enough behind to escape the primary thrust from the falling mountain of snow, but was still buried in several feet near the edge. It was fortunate for me that the entire event was witnessed by those who became my foster parents.

Seeing where I had disappeared, the man and wife began frantically digging, calling out to me for directions. At first, although totally disoriented and confused by what had happened, I was able to respond with weak bleats. As time moved on, I grew quiet and it took nearly an hour before my body was discovered and pulled out from beneath the snow. The couple who found me were both doctors from San Jose, California. He was a radiologist working for a hospital, and she was a dermatologist in private practice. When they pulled me from the snow my heart was barely beating, then stopped moments after being released from my snowy grave. Being physicians, they realized the situation immediately, and he began administering CPR while she took off like a flash for the Snow-Cat ambulance at the bottom of the slope. She was back with the paramedics driving a Snow-cat in less than ten minutes. My heart had stopped and the paramedic who took over administering CPR from dad worked on me until finally, he stood up pronouncing me dead. The snow track ambulance had a defibrillator and the lead paramedic decided to use it on me, anyway. Just to be sure. Before long, my heart began beating, and I started breathing again.

I was admitted to the Tahoe General hospital where I spent the next ten days. My parents' bodies were recovered two days after I was rescued and they were buried a week later. My dad, Cecil Butterfield, had been a big housing developer in Bakersfield, California; CB Developments Corporation. The clever motto on the side of all his construction vehicles was 'SEE B-for your next house.' My mom, Abagail, worked in a number of community and charitable organizations. The fairy-tale couple known around town as A B-C B was given a grand double funeral with all the local big-Whigs participating. Since they were both an only child with both of their parents deceased, and I their only sibling, I became an orphan with no living family members.

My next ten years are blank.

My body woke up there on the slope, functioning like the machine it is, but my brain never got the message. It seems that there are various coma levels. I was in what is often described as a walking coma. Kind of dream state. Some even liken this state to sleepwalking. I could see, walk, talk and respond to verbal comments, but my memory lasted only a few moments. For all practical purposes, I was in a vegetative state. Someone with their eyes open and able to talk but not awake. My body was alive, the lights were on, but nobody was home. The automatic part of my brain functioned running my body perfectly, but I was totally unconscious of my surroundings and thoughts. It is difficult to describe this state of being, and even now I am not sure that what I am thinking makes any sense. I cannot recall one event that happened during those ten years.

The San-Jose doctors, my principal rescuers, were Allen and Joyce Albertson. They kept in touch with the hospital and my medical situation. The hospital staff made a gallows-type joke of the fact that for somebody who had died, I was doing pretty good. It was assumed that my 'coma' state was only temporary and any day I would wake up my normal self. When my body had recovered well enough to leave the hospital, I was temporarily assigned to the Child Protection Service who maintained a house with appropriate accommodations until more permanent arrangements could be made. When the Albertson's discovered that I was an orphan without relatives, they petitioned to be my foster parents. Being childless, they thought having an eight-year-old son would give them the benefit of being parents without the inconvenience of diaper changing and babysitters. When learning about my coma state, like everyone else they assumed it was just temporary. They were wrong.

As it turned out, my real father had over ten million dollars in liquid and convertible assets that were put into a trust for me until my eighteenth birthday. Dr. Allen Albertson was named the managing trustee. I learned about my situation purely by accident, ten years after losing my life. No pun intended.

CHAPTER TWO
WAKING-UP

On a Wednesday morning, a short time after reaching the age of eighteen, I was scrubbing the entrance-way tile floors in the Albertsons mansion. They have an eight-thousand square foot home on five acres in the Santa Cruz Mountains. Daily chores printed for me were hanging on the refrigerator where I would be sure to read them and remember what to do next. Wednesday was floor day; vacuuming an acre of carpet, polishing the wooden dining room floor and scrubbing the patterned Egyptian entrance tile. I had a mop bucket with soapy water to dampen the tiles, after which I used a power scrubber with rotating bristle disks to do the actual scrubbing. The power cord on the scrubber was getting frayed by the plug and Allen had promised to get it fixed, but hadn't gotten around to it yet. I had the floor all wet and soaped up, but when I went to plug in the scrubber, I got the shock of my life. The jolt kicked me backwards off balance. Falling over my head hit the tile floor knocking me out. As consciousness returned, I woke up for the first time in ten years.

My confusion was overwhelming. Where was I? Where did I get this big body? Why does my head hurt? Where were my parents? What's with these clothes? I remembered shoveling driveway snow with my dad, and seeing the beautiful sparkling gun-barrel ski run, but those were the last memories in my mind. Of course, at this moment I didn't know I had died, only that my life was very strange.

My head hurt and I was thirsty. I went into the kitchen for a drink of water and saw a calendar on the fridge with my chores all neatly identified. Chores for all seven days of the week. When I glanced at the year on the calendar, I got my second big shock. The shocking discovery was that ten years had elapsed since that time in Tahoe with my parents. This explained my big body and the strange clothes I was wearing. It didn't explain why I was here and what had happened during those ten years. I found a bathroom to look at my injuries and almost fainted when I saw myself in the mirror. I saw a tall, well-proportioned man with a mop of dark brown hair. My eyes were the same blue eyes I remembered as a child, the same blue eyes of my father; but somehow, they looked much older. I don't mean ten years older; I mean really old. Ancient. I would like to say wise, but I sure didn't feel wise at that time. My cheeks are flat with high cheekbones giving me a face that reminded me of Lee Marvin. And my clothes. My God how I hated the dreary plaid polo shirt and thin shapeless faded Levi jeans that covered my body. How could I have been dressed this way? Would my mother really let me wear clothes like this?

For answers I went looking for an office and computer. I found Allen's office up on the second floor and his polished teak desk with a new Apple Computer. After fiddling around for a few minutes, I remembered how to operate the computer. Allen had not bothered using a password for his search engine. Going on-line, I put in my parents' names and read about the avalanche and their deaths. The story had details about their funeral and how I could not attend because of my hospitalization. In a desk drawer I discovered a folder which dealt with my status as a foster child and the Anderson's taking responsibility for my life while being named my foster parents.

Over the next few hours I learned about my medical condition. I also located a folder in Allen's desk with all of my trust fund information naming Allen as trustee until my eighteenth birthday. I am sure this was all determined before anyone realized that my vegetative state was permanent. At the time of my parent's death, their estate amounted to a little over ten million dollars. Even though it had grown to nearly twenty million dollars, good old Allen had been paying himself two-hundred and fifty thousand dollars a year for managing the trust. This was on top of the custodian fees charged by Wells Fargo Bank who did the actual managing. It also didn't explain why the state also payed the Albertsons an additional $1800.00 per month for my foster care. It didn't come as a big surprise that I had been kept out of school because of my condition.

I find it difficult to describe my emotional state adequately. I had just learned that my parents died ten years ago. I was an orphan. I was living with total strangers who were also the people who had rescued me, but ultimately made me their slave. I had no time to grieve, no time to understand my situation. I had chores to perform. It was with an aching heart and throbbing head that I went on with life.

In looking at my room and wardrobe along with the list of chores on the kitchen refrigerator, it was obvious that I had become the Anderson's live-in servant. I was expected to fix breakfast and dinner. Prepare weekly menus and grocery lists. Clean the house, do the laundry, make the beds and keep-up the yard.

My clothes, while clean and neat, were all discount items from Goodwill. The price tags and labels were still on a pair of pants and a couple of shirts. I couldn't be angry with the Andersons, they had taken me in, given me shelter and provided for my basic needs. However, I still couldn't help but be resentful for being made their personal servant. Even then, I wouldn't have been disappointed, except that they were being paid a quarter of a million dollars for my keep; they didn't need for me to be their slave. During the past ten years they had collected two and a half million dollars from my trust alone, plus an additional fifty grand from the state; all for providing me with a home.

I went downstairs and finished polishing the entry-way tile, being careful to avoid touching the bare wires. It was going to be an interesting evening. My newfound life was sure to be a welcome surprise, and hopefully a cause for celebration. Preparing the evening meal was one of my daily chores, and since I was sure the Anderson's had not made other arrangements, I began preparing a chicken-pot-pie plus a cranberry cake.

Chicken-pot-pie is one of the world's real comfort foods starting with the aroma coming from the oven. I always enjoyed the preparation phase. Chopping the veggies and chicken, adding the spices and making the crust. As I dumped sage dressing into the pie mixture, I couldn't help but be struck with the multiple meanings of the word. Besides being a spice, it means wise and having wisdom. Then to top it off there is the plant. With my new consciousness, memories of my youth returned and some of my favorites was walking in the foothills with my real father. I loved the smell of sagebrush. I would take a few leaves and crush them in my hand before holding them up to my nose for a real strong whiff. The scent wakes up your sinus cavities and puts visions of heaven in the brain. Then the spice itself always made me happy for some reason. Sage, a name to be remembered.

The cake, an unusual midweek treat, was made for our celebration that evening. I was sure there would be some kind of festive event recognizing my entrance back into the world of the living. The cake was just coming out of the oven when I heard Allen's car in the driveway. I waited for the garage door to open but it remained shut. Wondering what was happening, I went out the front door in time to see Allen just getting out of his new black Mercedes sedan. He was a short dumpy man with a beer belly, black eyes and sallow complexion topped by a bald head. Anxious to show him my new life I hurried out only to have him turn away from me facing the car as he issued me new orders.

"Herbie, wash my car and wipe it down inside with some ArmorAll. I have an important meeting with some associates tomorrow and I'll be giving them a ride. Want my ride nice and pretty."

With that he turned around and walked into the house, never once looking at me. I was crushed and left speechless. Not only did I hate the name Herbie, but my status as a servant was just made abundantly clear. The order to wash his car was not a request, but a command. No please, thank-you or could you, but simply 'wash my car.'

I did wash his car and wipe it down inside and out, fuming all the while. I hadn't known that for ten years Herbie had been my name. Named Herbert by my parents for my father's father who died shortly before my birth, Herbie was my nick name until I was old enough to raise a stink and change it forever. My real parents and childhood friends knew better than to call me Herbie; however, the Anderson's had no one to tell them of my name fetish. So, not only was I the Anderson live-in servant, they called me Herbie. Herbie is probably a decent enough name for an eight-year-old boy without a name fetish, but I was starting to hate my foster parents in-spite of their initial generosity in providing me with a home. I had not been eight years old for a long time. Except, perhaps in the Anderson's world I would always be eight.

Joyce got home a few minutes before I was through with Allen's car and went directly in the house without stopping to say hello. She was everything her husband wasn't. Trim with an athlete's body topped with long blond hair and flashing blue-green eyes, she was quite pretty. Her not pausing to talk wasn't unusual. After all, you needn't speak to the servants, other than to give an order. I hurried, finishing with the car before going in to fix the Anderson's their evening cocktail. He always had a Crown Royal over ice with a splash of water and she drank only Houdini Napa Valley Vineyards Estate Chardonnay, which had to be properly chilled in a special refrigerator that kept the wine at exactly 43 degrees Fahrenheit. These instructions were clearly printed on the refrigerator.

Joyce sauntered down the stairs from her bedroom dressed in a thin pink lacy pants suit with no underwear. Watching this, I saw it for the first time in an eighteen-year-old body. The attire I assumed was her usual evening wear when they were not entertaining. I suppose a male servant with the mind of a eight-year-old boy never noticed such a thing, but in my late teenager male body with raging hormones, it was very sexy. If my antipathy towards the Andersons had not been so strong, I might have been aroused.

This was her favorite lounging attire while sipping wine and talking with Allen about their day. She told a funny story about a man who came in with warts on his penis, while Allen, not to be outdone, described an x-ray taken on a woman who had three nipples. It was their usual practice to see who had experienced the most unusual case that day. Since neither doctor practiced what could be called emergency medicine; after their routine business-hour day, they settled into chairs with their cocktails and stories. They never told gruesome stories involving life and death situations. Their evening banter was strictly light-hearted and one would guess interesting and fun for them; although standing by the bar waiting for them to request a refill, I thought it was kind of sick.

Allen finished his Crown Royal first. "Herbie, would you refresh my drink? Oh, and put an extra ice cube in it this time." No matter how many ice cubes I put into his glass, he was never satisfied. It was always either leave out an ice cube this time or add another. As I walked past Joyce with Allen's drink, Joyce handed me her glass. "Herbie, be a good boy and fill me up again." Notice that neither person looked at me or uttered a please or thanks.

"Herbie, is dinner ready?" Joyce asked. "I'm famished."

"Yes mom, I can serve it whenever you are ready." I had been instructed from very early on to only refer to Joyce and Allen as mom and dad. This is what was so strange about my situation. I'm not sure how I remembered this or about some of their habits, as I could not even recall living here, much less being alive the past ten years. I suppose some Anderson's rituals must have made themselves programmed memories in my brain.

"In that case, why don't we finish our drinks at the table love," Allen suggested to Joyce, trying to sound as if that wasn't what they did every evening.

As they made their way to the dining room table I went into the kitchen and served a generous portion of chicken-pot-pie on three matching Royal Albert red rose-rimmed dinner plates; Joyce insisted on nothing but bone china. Dinner was always served with hot rolls and usually a vegetable, but since the pot pie was already loaded with peas, carrots and small potato chunks, tonight we skipped the extra veggies. After servicing the Anderson's and placing the heated rolls and butter on the table, I was allowed to join them for our evening meal. Breakfasts were more of a fast-order ordeal where I was too busy with their meals to sit with them and eat. After they left for work, I fixed my own meal, usually serving myself whatever I had made for them.

During the week we almost never had dessert after dinner as both were semi-conscious about their weight. On weekends I was expected to prepare a special cake, maybe a pie with ice-cream or something exotic like a fruit tiramisu or vanilla custard pudding. Tonight, I had planned on sharing the cranberry cake as a kind of celebration, but after finishing their meal both got up from the table to go about their evening plans. While they talked and joked with each other during the meal, neither one managed a look in my direction all evening. In the evenings Allen usually read a novel and Joyce went upstairs to watch television. Allen left without commenting, but as Joyce left, she had to make a statement.

"It seemed that the chicken-pot-pie was a little dry tonight, Herbie. Did you put in a full half-cup of sherry or dry white wine?"

"Yes, mom. Tonight, I used the sherry, although I agree it did seem somewhat dry. Perhaps my crust absorbed too much of the liquid. I tried out a new brand of flower which didn't work-up as smoothly as in the past. I won't use that brand again."

This was all b s as the chicken pie was frankly delicious and perfectly moist. It was standard practice for Joyce to find something negative about each meal, regardless of what I fixed or how perfect it might have been. There was no response to my answer as she was already halfway up the stairs.

I had been so excited to share my good news and have them see me fully conscious; yet neither one had bothered looking at me throughout the evening. I was just like a piece of furniture they looked past without seeing. I wondered if all servants were treated the same way. Of course, most servants are completely aware of their status. My question to myself, did that make a difference?

After cleaning up after dinner, I sat down by the kitchen counter and ate a big slice of my cranberry cake. The rest of the cake was left on the counter which I didn't expect them to see before tomorrow evening. I sort of wanted to let them know subtly what they had missed and how differently things might have gone.

My day was finished, yet I felt very uncertain about who I was, and what I was going to do about my life. As I wandered upstairs to my room grieving for my parents, I knew one thing for sure. I was through being the Albertson's servant.

Somewhere in my consciousness I could feel something stirring. I had these very unusual thoughts, there seemed to be strange feelings outside of my own, but I was too unfamiliar with myself or my mind to understand what was going on in my new found brain.

CHAPTER THREE
SEPARATION

I tossed and turned all night trying to figure out my future. In the early morning, by the time the Albertson's would be expecting breakfast, I had resolved to educate myself and catch up on events during the past ten years. I also decided to leave this house and life. Where I was going and how to begin a new life were questions to be answered after my morning chores. I didn't want my keepers knowing that I was leaving.

Weekday breakfasts were simple. Coffee, toast and a boiled egg, done easy. Albert and Joyce spent no more than five minutes at the table with their eggs and toast. Coffee went into travelling mugs for the road. By 7:30 they were both out of the house. Cleanup took no more than another few minutes and by eight o'clock I had packed a small gym bag I found in Allen's walk-in closet with the few clothes I might want. I owned one nice pair of dress pants, a long-sleeved white shirt and some nice dress shoes to wear whenever the Albertson's hosted dinner for friends or associates. The servant had to look like a well-cared for son. I say I owned the clothes I was wearing, although in this household everything was owned by the Andersons, including their servant. There was nothing else in that room that I needed or wanted.

Allen kept several thousand dollars in a hidden combination-lock bedroom safe. Since I was your ordinary idiot, he had shown me where he kept the combination so on the rare occasion when he wanted some cash and was otherwise busy, he would send me to pick up a few hundred or maybe a thousand dollars.

I helped myself to fifty-thousand dollars. I then took my personal files from his desk. I had passed my eighteenth birthday, so the trust fund was legally mine, and I wanted that file so I could make my own arrangements. I thought I might need the files giving the Albertson's legal rights as my foster parents so I took those as well. It might not be necessary since I was of legal age, but my previous mental state had made me dependent on their protection. It was not clear to me if

I would need to have a judge declare me legally sane or competent to handle my own affairs, so I packed those files just in case. I needed a ride off the mountain so I called for a limousine. After all, I was now a rich young man. While waiting for my ride, I wrote the Albertson's a note.

Dear Allen and Joyce,

You might have noticed last night that I finally woke up from my long sleep. I had an accident with the floor scrubber. The wires shorted knocking me out and in falling I hit my head. When I came to, I became alive for the first time in ten years. I had hoped for a celebration with the two of you with the cake I baked, but my status as the household servant interfered. With that said, I will be leaving your home forever.

Thank you for taking me in and providing for my well-being these past ten years. Allen, I took fifty thousand dollars from your safe. I figure this was little enough compensation for the servitude I was ordered to provide. I believe the two and a half million dollars you were given over the years more than makes up for whatever expenses my welfare might have cost.

I also took the files regarding my trust fund and foster care status. They might be necessary to establish my legal standing. Allen, you no longer manage my funds.

Please do not try to find me. I do not use the name Herbert (Herbie) Butterfield. I will never use that name again. As you well know, there is sufficient money in the trust my dad arranged to provide for my needs. I am not ungrateful for your protection; however, my status as your servant precludes me from ever being your son.

With thanksgiving,

???

I had kind of fibbed when using question marks as my new name. I remembered preparing the chicken-pot-pie last night and was intrigued with the name of Sage. From now on I would be Sage. Just Sage. No last name. I liked that it had several meanings. I did not feel wise or full of wisdom, but maybe that would come in time. It also felt reassuring to have a name for a bush that covers a great deal of the planet.

I had the limousine drop me off in San Jose at the Country Plaza Motel on N 1st street. I hailed a taxi and had the driver leave me in the heart of downtown at E 1st street. This subterfuge may not have been necessary, but in case the Anderson's decided to look for me, I didn't want to make it easy.

Using Allen's computer, I had located a motel nearby in a sick and dying part of town where I could rent a room by the week for $500.00. My attempts to establish a false trail was probably overkill since it was my thought that the Albertson's would never search for me in this ugly section of town; that is if they even went to the bother of looking at all. Without any clear plans for my future, I simply wanted alone time to figure out what had happened in my absence. I had to find out who I was, and what I was going to be. Strange feelings and thoughts kept occurring in my head, but as I was conscious for the first time in ten years, I was unable to appreciate their significance.

The Day's Inn was probably a nice place in 1950, but by 2015 it had clearly seen better days. Just the kind of place I was looking for. The white clapboard siding was warped and rust stained where the nail heads were exposed. There were five units on each of the three-sided U-shaped building. A foot-high red stripe had originally been painted around the top; however, the paint was so faded that it barely existed in spots. The asphalt in the parking slots had dead weeds in the cracks, some nearly twelve inches in height. A sagging cracked cement step led to a mildew smelling, cramped office space with worn lime green patterned linoleum floor just inside the office door. A partition with a plexiglass window separated this small entry way from an office. A small opening in the plexiglass had a shelf with a bell to ring for service. I punched down on the clapper button and waited. In a couple of minutes an older dark-skinned woman wearing a colorful Keffiyeh came shuffling in from some place in the back. I showed her five hundred dollars and asked for a room. She pushed a registration card through the slot. I registered as Sage with a fake address in Denver, Colorado. The lady took my money and the card which she shoved into a drawer without bothering to look at what had been written. She slides a room key through the slot and turned away without saying a word. The key looked just like an ordinary Swage house key attached to a large tear-shaped green plastic fob. The ugly fob had the number 5 written in faded gold paint. Picking up my small bag, I went outside and found room number 5. Opening the door, I entered my new home.

The bedroom was small with a regular sized bed. The room was surprisingly clean, painted with a light pastel green and matching bedspread. A picture of the Sierra Mountains mounted in a cheap unpainted wooden frame hung over the bed. The narrow front window had a dark curtain matching the worn carpet. The smell of stale cigarettes mixed with a lifetime of body odors and dust hung in the air. A small hanger mounted to the wall entering the bathroom was capable of holding a couple of suit-coats, nothing else. On one side of the bed a miniature nightstand held a black table lamp with a yellow stained shade. The small bathroom had a rust stained shower, commode and sink. What more could a man ask for? Dumping my bag on the bed, I left my new home to do a little shopping.

I was lucky to catch a passing yellow-cab and had the driver take me to the nearest Apple store. For a small financial incentive, he agreed to wait. I bought a new iPhone with a charger plus an iPad that would work with my telephone carrier. My next stop was the public library where I loaded up with books. Before my accident and death, I had heard about speed reading so my first project was to teach myself to speed read. Then I loaded up with books on history, science, metaphysics and astronomy completing this day's choices. I needed to sign up for a library card. Normally the library requires proof of residency before issuing a card. I provided a fake name and address for a wealthy community in the heart of the Santa Cruz Mountains. This, plus my abundance of books convinced the librarian helper that my forgetfulness was legitimate. I used the name Richard Miller and was soon issued my very own Santa Clara County Library card.

During the next month I left my hotel room on only a few occasions. One was to visit the local Wells Fargo Bank where my trust fund was located and managed. After showing them my birth-certificate, the Bank let me exchange my name for Allen's managing my trust. I occasionally visited the library to exchange one large stack of books for another equally large pile. My meals were mostly delivered. I didn't order a lot of fast food as there are many good restaurants in San Jose which delivered. I ate simple. With my preoccupation one meal a day was all I could handle. Reading didn't occupy all of my time. Using the iPad, I got caught up on events that had occurred during the past ten years.

My initial hope was that in one month I would be sufficiently well informed to rejoin the real world. After this first month of intense study, I believed I could carry on a decent conversation without sounding like someone's closet idiot. With my mind somewhat nourished, I really needed to work on my body.

Taking stock, I studied myself in the mirror for the first time since my awakening. The home style clip-job usually performed by Joyce had grown out so I needed a hair style to fit my new persona. Whatever that was going to be. I stood six feet one and weighed 185 pounds. I had light blue-green eyes, what some would call aquamarine. My curly hair was dark brown, nearly black. I thought my facial features were rather ordinary, but many people would later describe my face as chiseled and handsome. I did have flat cheeks with prominent cheek bones. During the past month in hibernation, my body had grown flax. I decided to join a gym and get my muscles back into shape.

I looked up hair salons on my iPad and chose one catering to men. During another taxi ride it occurred to me that I needed to learn how to drive so I could have my own car. The hair salon had pictures of famous men with various hair styles. I didn't look like Clark Gable, but we had similar colored hair and I liked the way he looked in Gone with the Wind so I had the stylist give me a similar cut. My next stop was the gym. Not only did I sign up for a membership, but I also joined their Karate club.

During the next month I had a personal trainer work with me every day in the gym getting my body in shape, after which I took Karate lessons. After two weeks I wanted more than Karate so I joined a Judo club. This led me to Taekwondo, then Aikido and finally Krav Maga. I couldn't get enough of the martial arts training. Not only because of the physicality each specialty developed, but the mental, spiritual and calm demeanor they promoted. The mental discipline this training required helped me later when I learned how to become invisible. I was just beginning to understand these strange feelings and thoughts that had been messing with my head. I was hearing other people's thoughts and reading their minds, feeling their energy. It was slowly dawning on me that this was a unique aspect of my being.

During my physical training I made it a point to read one book each evening. Each night was a different topic with Sunday's reserved for novels. Suspense became my favorite, although I like historical fiction and occasionally a detective story.

There are books dealing with the seamy side of life where I discovered it is possible to buy new identities. Researching this area on the web I learned about a local individual, Rosco, who provided this service for appropriate individuals who could pass his requirements and had the necessary funding. While Sage was the name I liked for social interaction with people like my gym and martial art teachers, I needed a driver's license to rent a car and for basic identification. It only took a few hours to convince my local source to fix me up with two different identities complete with drivers' licenses, social security cards and false addresses. Birth certificates and Passports cost more and while I didn't think I would be needing them, I bought them anyway. You never know what you'll be doing. I was not into travelling yet. That would come much later, after Sage became The Reader; and not at all as I might have expected.

CHAPTER FOUR
THE SECOND AWAKENING

Three months later I decided it was time to become more independent. I took driving lessons and learned to drive. Being ignorant about automobiles, it became my practice to rent a different car each week in order to determine the model that suited my fancy. Getting used to my status as a person outside the grid was becoming a habit that I found suited me perfectly. Sage was the name I used for people who interfaced with me regularly. These people never knew I had other names. I used a fake identity when I needed some kind of identification such as renting a car. Those people who knew me under one of my aliases never knew me as Sage. Having nobody know my real name or where I live became intoxicating. I liked the anonymity. Living outside the normal population has its advantages. You also have to be immune to loneliness. Of course, having the money to make this possible without living on the street is a great benefit.

In order to make myself truly impossible to find I was going to need some help. Finding a good corporate lawyer who also handled estates and trust accounts became my next project. While completing this chore, I discovered I was using my new talents.

After researching law firms on line and making several calls, I found someone in Palo Alto that seemed to match my requirements. In making an appointment I became aware for the first time that I had distinct feelings about the lawyer I was about to meet. Slowly it dawned on me that I had been having these feelings about people in my life for some time. Remembering, even from the beginning after I woke up, I had these strange sensations around the Albertsons. It was like I picked up their vibrations without any conscious action on my part. This awareness took me by surprise.

I remembered reading some advanced physics books about our quantum universe and how everything in this universe is just some form of energy. It's all vibrations, even this chair I was sitting in. Everything is vibrations, just different frequencies. Even our thoughts have vibrations and that's another form of energy.

It only made sense when understanding that I was picking up on these energy vibrations coming from the people I was meeting.

With increasing confidence, I took my trust and foster child folders for an initial meeting with my lawyer.

Neal Esposito was a third generation U.S. Italian. His office was on the third floor of a sparkling new ten story black glass encased structure. It looked like a futuristic picture you might see in a modern comic book featuring superpower beings. This kind of ostentatious showy image was exactly what I thought Neal Esposito Esquire represented. His office complex featured an elaborate eight-foot-high polished mahogany door which opened to a spacious waiting room with a thick white carpet. Completing the picture was a beautiful, well-built blond receptionist/secretary wearing a tight low-cut blue sheath dress with a narrow white belt. She sat behind a glass desk so it was possible to see her perfectly shaped legs. Sitting on the desk was a slim desktop computer and a polished new age phone. The entire scene almost perfectly matched my image of the lawyer I was about to meet.

I was kept waiting only a minute before being led by the sexy receptionist through another high-polished door into a long, beautifully carpeted hallway lined with pictures of the Sierra Mountains. The tour took me past a library stocked with the usual legal looking reference books and a glass fronted conference room with a large oval redwood table surrounded by a dozen tufted black leather chairs. At the end of the hall I was ushered into Esposito's large corner office with floor to ceiling windows on two sides and a five-foot, natural Golden Cane Palm tree in one corner. The other two walls featured large framed photos of the smiling lawyer in the company of the state governor, the United States President and other minor dignitaries including a few Hollywood entertainers. From the foyer past the library and conference room into the office it was a showy extravaganza meant to impress prospective clients with the lawyer's success and importance. Confirming my newfound talent, Esposito reeked of disingenuous behavior. I'm not sure how I knew, but everything I was feeling told me that Mr. Esposito was a snake in the grass. Exactly what I was looking for.

We exchanged greetings and before Neal got all wound up telling me how wonderful he was, I got right down to business. "I want to remain invisible to the world and I would like your help."

"Wow. That's quite and order." He responded flashing a mouthful of blazing white teeth. "Why did you select my firm to, what did you say, to ah... help make yourself invisible?"

"That's exactly what I said. Your advertisements suggest that you specialize in family trusts, estate planning, corporate law and various other aspects of legal representation. These are the special legal actions I believe are required to accomplish my goals."

Giving me another view of his perfectly white teeth Neal replied, "Those are a few of the specialized legal practices this office provides. What did you have in mind.?"

I explained that I recently recovered from a ten-year coma and had abandoned my foster parents. Not wishing to be found, I stopped using my given name and went by Sage. I told him about false identities and that I had obtained one to get a driver's license and social security card; all the proper identification needed to transact business in the real world. My aliases had fake addresses so I could remain invisible. I needed the same kind of isolation for my financial protection.

When mentioning my fake identities and addresses I couldn't help but notice a certain gleam in the lawyer's eyes.

"Do you have a plan outlined?" he asked.

I opened my Wells Fargo Trust folder from which I had blanked all references to account values. "This is my personal trust set up by my deceased parents. I want the funds transferred to an offshore family trust in another name. Wells Fargo is managing the trusts and I wish them to continue. They have a branch in Belize which should make the electronic inner-transaction very easy. I desire another offshore corporation located in a different country, say the Cayman Islands, to be named the trustee. The corporation will be solely owned by one of my ficitious identities. This trustee should be able to deposit and withdraw funds from the primary trust at will."

"Well," he said with a big grin. I could almost hear the wheels turning in his larcenous head. "You have come to the right place. Let's see the names you're thinking about."

After giving him the trust and foster child folders, I gave a brief summary of my history then gave him a chance to review the documents. When he finished the last folder, I looked him squarely in the eye so he would get my final message. "You will be the only person on this earth that will know of these arrangements. You are the only being who knows the relationship between my birth name and fake identity. I will hold you to the attorney-client privilege." I didn't see the need to tell him that I had another complete false identity.

Neal gave me kind of shit-eating, back slapping grin, "Hey, we know how to protect our clients," he said with all the genuine warmth of a carney barker. That was all right. My vibrations were telling me that we perfectly understood each other. I was beginning to like this power I felt. Knowing the thoughts and feelings of others is a sensation unlike no other. I was about to discover how this power could be used.

CHAPTER FIVE
LEARNING TO FLY

After leaving the lawyer's office I stopped by Marie's coffee shop on El Camino Real for a coffee and something to eat. It was a new chrome and glass building trying to fit into the hi-tech corporate world of Silicon Valley. The day's special was a tuna fish sandwich with melted cheese and fries. Not the healthiest meal, but after eating a lot of veggies lately I decided to splurge. Their counter looked pleasant, so I sat in one of the red leather stools with a padded back and ordered coffee while waiting for my sandwich. Before my sandwich arrived, I was joined by a harried looking man in a suit and tie. His clothing alone separated him from the valley's tech giants, probably a banker or insurance salesman I thought. Most techies I saw opted for the Steve Jobs look, levies and colored T-shirt. This loser had a poor fitting suit with a frayed yellow shirt collar. His portly five-foot eight frame with thinning brown hair and pinched face further divided him from a tech giant.

After exchanging pleasantries about the weather, he launched into a tirade about cheating wives. I really didn't care about his problems, but to be nice I asked, "are you having some marital issues?" I could already feel and see his problem. My newfound powers were starting to interfere with my peace of mind.

"I think my wife is having an affair," he practically sobbed. "Been married six years with two kids." His nose was dripping which he wiped on the sleeve of his suit coat before continuing; "hell, I give her practically everything she asks for," he sniffed. "Can't imagine why she would go and do something so stupid."

I was almost paralyzed with indecision. Why did this guy choose me as the audience for his sob story? And My Lord, what a performance. The man was wasting his time as a clerk. Showing that kind of fake grief complete with runny nose and whinny voice, quite an act. What was I supposed to do in this situation? I knew the truth, but should I just confront him or pretend to humor his performance?

Disliking the man who had joined my life, I was shocked to discover how much of his life was familiar, although we had just met. It was then I realized that in addition to feeling his energy, I was also hearing his thoughts and reading his mind. For quite some time I had been having these strange thoughts images and thoughts about people, ever since regaining my consciousness. Without really thinking about it I had tucked them in the back of my mind. With this new awareness, I gradually became conscious of the thoughts of everyone in the café. It was like I was a radio antenna picking up all the broadcasting stations simultaneously.

My God! I couldn't think. It felt like somebody, or something, had just pulled the plug releasing my consciousness. The noise in my brain was painful. There was so much gibberish in my head it was driving me crazy. I had to do something. The racket was starting to make me sick. In desperation, clawing at the counter with hands that must have looked like talons, I discovered that by focusing on just one person it was their thoughts and history that permeated my mind. Kind of like tuning in to only one station at a time. After this discovery I found by forcing my mind inward on my own thoughts and feelings, it was possible to blank out all other extraneous inputs. Blocking out the energy of other individuals was a terrific discovery for me. I didn't realize it at the time, but this was my first real lesson in becoming invisible.

Turning back to Dennis, a sales clerk at Macy's, I realized he was the one having an affair with a gal that worked in the woman's department of the same store and was terrified that his wife might discover the truth. His sobbing, slobbering performance was a defense mechanism to avoid facing his actions. By blaming his wife for cheating, he was trying to defer the blame and make himself feel better. He wanted someone, anyone, a stranger like me to honor his performance so he would have support for his sad life.

"I'll tell you what Dennis," I started saying before realizing that we had not introduced ourselves; he didn't notice. "I can know without a doubt whether your wife is having an affair. All I need is a chance to see her for a couple of minutes."

Making this offer caught me by surprise. Maybe at some level I did want to reassure him that his miserable life was fixable, but that isn't my normal response to someone with a hypocritical story. True, I didn't want him know I had already read his mind and knew the problem. I'm not sure why, maybe it was this secret identity fixation I had, not wanting people to look at me at though I was some kind of freak. The best explanation I could give myself is that discovering the full extent of my powers was throwing me off balance. I wasn't sure how to handle myself. What does a person do who can hear every thought in someone's head, know all of their intimate secrets, read their mind like an open book and feel their energy, just like you can feel the heat of a light bulb without actually touching the glass?

"Is it possible to really do that? He stammered. "I mean how can that happen?

"It's just a gift I have," I said in as passive a voice as possible under the circumstances. "After I meet with your wife, I will be able to prove to you that what I have said is possible. I don't even know what she looks like, right?"

A lie since I could see a perfect picture of her in his mind. A pretty lady, a bit overweight but with sadness in her eyes. Undoubtedly, she knew the truth.

"After seeing her, I continued, I can tell you everything you think you know about your wife. What kind of foods she likes, her favorite music, who her friends are etcetera? This will prove to you that my analysis about her faithfulness is not untrue."

Meeting his wife was totally unnecessary, but it was the only way I could of think of to get out of the quandary my offer had created. I already knew he was simply projecting. That was not something I felt like sharing at that moment. The fact that it might be possible for me to 'read' someone else did not register on his brain that just maybe, I could see into his own head.

"How could you make that happen?" He sounded both skeptical and petulant, like a child being told it cannot have another helping of ice cream. I suppose at some level he was afraid I would see the truth, although I'm also sure he was not conscious of that thought at the moment. It wasn't clear to me if he meant how could I read his wife's mind or how could I see her physically?

"You just tell me where you will be with her, say at a restaurant or out shopping, and I be there in the background so I can get a good look."

"I don't know where we'll be," he sniffed. "How can I tell you about something in the future?"

My good Lord, I was not sure at this point that he really wanted the truth. It seemed like he was intentionally putting up barriers. Perhaps subconsciously, but still fighting against some kind of disclosure. It felt sort of surreal. Here I was trying to sell myself to someone I had no respect for, and this man seemed to be having difficulty accepting my help.

"Look, you can give me a call on the phone and tell me where you are, or where you'll be, and when. I'll just be there and then we can find a time for me to give you the report."

It was at that moment I realized the trap I had set for myself. By giving somebody my phone number and name, my anonymity would be lost. This was a situation that must be only be temporary and corrected immediately if my privacy was to be protected. There would have to be some serious changes. It was too late to correct the situation with Dennis, but I was determined to learn from this mistake.

With reluctance I gave him my phone number and watched him write it down in a little notebook he kept tucked inside of his coat pocket. "What's your name?" He asked.

I guess I am not as smart as I believed myself to be. I should have anticipated this question, but it caught me totally by surprise. Without even thinking, I said, "you can call me The Reader." The name just popped into my head. I have no idea where it came from, perhaps when I was thinking about reading his wife; but in that moment my identity as The Reader became established. Dropping a twenty on the counter to cover my food and drink I got up and left after saying goodbye to my new 'friend' and giving him a reassuring pat on the back.

Why in the name of hell did I just volunteer to read his wife? Why did I volunteer my phone number? How in the devil's name was I going to get back my privacy?

It was a real pleasure to regain the relative quiet in the street after leaving the babble, noise and confusion of the diner behind with its dozens of thinking, talking patrons. Controlling my ability to read other people would take some time and practice. Something I would program into my daily activities. I was even thinking it might be fun to learn how to turn my powers on and off at will.

CHAPTER SIX
THE BUSINESS

After thinking about what I had done by giving my phone number to Dennis, I decided it wasn't all that bad. That number was for a telephone listed under one of my aliases with a fake address. I needed to buy a new phone with another number for my regular calls and get a new, unlisted, untraceable, throwaway, 'burner' phone using the old number I just gave Dennis. Sure, that phone number could be traced back to my alias, but there it would die. The burner would have no name or address attached and I would leave it turned off and only turn it on once a day for messages. I notified the Gym; the car dealership and utility companies about my new number. Now, theoretically, with my ordinary phone needs being met by a new phone listed to an alias and my old number on the burner, the only call I should get on the burner would be from Dennis.

The next day when checking messages, I did have one from Dennis telling me his plans for the evening and where he would be taking his wife and two sons. Hipster, was a hamburger joint where you can order just about any kind of jazzed up burger it is possible to describe, plus a vast array of fries, onion rings and chips. The place featured Hawaiian burgers with pineapple, South American burgers with peppers, almost any kind of burger a kid could visualize. It was a chore to find an old-fashioned all-American burger on the menu. Definitely not my kind of place, but perfect for what I needed to do to get Dennis out of my life.

I saw Dennis sitting with his wife and two children in one of the booths. Walking past their booth with my back to the wife so she would not get a glimpse of my face I signal Dennis to follow me into the men's room. Once there, I informed him that his wife was not having an affair. Since he was working 'long' hours and was often late getting home she had joined a couple of book clubs and volunteered at their local library. And just to be mean, I told him I knew all about his affair with the women from the store and suggested that he take his marriage and family a bit more seriously. Without bothering to say good-by, I just turned around and left him standing by the urinal. It was impossible for me to stand his reeking presence one more moment.

The days that followed were ethereal. My daily workouts, energy drinks plus high protein shakes had my skin and hair glowing, my spirits were soaring and I couldn't imagine being any happier. I had learned to shut out the noise of people's thoughts until, or unless I chose to listen for some reason.

For full disclosure, I will admit that from time to time I thought about women, but having virtually no experience with the opposite sex, and knowing how my missing ten years had left me ill prepared to join in the dating game, I found solace in my books and research. It was on one of these nights while reading about our soul body that I received a call on my burner phone. I usually checked the phone once a day just for the hell of it, but sometime in the past couple of days I had apparently failed to turn in off. Anyway, the damn phone started ringing which nearly frightened me out of my wits until I realized what had happened.

I finally found the blasted instrument and said a brusque "hello."

"Hello, is this The Reader?" The caller asked in a timid voice. Initially I was confused. Not only was the name Reader new to my ears, but I was slow to understand how the person on the phone had obtained my number. The only person who knew me as The Reader was Dennis, and he alone could have given away my phone number.

"Yes," I practically stammered, "I'm called The Reader." I tried to sound like the professional my caller obviously thought he was calling. "Who is this please?"

"My name is Earl Christensen. My friend Dennis gave me your number and suggested you might be able to help me out with a little problem I have."

"And what problem might that be?" I had to ask although I already knew the answer.

"Well, I'm not married, but I have been living with this chick for ten years and we've always been faithful to each other. We finally started talking about getting married and having some kids, but I'm getting the impression that she is having second thoughts and might be trying out some new partners. I really need to know for sure. Dennis said you can help me with that."

Earl had a thin tinny voice that was particularly aggravating. I could not remember if I ever heard chalk squeak on a blackboard when I was a kid going to school. Hell, I could not recollect ever seeing a blackboard; and why in the name of heaven are they called blackboards? Everyone I saw in the movies was green. Anyway, from my reading I concluded that was the sound of Earl's voice. I thought about it for a couple of minutes keeping ole Earl on the line while I waited. After thinking it through I decided on my answer.

"Yeah, I can help. Two hundred and fifty dollars; cash up front and another Two hundred and fifty in cash when I give you the report."

"But Dennis said you didn't charge him anything."

"Yeah, a mistake on my part. One I won't keep repeating. My time is valuable. You want to buy it, fine. If not, don't bother me again."

"Okay, I guess I can come up with that kind of cash," he whined grating on my nerves making me wish I had never answered the blasted phone. "What do we do now?" His voice was so painful to the ears that I nearly begged off, but in the end I relented. Even people with shitty voices sometimes need help.

"We meet at a convenient location. You give me the first two-fifty and we arrange for me to see you and Karla at another convenient location. I only need a couple of minutes in her presence to be able to give you a full report."

His problem had to do with Karla and I could not read her mind by talking to him. I was going to have to see her in person.

And this is how my business began. It turns out that Karla was indeed shopping around for a new roommate, but I told Earl to ease off on the marriage talk and perhaps she would rethink their relationship. During the next two years I managed about two calls a week and as the calls increased in frequency my 'reading rate' doubled. I was surprised when instead of a call about someone's personal problem there was a call on the burner from a real business.

Tired of living of living in an apartment the idea of renting my own house had been growing in appeal so I was looking at the real-estate adds for rentals as I picked up the burner listening for messages.

"Hello. Is this The Reader? My name is Cunard Verkla and I own a software start-up company, The Real Byte, with my partner Haskell Robinson. I'm beginning to think that Haskell is sandbagging our progress and siphoning away some of our working capital. I can't imagine why he would do that unless he wanted the entire business for himself, but then why wreck our business. Anyway, if you can help me solve this problem, I would be very grateful. Contact information to follow,"

To say that I was excited would be an understatement. Finally, a job that didn't involve some kind of domestic infidelity. Of course, we were still talking about cheating, lying and swindling, but I wouldn't have to listen to heart-broken tales about personal relationships. Instead of infidelity and adultery it would be betrayal and backstabbing.

I called Cunard back and informed him that my going rate for corporate disputes was five thousand dollars. Half up front when we met and the other half upon the delivery of my report. "Five thousand! I was told you only charged a thousand."

"A thousand dollars is my domestic affairs rate. Corporate business usually entails more time and investigation, hence a larger fee."

I could feel Cunard cringing on the other end of the line but he eventually agreed to my fee.

We did the usual meet and greet stuff where he gave me the initial twenty-five hundred dollars and arranged for me to visit his company as a prospective employee. I didn't know squat about programming so my interview would focus on marketing. I didn't know anything about marketing either, but hell, I figured I could wing it through an interview. According to Cunard, Haskell was the programming geek while he, Cunard, was more or less the business man. I wasn't sure how much marketing savvy a computer geek would have, but my suspicion was that he probably didn't have any more grasp of the subject that myself. Surprisingly, it was during this interview that I discovered the final secret to making myself invisible.

The Real Byte was located in a five-thousand square foot incubator slot of a small industrial park in south San Jose. There were twenty business slots in the park with everything from a machine shop to a carpet wholesaler. It was all tilt-up construction of concrete walls and floors, a front door and window and little else to recommend it for a business except the low rent. There was no air conditioning with nothing but air vents on the roof and fans to stir up the hot air. Nowhere in Silicon Valley was rent cheap, but these low-cost industrial strip parks offered the best rates for a startup company. Cunard and Haskell had not spent much money on interior furnishings. Second hand steel desks featuring two and sometimes three computer monitors were scattered around the room. They had ten employees who seemed to be preoccupied with the work. Like most startups, employees were given big stock incentives in lieu of high salaries. This is referred to as sweat equity in the business world. If the company makes it everybody goes home rich. Otherwise they try some place else unless they are cash strapped and need a real job. One corner in their building was an enclosed office. Inside the office there were two more steel desks for the company incorporators. The two managers had real black leather desk chairs although the leather was cracked with white padding oozing through the cracks. In front of the desks were plain brown metal fold-up chairs for guests. When I got there Cunard was in the office but Haskell was nowhere to be found.

Since I didn't need an interview with Cunard, I found an extra chair and sat back in a corner out of the way. While sitting there it occurred to me that the energy bodies that surround each living person is not fixed in size. I could remember not too long ago sitting in a car dealership when a salesperson rushed into a room in a blazing angry rage. Without even looking at the individual you could feel his negative energy. Likewise, I attend a lot of spiritual/new-age seminars and lectures where I am always struck with the quiet, calm demeanor projected by the presenter. In both cases you could feel the energy bodies from a long distance. Knowing that we all have an energy body surrounding our physical body, I began wondering if it would be possible to contract our own energy body; that is bring it close to our physical body, so it was not projecting.

I began focusing on bringing my own energy body in close while remaining perfectly still. Defocusing my eyes with mere slits between my eyelids I was able peripherally to see everything in the office while looking at nothing. Open eyes attract attention and they also project energy. Constraining my own energy body while limiting my vision, yet still absorbing energy from others was hard for me to accomplish with my eyes almost closed. It was during this time that Haskell came into the office. Cunard was busy at the moment and didn't look up to introduce me so Haskell sat at his desk and began working on his computer. Nearly five minutes went by when I stood up and walked over to Cunard's desk.

"Let's take a walk Cunard," I suggested.

"Where in the hell did you come from?" Haskell exploded.

"Sitting right over there," I said pointing to my now vacant chair.

"Bullshit," he responded. "I have been here for several minutes and there was no one sitting in that chair."

"Okay," I responded in as smooth and silky voice as I could muster, happy that my invisibility program was working. "I must be mistaken. Anyway Cunard, we need to talk."

Haskell was extremely agitated and thoroughly pissed off. "You can talk here," he growled. "We don't keep secrets from each other."

"Well that's fine by me. Maybe you should explain to Cunard where you got the money you just deposited in the bank to go along with the other hundred and seventy-five thousand you've managed to hoard away during the past few months. Oh, and while you're at it since we don't have any secrets in this office, tell us about that other little start-up you have going with that old college buddy of yours using the work product of those slaves in the back room. I'm certain they would also like to know what you're doing with their sweat equity. And since you don't keep secrets in this company everybody must know, right?"

I expected Haskell to act a bit sheepish, but instead he exploded.

"You son-of-a-bitch. You've been spying on me," he accused in a loud voice pointing a finger at Cunard. "Hiring private detectives…" he fumed unable to find the words.

"That's really rich you crooked bastard," I said sweetly. "Here you are cheating your business partner and all of your employees and you have the temerity to act outraged."

I stood by Cunard's desk with my hand out until he opened his center drawer and pulled out my final twenty-five hundred dollars placing it in my palm.

"Get a good lawyer Cunard," I advised. "You should be able to recover most of your money." With that said I turned around and left the two partners struggling to find something to say to each other.

That was my first real business job. I had no idea then that my safe little reading business would soon bring a hit team of special forces personnel intent on putting me in the cold hard ground.

CHAPTER SEVEN
8:30 A.M. MENLO PARK, CA.

Just north of Stanford University, off El Camino Real, in a small enclave, resides several of the world's largest venture capital firms. Samuels, Ratcliff, and Hamilton Inc. have been around since the days of Hewlett Packard. Race Samuels, the founder, made his first hundred million dollars financing HP. Joined by Sonny Ratcliff and Bruce Hamilton during the early years of the firm's existence. They have since become one of the most prominent venture firms in Silicon Valley. Race and his buddies are long gone, replaced by siblings, cousins, and new junior partners. Today the firm has over 100 billion dollars invested in many businesses throughout the western united states. No one knows for sure where the term Sharks came from, but the smart money bets on old Race and his buddies. They took the lion's share of nearly any company they invested in and insisted on several board seats, often the majority. Like most venture capital firms, they hope to score on one in every five investments. SR&H has done a little better over the years averaging about one and a half wins for every three and a half losses. One of their recent investments, Quantum Foam, was a startup in San Jose. Quantum Foam was undergoing start-up blues when they called for The Reader.

You can read a lot of books about the rules for starting a company, but most of them are wrong. Sure, everybody underestimates the amount of money they will need, and almost nobody plans for the right amount of time required to complete a project. The rule of thumb is double the money you think you will need then double it again. The same is true for the schedule. Assume it will take twice as long, then increase the time allotted once again. Yet the most significant reason most startups fail is greed. As soon as it looks like the company has a real winner and the chance to make a big score when the company goes public, the greed factor takes over. The infighting turns former friends and colleagues into adversaries, and even enemies. Usually, one or more of the parties hold out for more stock and higher salaries, often not showing up for work until it satisfies their demands. The obituary reads the company ran out of money.

Company engineers contend that without them, the company would have no product, so they deserve a more significant piece of the company. Marketing likes to argue that unless they can sell the bloody product, it doesn't matter what the engineers' design, so they should get a bigger slice of the pie. Programming, finance, and facilities all get into the act of demanding more stock. Sometimes one or more of the founders look for ways to take over the company and oust the other founders stealing their shares. Rampant discontent permeated the situation at Quantum when The Reader came in to find out who was sabotaging their company.

Every Tuesday morning at 8:30, the five partners and ten junior partners of SR&H meet to discuss their various investments. They assign each partner or junior several companies to follow and help guide. Besides all the companies in their current portfolio, every week, the firm receives, on average, another twenty business plans from new startups looking for financing. They assign a junior staff of employees looking to make a partner the task of reviewing each business plan. They pass those that look promising up to a junior partner for evaluation. If the new company looks promising to the junior partner assigned to evaluate its business potential and merits, they bring the plan up for review to the entire partnership during the Tuesday morning meeting. If enough partners agree that a new business plan is worth pursuing, the junior partner assigned to the company schedules a meeting to get together with the company founders to discuss their business plan. About one in a hundred business plans get funded, and nearly three out of every five companies funded go bankrupt.

Today, Honey Samuels, daughter of the founder and current CEO, calls the meeting to order. Honey is tall, standing six feet in stockings with a full head of dark brown hair. Perhaps helped with a little bottle of hair coloring, although her face and general demeanor made her look years younger than her real age of sixty-two. The first action item is a report by Gary Alexander, the junior partner assigned to monitor and guide Quantum Foam. Gary has a fair complexion topped by thinning brown hair turning grey. With pale blue eyes, dark eyebrows, and sunken cheeks, he gives the impression of being rather dull, but looks can be very deceiving. Gary is the company leader in new venture successes. Most of his companies look like winners with only two losers. Quantum Foam looked like it might join the losing column which made today's presentation even more significant.

"We found the culprits trying to take over Quantum and believe the situation is now under control." Gary delivered his assessment in a dry, understated tone that gave his one-sentence report less value than it deserved.

"Who were the bad guys, and how did you find them so quickly?" Honey wasn't impressed by Gary's dry delivery.

"Our company's CEO, meaning Quantum's CEO, that is Jim Bledsoe, heard about this guy called The Reader. I went down there yesterday to see what for myself, and I have to tell you this Reader guy is amazing. Within twenty minutes, he identified all of those plotting against Quantum, he named names, and what they were planning. When confronted, every person this Reader faced admitted their role in the planned takeover."

"How did he accomplish this amazing feat?" Honey asked. She made it clear from her tone that she was skeptical about anybody having this much success so quickly.

"I'm not at all sure," Gary responded, seemingly perplexed. "The man really can read minds. He also reads body language. According to The Reader, everybody has thousands of thoughts racing through their minds, and we are only conscious of a few. The Reader on the other hand, can access any thought of any individual out all of those ongoing thoughts he chooses."

"What is the name of this Reader?" Honey asked with more interest that the situation would warrant.

"Just, The Reader. That's the only name he gave," Gary replied. "I asked him for his name, and the response suggested that I could call him The Reader. That's the name all of his clients seem to know."

"So," Brett Burtenshaw, another partner interrupted, "this mind Reader found the bad guys in just twenty minutes. Is that right?"

"Yeah, that's about it," Gary said. It turns out the Vice President of marketing and one of the principal engineers thought they could steal the technology and start their own company without giving away stock to all the other players."

"How do we find this Reader person?" Honey wanted to know.

Everybody looked at Gary for the answer. He looked a little chagrined at having to explain that he had no idea. "According to Jim, he got a phone number from an old friend he knew who had a similar problem. The Reader solved that problem, and when Jim had drinks with his buddy, the buddy bragged about how quickly this man operated. When Jim asked how to get in touch with The Reader, his friend gave him a telephone number advising him that the phone for the number he to call never got answered, but a return call would come within a few hours. I will say that The Reader isn't cheap. He charges twenty-five thousand dollars a visit. All cash. Half upfront when you first meet and the rest after finishing the job?" No billing and no receipt.

Much to Honey's delight, another senior partner, Warren Beus, asked a follow-up question. Honey didn't want to appear more interested than already showed.

"What if he can't find the problem?" Warren asked.

"That doesn't appear ever to happen. When the Reader grabs hold of someone's mind, that mind becomes an open book." These questions were making Gary feel like an inquisition, and he was happy when they moved on to the next topic.

9:45 a.m. Menlo Park

Kurt Flinders, the oldest son of Sonny Ratcliff's daughter, was one of the senior partners for SR&H. Kurt managed Sawtooth Business Resorts, a ski resort in Sun Valley, Idaho. Sonny Ratcliff had made the initial investment of three million dollars for the ski resort's primary funding several years earlier. For several years the company had been grossing over a hundred million dollars a year, making SR&H a lot of money. Last year had been a banner year for skiing, yet the company had lost a little over two million dollars. They believed an insider to be responsible, but no amount of investigation could turn up the person or persons responsible. It was Kurt's job to find and fix the problem.

Wyatt West is the CEO of Sawtooth Business Resorts, known as Sawtooth Ski Resort. He was having a mid-morning coffee break being an hour ahead of west-coast time when the telephone on his desk buzzed.

"Wyatt, this is Kurt. You got a minute?" The question was rhetorical as CEOS always have a minute when a call comes in from the big money boys.

"Sure, what's going on?" He asked because subordinates always appear interested in what the boss wants.

"I might have a solution to our missing money problem."

"Yeah, what might that be?" a skeptical Wyatt responded.

"Grab a pen and write this number down. It's for a man who calls himself The Reader. He just solved a similar problem for us down here in the Valley, and comes pretty highly recommended."

"Okay, I've got a pen, but how is this guy going to solve our problem?"

"The number is 408-678-8896. The Reader never answers this phone; however, within a few hours, the Reader returns every call. This guy is a phenomenal mind reader capable of reading everybody's mind. He shows up, spends a few minutes with the people in your organization then points out the bad guys. I know it sounds kind of weird, but according to my local source, this guy is the real deal."

"So, you want me to call this Reader guy?"

"That's up to you; I'm just passing along an answer to our problem. By the way, he isn't cheap. If he takes your job, you must pay twenty-five large ones in cash. Half upfront and the other half when the bad guys are pointed out."

"Well, hell, I don't mind throwing twenty-five down the rat hole. It's only money. Besides, if this mind Reader really can fix our problem, twenty-five grand will be cheap."

"There you go," Kurt encouraged. "Give him and call and let's see what happens."

10:05 am Menlo Park

Rayess Investigations comprised just Khaldoun Al-Rayess, a private investigator who had been doing nearly all of SR&H's investigative work for several years. New company founders seeking funding, are routinely investigated for criminal backgrounds, plus all the other petty little jobs SR&H partners create such as looking into the kids their kids hung around with, and the boys their daughters dated. Rayess discovered years ago that Americans have a hard time pronouncing Khaldoun and always say Rayless instead of Rayess. He found it much simpler to go by the name Ray, which is how he answered the phone.

"This is Ray, go ahead."

"Ray, it's Honey Samuels. I need you to find everything you can about a man who calls himself The Reader. That is the only name I have. I need the information yesterday, literally. The only help I can give you is his phone number and the name of the last person he did business with."

"That isn't much, Honey, but let me have it. I'll see what I can find."

"Thanks, Ray, don't let any grass grow."

"I'm on it now."

CHAPTER EIGHT
THE MAKINGS FOR DISASTER

During the past couple of years, my life evolved into a routine of sorts. Every morning at six, I go for a ten-mile run at a nearby high school track. Without bothering to shower, I climb into my car and drive to one of three martial art dojos or Kwans that I frequent on a rotating basis. In the dojo, I change into a Tai Chi Uniform that I wear for all of my practices. I earned black-belts or their equivalent in three different martial art programs and nearing an upgrade in Taekwondo. I normally spar with the instructor or another black-belt if one is available. After my martial arts workout, I take a long hot shower, followed by a protein drink. At this point in my life, I am not interested in spending more time working out than now scheduled, but I want to maintain my proficiency. Besides, the mental discipline gained is worth the effort. Mental preparation is an excellent aid in my invisible practice.

I am happy with life and considering the purchase of a house in Los Altos Hills when I got the phone call that changed my life forever. In the late afternoon, after reading Hamlet for the third time, I checked my burner phone for messages.

"Hello, is this The Reader's number? If so, I would like to engage your services. My name is Wyatt West, CEO of The Sawtooth Business Resorts. Sawtooth is a ski resort in Sun Valley, Idaho. I got your name from an associate who works with Jim Bledsoe at Quantum Foam. I understand you did some work at Quantum. I need similar services here in Sun Valley. If you are available for this job, our company jet can pick you up in San Jose and fly you here at your convenience. Hope to hear from you soon. My phone number is 208-555-5565. Thanks."

I was curious about this Idaho job. Strangely, I had never left California since I woke up and the prospect of seeing a new country was appealing. I called the number right away.

"Hello, this is Wyatt."

"Hi Wyatt, this is The Reader you called?"

"Hi, mister Reader. I guess that's how I address you?"

"The Reader works for me. What can I do for you?" I was more than a little nervous as I didn't want to appear anxious, yet I wanted a plane ride having never been in an airplane in my life.

"My understanding is that you can help me find out why my business is losing money?" Wyatt sounded stressed over the telephone. Sage could sense the negative vibrations, but didn't know the source of his anxiety.

"I can't do anything about poor management," Sage responded. "I can only help if your problem stems from someone in your organization orchestrating your losses."

With relief in his voice, Wyatt answered. "I'm sure someone here is the source of my problems."

"If that's the case, I know I can be of assistance." It also relieved me as it looked like I might get that much-desired plane ride.

"That's great, Reader. When can you come here to Sun Valley for a visit? Our plane can be in San Jose in less than two hours."

"Why not now?" Sage could feel the adrenalin already pumping through his body at the thoughts of his first plane ride. It reminded him of the feelings he had when standing on a matt in the dojo facing his master while trying to earn his first black belt.

"Why not," Wyatt said. He also sounded giddy. 'The day is still young and there is plenty of sunlight left. I'll have my pilot pick you up at the general aviation terminal in San Jose. You know where that is, right?"

"I'm afraid not Wyatt, but I know I can find the terminal." Sage was already starting to get butterflies in his stomach at the thought of a real plane ride. "I have to admit that I have never flown in an airplane before."

"Wow. That's hard to believe in these times. These days everybody; their kids and dogs have all flown on an airplane. That's one of the reasons we have our plane. Our bosses in Silicon Valley refuse to fly commercial anymore. Too many crying kids and too crowded. First class is a little better, but even their parents let their kids run amuck."

"Well, I'm looking forward to the ride and meeting you," Sage said. "I can be at the airport in twenty minutes."

"Don't get too anxious, Reader. The plane won't land for two hours. Oh, and by the way. While we have a great resort here at Sawtooth, with some fancy rooms, I will have a limo pick you up and take you to the Sun Valley Lodge. It's only ten minutes away. I'll book you in the Lodge for a few days. I don't want anyone here at our lodge to see you before we have a talk and decide on our next step. Is that all right with you?"

"What's not to like?" Sage replied, trying to sound like he got booked into swanky lodges routinely. "The Sun Valley Lodge sounds great." He didn't have any idea what the Lodge was like, but if Wyatt was putting him there, it must be okay.

"Okay," Wyatt said, sounding relieved. "I'll plan on meeting you in front of the registration desk at nine a.m. tomorrow. Does that work for you?"

"Sounds perfect. Gives me time for my morning exercise."

"Oh, how will I recognize you?" Wyatt wanted to know.

"Don't worry about it, Wyatt. I'll find you." Not that Sage was reluctant to describe himself or what he might be wearing. He always aware of who he was meeting by feeling the vibrations of those in his vicinity. It was always easier to find his proposed contact than to exchange descriptions, which for Sage was unnecessary. "You know about my fee structure, don't you? All cash, no receipts, no bills, only money from your hands to mine?"

"Yes, my associates explained that. Until tomorrow, mister Reader. Oh, and enjoy your flight. I'll have a little surprise onboard for you since this is your first flight."

"Thanks, Wyatt. See you tomorrow. Bye for now."

4:30 p.m. Menlo Park

Honey Samuels enjoyed an office overlooking a small Japanese Zen garden complete with a little artificial brook, and beautiful hand-carved bamboo bridge painted bright red. She employed a full-time gardener who did nothing but tend to her garden planting colorful flowers, which her private gardener changed whenever the blossoms started to fade. White gravel and red sand appeared in an artful pattern providing graceful Zen symmetry conducive to meditation. Under a Flowering Dogwood was a beautiful white lace patterned bench Honey retreated to whenever she felt the pressure that comes with managing a hundred-billion-dollar portfolio run by a group of people with enormous egos. She was sitting on this bench, contemplating her next move in the saga that had suddenly engulfed her entire world when the very private phone by her side vibrated, alerting her to a call she didn't want to miss.

"This is Honey." Terse and business-like.

"Honey, this is Ray calling you back as requested. Sorry, it has taken me so long. I'm afraid there isn't any good news. I've checked every database in the United States starting here in California, and there is no information about a man called The Reader."

"This may be a stupid question, but did you talk to the people he worked with?

"Oh, yes. And that's not a stupid question." Ray was quick to respond. Although it was a stupid question, he wasn't about to say that to one of the most powerful women in the world. "I talked with your man at Quantum and the person who gave him the number for The Reader. According to Jim Bledsoe, The Reader showed up, spent about four hours talking with people then gave Jim his report. He asked Jim to call those responsible for the attempted coup into his office. They confronted each conspirator in person, forcing them to admit their guilt to Jim face to face. After that, he disappeared."

"But didn't Jim tell you what he looked like, and where we might find him?" She persisted.

"Sure. He's about six one and maybe a hundred and eighty pounds. It looks like he's somewhere in his early twenties, but Jim said he acts like a wise old man. Good-looking chap with dark brown hair and a very physical body. Looks like he works out. He didn't divulge any personal information to Jim, and the only name he gave was The Reader. The only contact that Jim has is the telephone number you already know. The telephone number is for a burner phone with no information who has possession or where the phone is located. Everything I have checked out leads to a dead end. There is no one named The Reader in any database."

"Dammit, Ray, I've got to find that bastard. Do you have any ideas for me.?"

"Well, I can start checking out the gyms in the area. There are only about two hundred," Ray added facetiously. "He's bound to be working out in one of them. Unless he has a gym at home. I can start checking them out for you," he blurted, hoping to erase the sting from his factious remark, "but that will take some time."

"Did you get the impression from your talks with Jim and the other people Reader did business with that he can read minds, for real?"

"Oh, Honey. From everything I've learned, this guy is the real deal. It's kind of scary to realize somebody is running around who is privy to every one of our private thoughts."

"Okay, Ray. Thanks for the report. Send me your bill. If, by chance, you learn anything new, please call me immediately."

"Sure, Honey. Sorry, I couldn't be more helpful and forget the bill. This one's on me."

"Talk to you later, Ray. Goodbye."

Honey sat back on her bench, contemplating the bad news. If this Reader guy crossed paths with one of the many individuals she was conspiring with in Silicon Valley, it could be the ruin of everything. Her own life could be in danger, plus her company might be forfeit. As luck would have it in only a few more days, it would all be over, after which it wouldn't make any difference.

CHAPTER NINE
A PLANE RIDE

I was more than excited anticipating my first plane ride. And on a private jet. I showed up at the airport early to find the General Aviation terminal. I knew about general aviation from my reading, but there had been no reason to explore the facility in person before now. Unsure just where the terminal was or where to park my car, I took a taxi to the terminal. The San Jose general aviation terminal is a large white V-shaped building with double rows of black windows surrounding the entire building. The windows give the terminal a new space-age look making the whole terminal complex feel like some futuristic building you might expect to see in another hundred years. As the taxi pulled up to the entrance, I felt filled with wonder, totally entranced. It reminded me of a scene in an old movie where I experienced the feelings, I imagined Peter Finch must have felt when he first saw Sangri La while portraying a survivor in the movie Lost Horizon. A paradise beyond description.

I paced the terminal like a caged tiger waiting impatiently for my airplane ride to arrive. The counter attendant had assured me she would call me as soon as the airplane from Sun Valley arrived, but I could not sit down and relax. Pacing by windows in the second-floor observation lounge imagining every plane that came to be my plane helped a little. But barely. I was like a six-year-old child waiting for Christmas. Having missed so many Christmas's over the years, I took exceptional pleasure in anticipation. The event seldom lived up to expectations, but this didn't stop me from daydreaming. This time, it might be right.

A sleek blue twin-turboprop pulled up behind the building, and I wondered if this could be my plane. But wait, a turboprop isn't a real jet, is it? I wasn't sure, but it didn't feel right. While waiting and pacing, several Cesena's, a Beechcraft with retractable landing gear, and two jets, including a Learjet and Beechjet, all taxied up to the apron. While waiting with mixed emotions, running from uncontrolled excitement to pure joy, my anxiety grew while the counter never called my name. When I had about given up, a vision in pure white with a blue stripe running down its full length from nose to tail taxied up to the rear gate – a Gulfstream G650. When they called my name, I felt like my heart would explode. Never in my life had I ever expected to ride in such a fantastic airplane. One of the fastest private commercial jets in the world with an unbelievable range; this plane was the fantasy of nearly everyone who flew private jets. The only thing keeping the masses away from owning this plane was its price tag; 65 million dollars for starters, with no top end.

I ran down the airport stairs hustling outside to the walkway leading towards the loading apron. The door to the G650 opened, dropping the stairs to the tarmac. A beautiful female vision in white appeared at the airplane door and descended the stairs waving at me. I hurried towards the lady, only halting when reaching the bottom of the stairs.

The vision in white was a spectacular looking brunet with long dark hair reaching her waist. The white uniform was a form-fitting jumpsuit that hugged her full-figured body like a tight-fitting glove. Sparkling brown eyes in a smooth oval face with the complexion of pure cream only accentuated her bright smile and shining white teeth. With spectacular long legs giving her a full five foot eight inches in height, she was only a few inches shorter than me and able to look me in the eyes. She was standing holding out her hand in that classical female pose you see runway models hold as they first enter the stroll walk.

'Hello," she said speaking with a friendly smile flashing brilliant pearly whites. "Are you The Reader?" she continued holding out her hand.

"Yep, that's me," I replied, taking her hand in a firm grip. "Are you my ride to Sun Valley?"

"Well," she replied with a coy smile. "That remains to be seen. I'm here with the plane which can give us both a ride. By the way, my name is Anita. I am a hostess at Sun Valley Lodge and hired by Wyatt over at Sawtooth Resorts to make sure you are well taken care of while traveling to our fair city."

"He mentioned having something of a surprise for me. I have to say Anita; you are a delightful surprise."

"Well, thank you, kind sir, let's climb aboard and start our journey," she teased in a pleasing voice with that same coy smile waving her hand for me to enter the plane.

"I lost his breath when stepping into the G650. The inside was another vision in white with large soft white leather chairs and couches. The seats looked like Ashley recliners with padded armrests and deep-cushioned back supports. Pure white deep carpeting completed the picture. I wasn't sure whether I should take off my shoes until Anita gave me a little shove from behind ushering me into the cabin.

"You can take any seat you want, mister Reader, as we are the only two passengers." She had barely finished speaking when the plane began to move. The experience of being in an airplane was unbelievably exciting. Going for a real airplane ride had my heart pounding while my muscles were strained in a state of paralysis."

Sensing that something was happening to her passenger, Anita stepped in front, and taking his hand led him to one of the beautiful soft leather seats.

"You have to forgive me," I stammered. "This is the first airplane I've been in during my entire life. It's just that I expected nothing this luxurious. From the movies and TV shows I've watched, I thought it would be more like a cattle car."

"You have to be kidding, right?" Anita said, surprised. "At your age, I would expect that you would have flown a hundred times already."

"I haven't had what you would call a normal life," I responded with a chuckle and wry smile. The grin on my face combined with the overall experience of being in this fantastic plane made me appear like a love-struck teenager.

"You must tell me about that during our flight. The pilot is about to take off, and we need to be in our seats.

I felt like a teenager must feel going into an ice-cream shop. There are so many choices that all seem so tempting it's hard to focus on any item. You want to experience everything all at once, yet our senses are limited, forcing us to abandon ourselves in an orgy of pure delight. That was me, sitting in my virgin white soft leather chair, trying to absorb every aspect of my first flight. Oh, the sounds. The feeling of the plane hurtling down the runway. The scenes outside the windows flashing by ever so fast. And the scent. A new-car smell was filling the airplane. And Anita in her form revealing jumpsuit sitting across the aisle. I could not help but feel the heat and pressure in my groin. All alone, this close to an extremely sexy, beautiful woman. Would heaven be any better?

"What does a hostess do at the Sun Valley Lodge," I asked to gain control over my senses. With perhaps a little hope thrown in for good measure.

"Usually whatever our guests requests," she responded with that maddening coy smile. "We have guests from all over the world, so it requires us to speak many languages. There are ten of us hostesses at the Lodge speaking over sixty languages. Able only to speak five languages makes me kind of a novice. Anyway, we escort our guests around the lodge property. The resort village is large, with many different features, much like a small city. There are always several activities taking place, and there is the town of Ketchum close by down the road. Ketchum is everybody's dream of small-town USA. It's always a pleasure to take our guests to Ketchum for sight-seeing and a great dinner or lunch."

"Wow. You make me feel like a real hick. I can barely speak functional English," I quipped.

"I doubt that you are the hick you pretend to be. Even if this is your first airplane ride."

By now, the plane had lifted off from the runway clawing at the air in a steep climb. I couldn't be sure which I enjoyed most – the feeling of being in this fantastic plane reaching into the sky, or looking at Anita.

Sensing his interest, Anita asked. "Is there anything I can get you? A drink perhaps or I could make you a sandwich. I'm sorry, but on a flight this short, we don't stock any heavy meals. I make a great PBJ," she joked, flashing a beautiful smile."

"Sure. A PBJ sounds almost perfect," I responded with what I hoped was a great smile of my own. "But, serving it with a smooth scotch and water would make it truly perfect."

"A scotch and water it is," she said, getting up from her chair. While standing, she gently brushed Sage on the shoulder in what might have been an accident, but it might have been intentional. I could only hope. "We're joking about the sandwich, aren't we? Are do you want a PBJ? Oh, sorry about that, but we don't have those ingredients," she added with a teasing smile. "I can, however, make you a fantastic ham and swiss."

"Forget the sandwich, but I will take the drink." I felt the brush on my shoulder and could feel myself getting even more aroused. Was that an accident, or was it a message?

Stupid. Stupid to even think like that.

I had never been with a woman in my life and did not understand how to proceed. She said whatever the guest requested. But that could have been a figure of speech. Better to enjoy the flight and forget about the girl.

Palo Alto

Honey was in a meeting at her private club, The Bay Breeze, in Palo Alto with fellow Silicon Valley coconspirators when her private phone buzzed. Glancing at the men and other women in the room, she grimaced while saying, "I have to take this call."

"This is Honey."

"Honey, this is Ray. Sorry to disturb you again, but I found out The Reader is on his way to Sun Valley Idaho on a private jet. I'm not sure if this is of interest; but you said to let you know about anything I learned."

At first, Honey didn't understand the content of the call, and when its significance dawned on her she became extremely concerned. "Do you know when he left and who picked him up?" She demanded using the stern ironwoman voice used when failing to respond was not an option.

"He left about an hour ago on a jet owned by Sawtooth Business Resorts." Ray understood from Honey's tone that something was disturbing her, and he did not know what it could be. He only hoped it wasn't something to do with him. He did not know that Sawtooth was one of the company's portfolio champions.

"Do you know where he is staying in Sun Valley?" She asked in that same demanding tone.

"Sorry, Honey. I don't, but I will try and find out."

"Let me know as soon as you learn something." The phone was abruptly turned off without saying goodbye.

Turning to the other men and women in the room, she quietly said, "we may have a problem."

CHAPTER TEN
ANITA

Anita returned to their seats, handing The Reader a Waterford crystal tumbler filled with a glowing amber liquid. Sunlight from outside lit up the cut-glass and ice cubes floating inside, giving the drink and ethereal sparkling quality. "I hope this is all right," she said, handing Reader the glass. "Johnny Walker Black is the only scotch on board."

"Oh gosh," I sighed dramatically. "I guess I'll just suffer and make do."

Rainbow colors from the cut-glass prisms kept flashing around inside of the plane, giving me weird mixed feelings of excitement and fear. It took me a few moments before realizing that in my mind; I was standing at the top of gun-barrel with my parents looking at a field of diamonds. Shaking off the memory, I tried hard to focus on the vision in white instead.

Anita sat on the padded arm of my chair and leaned into me a little for support. Precisely the diversion I needed to get out of the past. "There are a little less than two hours for this flight," she said. "I could put on a movie if you would like, or perhaps you would like a great massage."

I could sense Anita's presence, which she could tell. Struggling to keep my voice from breaking into a squeak, I said, "and besides being a world-class polyglot, I supposed you're a licensed masseuse."

"Absolutely. Part of my job requirement." Anita could tell she was making The Reader uncomfortable and for reasons that made no sense. Here he was a handsome man with a great body and winning smile. Surely, he could not be nervous about getting a massage.

"I guess this is my day for divulging secrets," I responded with what I hoped passed for a chagrined look on my face. "I've never had a massage."

"What," she demanded in fake horror. "You have never ridden in an airplane, and now you say you never had a massage. What else are you been missing in this mysterious life you lead? And tell me where you have been all your life."

"Oh, God, Anita. You wouldn't believe me if I told you," I said, taking a long drink from my crystal tumbler watching rainbows fly around the plane, but this time without fear and excitement.

"Well come on stud," she said, getting up and grabbing his free hand. "It's time you had a real massage."

She led him towards the back of the plane where she pushed a button on the side of the airplane wall, releasing a fold-down massage table already made up with a white sheet. A cabinet next to the table held towels and massage oils. Handing Sage a towel, she instructed him to take off his clothes and wrap a towel around his body then climb on the table face first. Anita pointed out a place at the head of the massage table next to the plane's outer wall for his head.

I handed Anita my drink then turned around to get undressed. By this time, the experience of being with a beautiful, sexy, well-endowed woman had me completely aroused, and I received the instructions to lay face down on the table with gratitude. Embarrassed by my erection, I didn't want to expose my excitement. My attempts at modesty were unnecessary as Anita could sense my body's reaction to the new experience. I glanced back over my shoulder to see if Anita knew of my condition, but she had her back turned, giving me a little privacy to undress.

Wrapping a towel around my waist to hide my excitement, I climbed on the table grateful to be lying face down. Unfortunately, my aroused state made this position very uncomfortable as they do not design the massage table to accommodate this situation. I had barely made it on the table and situated myself as comfortable as possible when Anita poured a little oil into her hands to warm it up and then applied it to my shoulders. Rubbing the oil into my muscles, she instructed me to relax.

"Oh my," she said. "You are carrying a lot of tension in your body, mister Reader. Try to relax as I work on your muscles, relieving the strain and pressure. I can tell you are holding a lot of tension in your shoulders."

To me, it seemed like mere moments before I could feel the tension leaving my body as Anita worked her magic with knowing hands. I had never experienced a massage, but was comforted by the woman working on my back who convinced me she had been highly trained with extensive experience besides being extremely skillful. The pressure from my erection was subsiding, which was a total surprise. When she could feel the Reader relax, Anita moved up to his head and neck then began working her way down both arms and his back. The experience was so relaxing that Sage found himself in a state of drowsiness. A few minutes into the massage, Anita said, "I knew from looking at you in your clothes mister Reader that you had a remarkable body; however, in the years I've been doing this, I have never worked on anyone one so superbly conditioned." By this time, Sage was like a limp noodle and almost asleep, unable to think of any response.

Palo Alto

Honey had figured out by herself how The Reader came to be in the plane owned by Sawtooth flying on his way to Sun Valley. She discussed the situation with her fellow conspirators before placing a call to someone she thought was to Washington, D.C. She was one of just five people who had the secure private number for Roger Horowitz, the Secretary of Defense. All calls to this number were highly encrypted, yet it was only prudent to scrutinize what was spoken by either party.

The phone was picked up on the first ring. "Hello." The salutation was brief, as whoever had this number already knew who would be answering.

"This is Honey Samuels. We might have a serious problem."

"Go ahead."

"A man is heading to Sun Valley as we speak. He can read the minds of every person he meets or passes on the street. I know there is a major gathering of important government officials taking place in Sun Valley who could be out and walking around town or eating in a restaurant when not in a meeting. If one of them ran into this man called The Reader, he would know everything about our plans instantly."

"Does this Reader fellow have a name?"

"Not that we have been able to find. We have exhausted every database in the country, and there is no one called The Reader. We don't have his picture, but we have a description of what he looks like."

"What is it you suggest, Honey."

"We know that he has a meeting with Wyatt West, CEO for Sawtooth Business Resorts at 9:00 a.m. This meeting will take place in front of the registration desk at the Sun Valley Lodge. I can provide you with a picture of Wyatt. Our only chance of catching The Reader is to make certain there is someone watching to see who Wyatt meets."

"Okay. I've got the message. I'll see that we solve our problem; that is if this Reader fellow doesn't stumble across one of our principal members before tomorrow morning."

"He lands just a few minutes before sunset and may decide to get something to eat before checking into his motel. Unless he runs into one of our party at dinner, we're probably all right," Honey said.

"Where is he staying? Maybe we can solve this little problem tonight."

"We don't know. There are no hotel or motel reservations anywhere near Sun Valley for anyone named The Reader. He must be staying under some other name, perhaps staying with an acquaintance, or maybe he hasn't yet made a motel reservation. We will watch to see if his name pops up, but I wouldn't count on that happening."

Roger thought about what he had heard before replying. "I'm in Sun Valley now with almost all of our principals. I'll have dinner catered tonight and make sure everyone stays off the streets. Most of our members are staying in various motels and lodges around town, and I'll advise everyone to go straight to their rooms when retiring for the night — no carousing around town or bar hopping. We should be okay before tomorrow morning. Thanks for the warning, Honey. I'll talk to you tomorrow."

"Goodnight, Roger." Honey clicked off her portable phone, feeling at unease with the entire situation. Not being able to identify or find The Reader was unsettling. There had been enough reports about this strange individual and his formidable powers to be worried. She was, however, confident in Roger's ability to solve their problem if The Reader didn't cause them any difficulties before tomorrow morning. Honey knew it would be a long restless night until hearing from the Secretary tomorrow after they had resolved the problem.

•   •   •

Slapping Sage on the butt, Anita told him to turn over so she could do his front. She held the towel over his private area for modesty as he rolled over. In turning over, Sage noticed for the first time that Anita was naked. And such a beautiful naked body it was. Sage felt himself getting hard again before getting on his back. He blushed and assumed he must be glowing red from his head to toes. Anita pretended not to notice the towel rising over his crotch before it became too obvious to ignore.

Trying to maintain some dignity, Sage asked: "how come you're naked, Anita? I thought I was the one getting the massage."

"Normally I wear a shift while giving a massage, but this was unexpected, and I didn't bring one. I took off my clothes so I wouldn't get oil on my uniform."

Unable to avoid the embarrassing situation, Sage blurted out, "I'm sorry about this," he said, motioning towards the rising tent over his crotch. "It's just that I've never seen a live woman in the nude before. I mean a real live woman, in person. Sure, I've seen pictures and some television, but never in real life." Even to himself he sounded like a stammering adolescent.

"You aren't gay, are you?" Anita asked as an excuse to stall as she was sure about the answer to the question and unsure about how to proceed. She had never experienced this problem before.

"Err, ah...no. I mean, I don't think so. I find myself attracted to women as you can see."

"How is it you have never seen a naked woman, Reader? You're not some awkward, shy teenager."

"Oh, hell. I guess I have to confess another of my secrets. I've never made love to a woman Anita. I don't know how." My whole body must be a deep red by now.

"My God! You must be kidding. At your age? You should have had several dozen conquests by this time. How come?"

"It's a long sad story which I can tell you sometime. There was an accident when I was eight and for the next ten years I lived in a coma. By the time I woke up, I had missed all the teenage dating, dancing, and making out stuff. Since then, I've just been too shy for a romantic relationship."

"Oh, you poor thing. How sad. I'll tell you what mister Reader. There is only one first time for anything, and your first experience with sex should be memorable. If you let me, it would be a real pleasure to instruct you in the fine art of making love. I can teach you all the ways to pleasure a woman, thereby pleasuring yourself."

Sage was too dumbfounded to answer. Nodding his assent, he held out his hand to Anita, who had extended her hand. Leading him off the table, she took him back to the main cabin where there were big full soft leather couches. Sage lost himself in a world he was unaware even existed and was surprised when the pilot announced they would touch down in ten minutes. Anita said, "we must hurry. There is a small shower in the back where we can rinse off the smell of sex. Come with me, and I'll clean up both of us."

We were both dressed, barely, when the wheels of the plane squealed as they touched the runway. There could be no denying that my emotions were on the cusp of being out of control — first plane ride in a magnificent airplane: first partial massage, and first-ever trip to heaven.

I had no way of knowing then that gut-wrenching fear and equally strong feelings of a different sort would soon replace these grand emotions.

CHAPTER ELEVEN
KETCHUM IDAHO

The pilot never left the cockpit while Anita lowered the stairs and escorted me outside into the fresh Idaho mountain air. Living in Silicon Valley, I had forgotten how fresh air looked and smelled. The sky was dazzling blue, and the mountains were impressive. My home is in California, and I had not returned to the Sierra Nevada Mountains since that fateful day when I was eight years old. My memory of those majestic mountains was forever gone, but the pictures I had seen showed them to be spectacular. Yet, it was hard for me standing there in the bright Idaho sunlight to believe any mountains could be more beautiful than the Sawtooth Range. Anita guided me to a Lexus SUV with the words Sun Valley Lodge painted on the side. I whistled at the sight of such a luxurious ride, wondering why I was riding in a Sun Valley vehicle before remembering that Wyatt had told me he had booked me there for the night to avoid meeting any of his people. Anita ushered me around to the passenger seat while explaining that Sun Valley only used the four-wheel SUV's because of the winter snow. It surprised me when she went to the driver's side and climbed in behind the wheel. "I get to be your chauffeur today," she explained. The lodge gave me one of their guest rides to fetch you into town. "You should feel honored. With all the Washington big whigs in town, getting our own limousine is a miracle."

Used to those long boat Cadillac and Lincoln cars that looked like they are a block long, it surprised me when she called the SUV a limousine. "You call this is a limo?" I asked out of pure curiosity.

"These cars are the Lodge's version of a limousine. They need a place to stow their guest's skis and equipment plus offer a luxury ride. The Lexus SUV is their answer."

We were quiet for a few minutes as Anita guided us out of the small airport and onto the highway leading into Ketchum. I couldn't help but gawk at the scenery, feeling comfortable with the experience of just being there, no need for conversation.

Anita broke my reverie. "If you would like to see a little of the area before it gets dark, I could drive you around Ketchum and along the river. You can check-in after our ride and before dinner, or we could eat first and then check-in. Your room will be waiting."

"I want to see everything," I said, grinning like a fool. Still in sensory overload, I was trying to take in all the new sights, sounds, and smells. While I have traveled little since I woke up, my limited traveling always surprised me when I went to various sections of San Francisco or San Jose. The scents of China Town in San Francisco were so different from what you got down along Fisherman's Wharf at the waterfront. No matter where I went, the smells and sounds were my first impressions of the new local. Here in South Eastern Idaho, for the first time in a very long time, I realized I was smelling something similar to the day I died.

As we entered the outskirts of Ketchum, Anita touched me on the arm to get my attention. "Hey, mister Reader, I want you to notice something. Ketchum is still considered a village by the residents; however, in my humble estimation, it is more like a small town, although a very charming small town. The first thing you should notice is that you never see a fat person in Sun Valley or Ketchum unless it is a tourist. The lifestyle here is so healthy, and everybody is so active with skiing, jogging, bike riding, hiking, kayaking, river rafting, swimming, ice skating, etc. that people living here never get fat."

The windows of the SUV were down so we could enjoy the fresh air, and as we drove slowly down the main street passed the restaurants, bars, boutiques, and art galleries, her statement was true. There were few people on the sidewalk, but those I saw looked in excellent shape, even though many were well beyond middle age.

"I'll take you down to the Big Wood River and show you some property," she said, turning down a side street. "Some ole prospector or sheepherder bought these lots almost a hundred years ago. Over the years, many people have tried to buy them, but no one could find the owners, even though the property is listed in county records, and the property taxes paid on time. All the inquiries about the land have been returned as undeliverable, even though someone kept paying the taxes. Last week I escorted this 90-year-old lady from Tennessee. It turns out she owns this property, which has been in her family all of her life. She told me a great uncle of hers bought the land for a sawmill, but he was killed by a bear before building the mill. None of his siblings wanted the property, and it got passed around to various relatives over the years. Over seventy years ago, her aunt got the property then moved to Tennessee. The aunt had no children of her own, and upon her death bequeathed the land to me, the Tennessee lady told me. 'I guess I took after my aunt,' she said,' 'as I had no children either. 'All of my siblings and parents are dead,' she continued. 'I was curious about this property that has been in the family and I decided to come see what they had owned for such a long time.'"

Anita kept telling me about the woman. "After seeing the property and looking at the work, the property needed before they could develop it, such as a bridge across the river, she asked me to find her a real estate agent or a buyer," Anita concluded the woman's story. "I've been too busy since she left to follow-up with her request. I will show you the land as it would make a fantastic home site right here in Ketchum. You could get an excellent deal on the property if you were interested."

Sure enough, the property looked spectacular. Just off the road was the Big Wood River. Pointing out the land across the river, Anita explained, "The land is a little over seven acres, most of it across the river which means you would need a bridge." Large Western White Pine trees were prevalent with a few scattered Aspens close to the river. From what we could see from the car, the land was flat before rising towards Bald Mountain. While fascinated, nay mesmerized, by Ketchum and environs, I wasn't sure in my heightened state of fascination if Ketchum was my future home. It wasn't until driving back into town near sunset when that observation changed as I spotted a dojo on the side street, we were on about a block from the main highway.

"Hold on," I yelled at Anita. "Stop the car. I want to check this place out."

"What? What place," she responded.

Pointing to the dojo, we had just passed, I said, "pull over here. I'll only be a minute." As soon as the car stopped, I hopped out and hustled over to a building with black lettering on the windows, MARTIAL ARTS. Going through the door, it amazed me to see a layout very similar to my favorite dojo in Santa Clara. In the center was a padded exercise floor used for classes and matches surrounded by reed mats. At each side were smaller workout areas where two fighters could square off and practice with each other. A small bleacher section was at one end of the mats where people could watch the matches. Looking around, I searched for the Sensei, a title of respect for the master. Not seeing anyone who fit the description, I approached two men practicing throws on one of the side mats.

"Can you tell me when I can find the Sensei?" I asked, bowing to them both.

"There is a small meditation room in the back behind those bleachers," one of the men told me, pointing the way. "He is called Daiki," he added before resuming his practice.

I knew that Daiki was a name of respect, meaning exceptional or valuable. I doubted that was his given name, but most dojo masters or trainers adopted another name, much like westerners use nicknames.

The door to the meditation room was open, revealing a small plain room painted white with tasteful Japanese brush pictures on the walls. Sitting in the lotus position on a matt in front of a small altar with a burning incense stick, I saw an old Japanese man with thin white hair and a wispy beard. Upon seeing me outside of the door, he stood without using his hands, much like a teenage gymnast, and walked towards me and the door. I bowed in the traditional greeting of the Japanese and inquired if he was the Sensei.

I could see him looking at me carefully, appraising me and my question. Satisfied that he would not be wasting his time, he nodded while saying, "Hai." Yes.

Explaining that I lived in California but was thinking of moving, I asked if he was accepting new students. "Hai, if you qualify," he said with a wry grin. I could tell he was playing with me. He had observed me closely, and it must have been clear that I would qualify.

"Would you tell me what you teach?" I asked as politely as possible. There was no sign of his specialty I could see on the walls or windows.

Mounted on the wall just inside of the meditation room was a smallholder with a half dozen colored Tri-folds. The Sensei handed me the brochure, then turned his back and went back to his matt and meditation. He wasted no motion in discussions and explanations. From his perspective, if I were interested, I would return with further inquiries. If not, there was no need for additional talk. I glanced at the red-bordered brochure noticing that his name was Asahi Saito, a world-recognized martial arts master, considered the leading Kung Fu expert in the world. Not only was the sensei a master of Kung Fu, but he was a recognized master in other martial arts, including Aikido and Taekwondo. Why such a master had chosen to live in Ketchum was beyond my ability to fathom; however, if it was good enough for this Sensei, it was certainly good enough for me. Sticking the brochure in my pocket, I bowed again to the old Sensei and returned to Anita and the Lexus.

Getting into the car, I could see the curiosity in her face, but before she could ask me a question, I said, "okay, Anita, let's talk about that property down by the river." During the next few minutes, we discussed how she might go about getting an asking price and the steps I would have to take to become a property owner. There was no way at this point in our relationship; I could tell her an offshore shell company would purchase the property, and the only tenant would be a caretaker with a fake name. I almost told her the name my associates called me was Sage, but something held me back. Not distrust exactly, and the name Sage by itself said nothing about me; still, I hesitated. I had developed a strong trust in my intuition, and my brain was screaming to be silent. Good advice as it turned out.

Kim's Sun Valley home

Christopher Kim is the senior Senator from Hawaii and having served in the senate for over thirty years was one of the highest-ranking members earning him chairmanship of the Armed Services Committee. His distant relatives were friends with the missionaries who first went to Hawaii preaching salvation. As the ministers took control of the land and began accumulating wealth, so did the Kim clan. Today the Kim's are one of the wealthiest families in Hawaii with houses in California, New York, London, Paris, and Rome. One of Christopher Kim's properties included an enormous house and parcel about ten miles north and west of Ketchum by Adams creek just off Adams Gulch Road.

His house, some call it a mansion, is 40,000 square feet of natural Quartz and pine built like a European castle. It has ten bedrooms with twelve bathrooms plus an outdoor and indoor swimming pool. The property boasts several guest cottages, a stable and housing for his maintenance staff. Current residents besides Kim include the U.S. Vice President, several ranking committee chairmen and women, a few of the President's cabinet members, one Supreme Court Justice, and two other senators. Wandering in and out glad-handing and exchanging platitudes are many additional senators, several members of the House and House committee chairs plus some Generals and Admirals staying in Ketchum motels and inns. However, the most distinguished guest, including the Vice President, is Roger Horowitz, the Secretary of Defense. The only person with more power has yet to join the group, but he is expected to arrive soon. Horowitz has been calling in favors all day long, and it is about to pay off handsomely.

The telephone rings in Colonel Hill's office, commander of the Mountain Home Air Force Base. Located forty miles southeast of Boise in a remote valley close to Arco. Mountain Home AFB is the home of the 366th Fighter Wing, better known as the Gunfighters. The Gunfighters are a shit-kicking, take no prisoner group of airmen and support personnel who are almost always in perpetual training when not on active duty. Across all military units, there is a standing policy regarding career officers and select service members who have only a few months left to serve before retirement. When a team member of these trained specialists finishes a tour of duty, and they have less than six months before opting out of the military, they are assigned service at one of several military bases in the United States mainland. This policy also includes those special forces men who have the most sophisticated, rigorous, and advanced training of all military personnel. At present, there is thirteen of these special force personnel from a mixed background of service units at Mountain Home awaiting retirement.

Disturbed while studying his list of base personnel trying to figure out how best to use their services, Hill groans while picking up his red secure telephone.

"This is Colonel Hill speaking."

"Colonel, this is Roger Horowitz, I need a small favor."

Upon hearing the Secretary's voice, Colonel Hill sat up straight in his chair, back ramrod stiff, as if the Secretary could see him. "How can I help you, mister Secretary? If I can do it, the favor is yours."

"I need you to fly a team of your special forces personnel down to Sun Valley tonight. We have arranged for the FBI to provide you with one of their advanced armored vans loaded with sophisticated communications equipment, weapons, and GPS systems. The van will be at the Sun Valley airport in about two hours. An FBI agent will meet your men on the tarmac, show them the van and equipment then disappear. The van is yours for the mission, after which it will be returned to the FBI, undamaged, hopefully." The secretary couldn't help but issue a small chuckle after the last statement.

"Do I brief my men on the mission, or will that happen in Sun Valley?"

"This is a wet job demanded for national security. I can't go into specifics over this line even though it is encrypted and hack-proof. Your men will be briefed on their task when they land and take over the van. This mission, although serious and of extreme importance, will be short. Your men should be home tomorrow night,"

"How big of a team are we talking about mister Secretary?"

"Oh, the job is simple, although it's these simple little jobs that wind up biting you in the ass. I'd say you better send four men, even though that might be overkill. Better safe than getting surprised later."

"I'll have the men in the air within ten minutes, mister Secretary. Anything else."

"No, that's it, Colonel. Thanks. I'll let you know if we need anything else."

"Your welcome, Mister Secretary." Hill almost gagged at being pleasant to the demanding Secretary. While he didn't have much contact with Washington politicians other than the occasional boondoggle visit from a congressman, he had observed the secretary giving press briefings holding forth with so-called investigative reporters. Hill always thought the Secretary overbearing and a total sycophant. Hill was also smart enough to keep such thoughts to himself.

•   •   •

Anita took Sage to the Pioneer Saloon for Dinner. One of Ketchum's oldest eateries where there is always a waiting time for a table. Serving the best steak in Idaho, it has been a local favorite since the 1940s. It is difficult to get a seat at the bar while waiting for a table, but there are couches and comfortable chairs around a coffee table with bowls of corn chips and salsa to ease the waiting pain. Sage had his favorite Johnny Red scotch while Anita ordered a Beefeater gin and tonic.

Dinner conversation was light as Sage was still processing his extra-ordinary day. Anita, sensing his mood, plus being weary from her demanding hostessing week, was happy to let Sage take it easy. Their dinners were superb as always at the Pioneer, and all too soon, they were on their way to the famous Sun Valley Lodge.

Sun Valley Lodge is the featured establishment of Sun Valley Village, an actual village unlike Ketchum, which is a small town. With fifteen hundred year-around residents, the Village supports an opera hall, a pro-links golf course, a deluxe shopping center, a lake, several private houses, and condominiums, both and outdoor and indoor ice-skating rinks, an Olympic swimming pool and tennis courts and so much more. Anita drove Sage around and through the Village showing him the number of facilities he could explore later if he had the time.

Built-in 1936, Sun Valley Lodge is a rambling three-story red brick and lodge-pole construction that shouts prestige, money, luxury, and comfort. Photographs of movie stars, United States Presidents, governors, Senators, Kings, Sheiks, and

Olympic athletics line all the hallways. It seems anyone famous has stayed at the Lodge at least one time. There is even a picture of Arnold Schwarzenegger complete with cast and crutches. They decorated the main lounge with many interesting conversation groupings. It was in this lounge that Sage would later discover his fate. Couches, high-back chairs, reading lamps, end tables, and coffee tables were all pleasingly arranged. The high ceiling is rimed with polished walnut molding three feet wide, adding elegance to a room that, while expansive and lush, was still homey and comfortable.

Entering the lobby, Anita went to the registration desk and picked up the key to Sage's room. Sage only had a small gym bag for luggage, so valet or bellhop services were not required. His spacious accommodation was a magnificent suite with King sized bed, an adjoining sitting room with blue couches and a fireplace and the most luxurious bathroom Sage had ever seen. Mirrors, heated towel bars, carpet, televisions, telephones, and fantastic décor lamps seemed to be everywhere you looked. It made Sage wonder what people did in the bathroom that required so much extraneous hardware. For him, it was a place to relieve himself, take a shower, and brush his teeth — none of which he wished to accomplish while talking on a telephone or watching television. As Anita showed him around, she was expecting some reaction, so Sage pretended to be impressed. While the facilities were outstanding, Sage didn't care much for the sights. He was more interested in Anita and her plans for the evening. He needn't have worried. Anita took him in her arms and planting a kiss that included some deep tongue leaving no doubt as to her evening's plans. Wasting no time, the pair was soon in bed carrying on what they had started earlier on the plane.

It was four o'clock in the morning before becoming exhausted; they fell asleep. Sage was up at six a.m., getting ready for his early morning run. Searching around for his clothes and bag, he disturbed Anita, who turned over, yawned, and asked, "what time is it.?"

Sitting on the edge of the bed, Sage explained, "it's six o'clock. I go for a little run in the morning before doing my exercises. I'm sorry for disturbing you."

"No, it's okay. I should get going, anyway. A long day ahead."

Saying this, Anita got out of bed, letting the sheets drop, exposing her naked body. After spending the night making love, there was no point in trying to act modestly. "I've got a bunch of wives to shepherd around today. I need to go home and change clothes."

Watching Anita get out of bed, showing off her incredible body, I could feel myself getting aroused all over again. "Will I see you this evening?" I asked hopefully. Never in my life had I ever experienced anything close to the ecstasy found and enjoyed with Anita.

"I'm sorry, Reader, but for the next couple of days, I'll be off-limits. There is this large assembly of Washington bigwigs in town for some big meeting. They booked all the hostesses solid. The other girls had to cover for me yesterday, and they were not happy. Everyone is busy, busy, busy. Also, today and tomorrow, there is the ice-skating show, and naturally everyone wants to go, and they all want the best seats."

"Ice skating show? In the middle of summer.?" Sage seemed perplexed.

"Oh yeah," she replied with a little excitement. "The Lodge has several ice-skating rinks, both indoor and out. Many of the Olympic and world champions lived and trained here. The current world champion, Katrina Novalotski, is in town with her troupe doing their ice-skating show I mentioned earlier."

"I remember seeing her picture on a poster in the lobby when we checked in last night." I've never seen an ice-skating show. Maybe I'll see you there tonight."

"Oh, Lord. Whatever you do, ignore me should we meet." I might lose my professional cool if we should run into each other." She sounded serious, but the words came with a smile. Kiss me, and maybe we can touch base in a couple of days. I'll check out that property for you as soon as I get a chance."

Grabbing the naked woman, Sage placed a gigantic sweet kiss on her lips saying, "sure; I'll be in touch. And thank you, Anita. For everything."

With mixed emotions, he looked back over his shoulder at his beautiful teacher. With a strange sense of wonder and hope, Sage left to start the most stressful, memorable day of his life.

CHAPTER TWELVE
KILL SAGE

Following the road Anita took when she drove me around the Village, I began my ten-mile run. I never use a pedometer but had timed myself on the track, so I knew approximately how long it would take me to run ten miles. Eighty minutes was my average run time, so I used my watch to keep track of how long I had been running. Being outside on my feet gave me a whole different perspective of Sun Valley. There were very few people out and about this early in the morning; still, I was surprised when I met a man and later two women also jogging going in the opposite direction. We just nodded to each other while continuing with our run.

Getting back to the lodge in the lobby, I noticed the big life-size cutout of Katrina Novalotski, the reigning woman's world ice-skating champion. A petite brunet in a robin-egg blue form-fitting shift that had slits from her waist to hip. The pose showed her getting ready to jump, looking back over her shoulder. With the lighting and shadows on her face, it was hard to discern the color of her eyes, but they looked dark, perhaps a dusty brown. Her perfect body was that of a figure skater, trim smooth and curvaceous. She was beautiful to behold and almost made me forget about Anita. Almost.

I showered, shaved, and got dressed for my meeting. I don't own a necktie and never plan on wearing one. My pants were a light grey cotton blend with straight legs that barely reached the top of my black slip-on loafers. For a shirt, I wore a new black Ralph Lauren Classic V-neck. My goal was to look casual but not cheap. I packed my gym bag with the few items I had with me and left it by the door to my room while I went downstairs to eat breakfast. Generally, I avoid coffee, but today it seemed like something I would enjoy, so I ordered a bold French roast to go with scrambled eggs, house-made gourmet sausage, and rye bread toast. Finishing breakfast, I had a few minutes to spare, so I took a chair facing the registration desk. Most of the conversation groupings in the vast lobby had soft armchairs and couches with the armchair backs reaching shoulder height.

In the center of the hall was an arrangement of chairs and sofas featuring chairs with high backs offering a headrest.

The chair I chose featured a soft dark leather cushion and padded back with high armrests. As I sat in the chair, it seemed almost to swallow me up, which gave me an impulse to become invisible.

Becoming invisible is difficult for most of us to master, but once accomplished, you become nearly impossible to detect unless the other person seeing you is exceptionally perceptive. It all starts with being motionless. You must be absolutely, perfectly still. It is preferable to blend into the background, like a big comfortable chair, but I have been invisible standing straight up in the middle of a room. We all give off vibrations, so to be invisible, you must reign in your vibrations while remaining conscious of the vibrations of others. Controlling my vibrations, was for me, the most difficult aspect to master in learning to become invisible. People feel your eyes on them so it is imperative that you do not look at anyone. Besides, the whites of your eyes seem to attract attention. By closing your eyes to mere slits and defocusing your vision, it is possible to see everything in front of you while looking at nothing. If you detect some energy of particular interest, it is possible to see that person without looking at them; in the meantime, you are processing all of their energy vibrations. It is also possible to focus your attention on the energies or thoughts of a particular individual while being invisible without arousing their attention.

Sitting there, practically invisible, unless one looked closely, unmoving, with my unfocused eyes mere slits, no one passing by noticed me sitting in the chair. Katrina passed me twice, looking as though she was expecting to meet someone. Wearing faded jeans, flip-flops, a loose-fitting white tee-shirt, and no makeup, she looked fantastic. Her aura glowed like the sun, and she moved with liquid grace. I saw her glace at my chair both times as she passed by, and there was no recognition in her eyes. For some reason, she sat opposite me on one of the two leather couches that comprised the conversational grouping where I was situated. She sat there for about five minutes, glancing around the room and looking at my chair from time to time before she noticed me. As soon as I knew of her attention, I opened my eyes and winked.

"Would you teach me to do that," she asked.

"Do what?" I almost smirked, pretending I didn't know what she was asking. "Sit in a chair? It seems to me you already mastered that art."

"No, silly; be so still people never notice your existence." While speaking, she arose from the couch and moved over next to my chair. "I must have looked at that chair a half dozen times." She continued; "I knew there was something different about your chair, but I couldn't see what. And then I saw you. I know you were making yourself hard to see. I want to know how to do that."

"I could you teach to that," I said, being semi-serious, "but it's gonna cost you," I added with a smile. "Becoming invisible is difficult for most people, but with you, it will be an easy task. I would love to be your teacher."

"And what, pray tell, is your price?" She was serious and wasn't about to be dissuaded by my light-heartedness from her quest.

"You will have to agree to have dinner with me," I explained, with the same seriousness she was displaying.

"Done," she said, somewhat excitedly. "How about tonight? I already have plans, but I can cancel them."

"As it turns out, miss Novalotski, I happen to be free this evening."

As fate would have it, at that time I saw Wyatt enter the room headed towards the registration desk. With beautiful Katrina sitting next to me, bubbling over with energy, I would not usually read someone that far away from me. Still, Wyatt was putting out powerful vibrations in anticipation of our meeting. I was about to stand up when I noticed a second man enter the lodge who was following Wyatt. He also was radiating powerful vibrations, although of a vastly different kind. Reading his mind, I learned he was looking for; The Reader. Not knowing what I looked like exactly, he was waiting for my meeting with Wyatt to identify me. I also learned from reading his mind that he intended to call in his friends from outside when he had seen me, and together they would muscle me out if I didn't go peacefully. The most frightening thought in his mind was his firm intention to kill me and dispose of my body.

Turning to Katrina, I whispered, "Katrina, you do not know me, but I must ask you for a huge favor."

She looked at me inquiringly, "You seem to know my name, dear sir, but what favor could you ask of a perfect stranger."

"My dear lady, your picture is all over the lobby. My business contact just entered the room, followed by a man who wishes to do me harm. Since motion attracts attention, which is why I was sitting with my eyes practically closed and not moving, I would like you to get up and stand in front of my chair. Your movement will attract his attention, but your back will be towards the door, and since you are a woman, he will lose interest. Not because you are unattractive, but because you are not meeting with my business contact."

"And just how do you know this man wishes to do you harm?" she asked, purely mystified.

"That, my dear, is a very long story which I will share with you during our forthcoming delightful dinner, but please take my word for now. I know that this man wishes to see me dead. I do not understand why. I must find out why he wants me dead if I am to stay alive. That is also why I would like you to stand in front of me now, so I can stand up without being noticed. Then you will act like my girlfriend. I'll put my arm around your shoulder, and together, we will exit the lobby through those doors leading away from the lobby towards the ice-skating rink."

"Well, okay, sweetheart," she responded in a sweet voice but with a look of alarm in her eyes. Standing, she moved in front of my chair. As I stood up in front of her, I stooped over so my silhouette would be no higher than hers. Throwing my arm around her shoulder, I leaned over as though whispering in her ear as we made our way out through the doors. Steering her towards a grouping of Aspens, I let go of her with a grateful thank you.

"I need to ask you for one more small favor Katrina," I said, feeling bad about imposing on this young woman after we had barely met. "The man I was supposed to meet will undoubtedly still be standing near the registration desk looking for me. He is a tall man, about six-six wearing light tan khaki pants and a red polo shirt. He should not be difficult to spot. His name is Wyatt West. I would like you to go up to him and repeat this phrase."

"The Reader sends his apology, but circumstances have prevented him from meeting you at this time. He will contact you soon."

"That's it? The whole message?"

"Yes, please, and I don't know when I'll be able to meet you for dinner, but I promise that no matter where you are, I will find you and deliver on my promise."

"That's your name? The Reader?"

"Only for business associates," I explained. "I'll tell you my real name when next we meet. Are you sure you remember what I asked you to say?"

Looking at me as though I had recently fallen off the back of a horse-pulled hay wagon, she merely nodded. With that, I gave her a brush kiss on the cheek and took off going around the lodge towards the far side.

My nightmare was about to get much worse.

CHAPTER THIRTEEN
THE SEARCHERS

Colonel Habib Rucinol was assigned to assist Roger Horowitz, the Secretary of Defense. As an assistant to Horowitz, Habib knew the secretary's plans and was sent to meet the helicopter from Mountain Home Air base carrying the four senior Special Forces personnel chosen by Colonel Hill led by Captain Critt. Upon landing the four Special Forces men were given their instructions by Colonel Habib.

"Find the man who calls himself The Reader and make him disappear, permanently. This Reader is supposed to meet with Wyatt West, at the registration desk of the Sun Valley Lodge at 9:00 a.m. Here is Wyatt's picture"- which he then handed over to the team. "He is the manager of a local ski resort. What we know about The Reader is that he is a mind reader, stands about six feet weighing roughly 180 pounds with a medium build. Caucasian with dark brown hair and blue-green eyes. Do whatever is required to make sure he does not come in contact with any of our people from Washington who are here for an important meeting. Reader is considered a national security risk and must be terminated and made to permanently disappear immediately".

They were given a piece of paper with instructions to call the number written on it when they had completed the mission.

With Colonel Habib was FBI special agent Scott Cardon, senior agent of the Twin Falls FBI office. Cardon had brought the latest fully loaded FBI van for the military agents assigned to the current case. The custom Ford F350 van was built like an armored truck with puncture proof tires, blacked out bullet resistant windows and a modified 450 cubic inch motor. The FBI van was loaded with automatic riot guns, stun guns, armored vests and a built-in cabinet fully stocked with electronic listening equipment, prisoner restraints, communication gear and knock-out drugs. It was Cardon's job to show the Special Forces men the van and equipment after which he disappeared along with Colonel Habib.

Captain Critt Rayess was a twenty-year Special Forces veteran with six weeks of active duty left before leaving the military. Having seen his buddies and comrades blown apart, lose their arms, legs, sight and hearing; watching women and children blow themselves up in order to kill infidels for most of his life, any resemblance to a sense of humor had been burned from his system. Standing six feet in stockings and weighing 220 pounds of well-conditioned hard muscle and bones, he was all business all the time. A square face with buzz-cut blond hair and black unsmiling eyes, the Captain was team leader for the present mission; making The Reader disappear. Wearing civilian clothes, jeans and black tee shirt; his combat boots were the only clothing items that said military. His size, battle-hardened body and eyes, made anyone in his general vicinity avoid contact if at all possible. If you were close and very observant, you might see the communication device plugged into his right ear.

The three sergeants assigned to Critt for this mission were also seasoned veterans with only a few weeks left in their military careers. Kyle Gunning at five foot eight inches was the shortest man on the team, but what he lacked in height was more than made up for in attitude. Sensitive about his height he wore a large chip on his shoulder daring anyone to try to knock it off. His specialty was communications and like all members of Special Forces he was cross trained in all disciplines. Peter Julien was the team medic whose experiences treating those torn up in battle made him sick of life and everyone in it except for other combat veterans. Brian Pugh was tall, almost six feet six, and weighing over 250. His size, muscular build and attitude kept people at bay. Brian was a weapons specialist who over time had come to despise everyone not associated with the military. He had killed so many people his nightmares left him perpetually weary, on edge and barely under control.

     •   •   •

Unknown to him, Wyatt West had been under surveillance for several hours. The hit team had West's picture, but knew only vaguely what The Reader looked like and that he was in Sun Valley to meet Wyatt.

While his comrades kept watch outside, Critt Rayess focused on Wyatt as he enter the Lodge, and then waited two seconds before following him inside. Wyatt was approaching the registration desk, his head on a swivel looking around for somebody. Rayess stood just inside the door watching the action unfold.

Wyatt stopped a few feet in front of the desk and just stood, waiting for something to happen. Several minutes went by and Wyatt was starting to get really pissed. He had flown this asshole up here first class in a private jet, put him in a great room. And this is what he gets. He was about to approach the counter demanding some answers when this attractive young woman approached him. "Excuse me, are you Wyatt West, the man waiting for The Reader?"

Wyatt was astonished by the girl and the question, but nodded his head while admitting, "why yes. How did you know?"

"This Reader man, asked me to give you a message."

Stunned by the strange appearance of this beautiful girl and her bizarre question, he could only nod and say, "yes?"

"The Reader sends his apology, but circumstances have prevented him from meeting you at this time. He will contact you in the near future."

She delivered the words exactly as heard while giving him a shy smile indicating that she didn't understand it either.

Wyatt didn't know what to say or how to react. He had been so angry at this 'Reader' man a few seconds ago, and now, knowing that The Reader might be in trouble, he finally managed, "thank you. I appreciate the message."

Turning around and walking back to the front door, a troubled Wyatt was deep in thought. Somehow, he knew instinctively that the problems Reader faced were directly related to his Sun Valley visit. The only people who knew he was meeting The Reader were his own people. Walking out of the lobby Wyatt saw a tough-looking man standing next to the open entrance, obviously someone in the military. The valley was saturated with Washington elites and their armed guards. All the major ski lodges had a few of these special guests and their body guards, including Wyatt's Sawtooth. Lost in thought as he was leaving the building, Wyatt missed the intense glare from Critt as he walked past.

Critt was watching Wyatt standing and fidgeting while growing angrier by the second when a beautiful woman in faded casual clothing approached him with a question. Too far away to hear their conversation as they were speaking softly, Critt saw Wyatt nod his head, saw the woman say something and Wyatt hesitate before speaking, then walking back towards the door directly towards him. Unable to move without drawing attention to himself, he focused on a cardboard cutout standing in the lobby. To his amazement, this poster of an ice-skating champion was the girl who had just met with Wyatt. Since Wyatt was obviously not meeting with The Reader, the girl must have passed him a message and this could only have come from the Reader himself. Therefore, this girl must know what Reader looked like.

The girl went back into the Lobby and sat down with Critt right behind her all the way. Critt managed a seat close to the girl and tried his best to appear casual and unthreatening, although he knew his looks would betray his attempt at friendliness.

"Excuse me, miss, I couldn't help but notice your conversation with mister West. I know your conversation isn't any of my business, but I was supposed to meet with a man who calls himself The Reader. He was going to give me and mister West a briefing. Is it possible that you happen to know what happened to the Reader?"

While the man was speaking, obviously trying to appear friendly, Katrina could not help but pick up his strong negative vibrations. His very presence appeared menacing. On the other hand, the message seemed innocuous and if telling this man what she had repeated to Wyatt would get him to leave her alone, then she would tell him. It wasn't like the Reader had told her it was confidential information.

"Why no. I don't know what happened to the man you call Reader. I met him here in the lobby just a few minutes ago very briefly. We barely said hello when he asked me to deliver a message to mister West." With that preamble she proceeded to tell Critt the same exact message she had just delivered to Wyatt,

"I see," Critt acknowledged, trying vainly to offer a friendly smile. "I don't suppose you know what those circumstances are that prevented him from our meeting?"

"I'm sorry, no. Like I said, we barely met." Katrina was sharp enough to know when she was being interrogated; and Critt's attempt at a smile was so pathetic she could have laughed, except the man was truly terrifying.

"Well, thanks for telling me the message." As he was standing up apparently to leave, Critt asked the question he had been dying to ask from the beginning; "Could you tell me what the Reader looks like? What he's wearing? You see, we've never met, and I don't want to miss him if he is still around the Lodge someplace."

Already on edge and distrustful of this intimidating man, Katrina shook her head from side to side. "I'm really sorry, but I hardly paid any attention to his looks. Like I said, we barely met. He was about average height, with a chiseled face and light-colored hair. Young. I didn't pay any attention to his clothes."

Not truly believing that the woman didn't remember his clothes, but unwilling to make a further scene, Critt turned to leave, "Oh, one final question. Is the Reader a white man?"

Unable to lie, she responded. "Why yes. I think so. He certainly had light colored skin."

Walking out of the lobby, Critt spoke into his button microphone. "Did you guys copy that?" he asked.

Affirmative came back from three other men. "Male Caucasian, average in looks. That certainly narrows our search," quipped one of the team.

"Okay, stand down for a few. Let me make a couple of calls. We should pay this West character a visit. He was the one who arranged the meeting. I want to find out just what he knows. The ice skater just met the Reader so we know he is on the property. We just need a better description."

Wyatt was sitting in his office drinking his third cup of coffee; trying to decide what to do? How to precede? Who to call? That someone of influence in his company wanted the Reader out of the way was obvious. At this point he didn't know there was a termination order on the nan. Since he had arranged for the visit, did the Readers problems have anything to do with the shortages that were showing up in his company? Was he personally at risk? Were they, whoever they were, trying to get him out of the company? As he was contemplating these questions, his secretary buzzed him announcing a number of men on their way to his office. That she had not asked him if the visits were expected spoke volumes.

The door to his office was opened without ceremony and four tough-looking men marched in led by the man he had noticed standing by the door at The Lodge. The four uninvited guests stood in a semicircle in front of his desk. Critt decided that a show of force would do more to make Wyatt talk than any carrot he could offer.

"Mister West," Critt sneered the name. "You invited a man named The Reader to pay you a visit here in Sun Valley." It was a statement, not a question. "We know why you invited him here and don't care about that. All we are trying to do is locate this man. Do you have any information concerning his whereabouts?"

Wyatt was not easily intimidated, but these four tough men with fierce unsmiling faces and dark glaring eyes filled him with fear. Considering his mental gyrations of the past few minutes, he knew there was some serious shit coming down, and he didn't want to be the recipient.

"I'll tell you all I know," he pleaded. He felt disgusted at his own cowardness. "I don't know this Reader man. I was given his name and invited him over the telephone to come here to Sun Valley. We have never met."

"Is it true that you arranged to fly him here in your company plane?" Critt's accusing tone was menacing to go along with the fierce look in his eyes.

"Why yes. Is there a problem?"

"We lost track of the man and need to find him at once. Unfortunately, we do not know what he looks like. Give us the name of your pilot and where we can find him." It was obvious to Wyatt that any failure to answer the man would only result in some very unpleasant business.

Wyatt provided Critt with the information and was only too happy when the four intimidating men trooped out of his office with their glowering faces leaving the door wide open. He felt a small victory since they hadn't asked about a hostess and he had not disclosed Anita's involvement.

The pilot was not hard to find. He was at the airport seeing to the stocking and servicing of the G650. Critt and his fellow hunters descended on the pilot with their questions about The Reader. Unfortunately for them, the pilot had never laid eyes on his passenger. Explaining about Anita and her hostess duties and how with her aboard there was no reason for him to leave the flight deck. In order to give them both privacy, the main cabin door remained closed for the short two-hour flight. "Sorry," he said, "I can't help you."

Critt and his team returned to the Sun Valley Lodge. They knew that Anita had spent at least two hours, and possibly many more with this mysterious man. They just needed to find her and get his description. The pilot had explained about Sun Valley Lodge's use of hostesses to help guide visitors around the Village and the town of Ketchum. In order to find Anita, they needed to talk with the manager at the Lodge.

Taking one look at the four men demanding to know where they could find Anita, Ryan Drescher, the wimpy Lodge manager had no trouble at all telling them that she was conducting a tour of the Village for wives of visiting dignitaries from Washington D.C.

The four men knew all about the visiting dignitaries from the Nation's capital, which was their primary reason for being called upon to dispatch this nuisance of a mind reader.

While touring the Village or the Town of Ketchum, each hostess wore a communication unit to talk with someone back at the Lodge if anyone in her group had a question she couldn't answer. Using this system, Drescher called Anita and told her to return to the main Lodge at once. She would only be tied up for a few minutes after which she would be free to continue with her tour.

Anita had no idea why she was being summoned back to the office. As far as she knew, she had done nothing wrong to merit such a demand. True, she had spent the night with The Reader, but that was not against the rules. After their official hostess duties were finished for the evening, each girl is free to resume her personal life and make her own sleeping arrangements. Sleeping with Lodge guests was not a requirement for the job. It was discouraged as the Lodge did not want to garner the reputation of a whore house. If they chose to sleep with a guest, either for money or just sex, it was their own business. They were just cautioned to be discrete and not wear any revealing clothing around the Lodge.

Anita opened the door to Ryan's office and one look at the assembled group of menacing men indicated a friendly meeting was not in order.

Without any preamble Critt demanded, "did you spend yesterday on an airplane with a fellow who calls himself The Reader?"

"Yes, Is that a problem?"

"Just tell us what he looks like and you can go." Critt's face and tone left no room for evasion. Only an honest answer would suffice.

"He stands a little over six feet. He's what women would call attractive. Dark brown hair. Yesterday he wore jeans and a V-necked tee shirt. I have no idea what he is wearing today."

"How old is this man and do you have any idea where he can be located or where he is staying?" Critt demanded.

Anita looked at Ryan for guidance but the office manager was busy studying floor. Deciding to risk a lie, she replied, "why no. He didn't tell me his plans. He is probably in his mid-twenties or so, but he acts much older."

"As a hostess, isn't it your duty to show new customers around the area?" Critt continued.

"Generally, that is our practice," she replied. At this point she had to continue lying, "however we landed just before dark and he appeared anxious to be somewhere. I had a car from the Lodge prepared to give him a lift, but someone met him at the plane. I don't know who. He was on the telephone for most of the plane ride. I made him a scotch to drink, but he barely touched the glass. It's a shame, since it was Johnny Walker Black." Having opted for lying, Anita intuitively felt a few embellishments would make her story more convincing.

"Six feet tall. Good-looking. Black hair. Anything else you can tell us? Is he fat, thin, big boned; any distinguishing features you can recall?" Critt toned down his menacing voice and looks as it appeared the woman was cooperating.

Anita was tempted to make up more stories like how the Reader was covered with tattoos, but she feared that if it was discovered she had lied it might really come back at her with unpleasant recriminations. "He seemed very fit," she said truthfully. "I don't recall anything that stands out particularly. Like I said, he spent most of his time on the telephone. He is a good-looking man, and I thought we might have dinner together, but that didn't work out. I'm sorry." She was tempted to tell them about the callouses on his knuckles, but something held her back. Even if they discovered this for themselves at a later date, they could hardly fault her for not noticing this physical aberration.

"Did he tell you his name? Anything besides The Reader?" Critt demanded.

Surprised by the question, it was still easy to give an answer. "Why no. The Reader is the only name he gave."

Deciding that they could gain nothing more of value from this woman, Critt turned about face and left the room without saying thank you or goodbye. He and his men just left.

After the men left his office, Ryan perked up and looked at Anita. "You didn't tell them that you brought him here. Was that wise?"

Anita knew the office manager had no backbone and would sell her down the river in a heartbeat to save himself. She had no shame in playing to his fears. "I didn't think you would want them tearing up his room searching for God only knows what," she responded.

"Oh, right. Good thinking, Anita. I guess you can go back to the guests you left wandering around."

Armed with a somewhat vague description of The Reader, Critt had his team split up to scour the grounds looking for him. There was still a chance the Reader was still somewhere in the Village. They were looking for a handsome six-foot man, around twenty-five years old with black hair and a good body. How many men like that would you expect to see in this area at any given time?

CHAPTER FOURTEEN
THE HUNT BEGINS

Watching Katrina walk away I had to find a quiet place where I could relax for a brief time and try to figure out a plan of action. Looking around, I saw a few spectators or perhaps just visitors sitting in bleachers over by the outdoor ice rink. Ambling over doing my best to appear casual, I took a seat a couple of rows back and leaned into the sun. My killers did not have my picture, at least I didn't pick up that thought from the man in the lobby, but they may have my description. My thought was that in the bleachers I would look just like another nonchalant visitor soaking in the sun.

Why does somebody want me dead? It made little sense. I wasn't aware of any enemies. How many men were with that killer in the lobby? My primary advantage was that they didn't know what I looked like. Now that I was free from Wyatt and identification by association, it should be possible to locate the killer's programmers and determine their motive. As far as I knew, the only people in the entire area familiar with my looks were Anita and Katrina. How long this situation would last was uncertain, and before they found me, I needed to know a lot more than I did at the present time.

My options were not unlimited. I could just catch a taxi to the airport and fly home. That however might only be a short-term solution as I still did not know who wanted me dead and why. This insane quest could follow me home. It was also possible to get a ride into Ketchum and rent a motel room under one of my fake identities. Lying low for a few days, my killers would assume I had left the area and it would be possible for me to surface. But that still left me not knowing anything of value and was no guarantee that the killers would not resurface sometime in the future when I might not be warned of their presence. Besides, as I thought about my options, they all seemed like running away and I was damned if I would let them be the architect of my life. I had not been working on my body and mind studying martial arts for the past two years to run from troubling situations. One faced one's challenges, not run away. It was time to put a new hunter in the game. Having decided to stay and fight; I needed a strategy.

Fortunately, I had some advantages over my enemies. I could read their minds and they did not know for certain what I looked like.

They also knew something thing about me; that I could read minds. They certainly did not know if I was educated or ignorant, or if I had any kind of training.

One of my many reading pleasures was The Art of War by Sun Tzu. I found it a tremendous aid in my martial arts training. To me its entire philosophy boils down to this; act simply, live impeccably. One chapter dealt with advantages and disadvantages.

'Advantages and disadvantages are interdependent. First know the disadvantages, then you know the advantages.'

Good advice. Getting cocky over my advantages could have severe consequences. These guys were professionals. One quick glance at my killer as he entered the Lodge's door radiating this fierce hunter countenance; with a body that showed powerful conditioning, I knew he was a real pro. His vibrations were off the chart. I could only imagine that his comrades were of the same caliber. Okay then, what are my disadvantages?

I don't know how many men are after me. I don't know their motivation; or how dedicated they are to accomplishing their task, whatever that might be, besides my death. I didn't know who was responsible for ordering these men to kill me, or if they could, and would, send reinforcements if this present group failed for whatever reason.

I only knew that for some unfathomable reason, there were an unknown number of men in the vicinity who would kill me on sight.

Unfathomable. That was the key I needed. One of Sun Tzu's central teachings and foundation for my martial arts is this teaching:

'In martial arts, it is important that strategy be unfathomable, that form be concealed, and that movements be unexpected, so that preparedness against them be impossible.'

For now, it would be easy to conceal my form since they did not know for certain what I looked like; therefore, I could move against them unexpectedly. Thus, my enemies could not be prepared. The strategy stuff would have to come later. After I had a chance to talk with one of my would-be killers.

I needed to get the leader of this pack of killers alone, and temporarily out of sight from his associates. They were undoubtedly using some kind of advanced communication systems such as an ear piece microphone. If I was clever, I could use that against them, but the risks were obvious. If I screwed up, his partners, however many, would know about it and our exact location.

I watched for my killers who periodically patrolled the grounds between the lodge and ice rink. In thirty minutes, I knew there were at least four men. Every trained killer is proficient. Since they were looking for someone, they must have somewhat of a description. It was only my innocuous sitting in the bleachers with a few other people, on the opposite side of the ice rink from them, that momentarily saved me.

CHAPTER FIFTEEN
GOING TO WAR

I must conceal my form. My movements will then be unexpected. I took notice of my form. After spending a few minutes observing the movements of the men who would kill me, it became obvious they had this idea regarding the man they were looking for. They must have gotten to Anita or perhaps Katrina. This realization gave me a brief pause. I knew there was the potential for physical damage to one or possibly both women. My brief view of Critt and understanding the mentality he and his team must have suggested that any interrogation of the women might not be subtle. Given my present situation there was nothing I could do about it now except offer a silent prayer for their safety. Okay, back to form; I must conceal it. This meant I had to change my appearance. A visit to The Gold Mine seemed in order. One item of interest about Ketchum Anita had mentioned while giving me a tour of the town was The Gold Mine. The name alone is enough to pique interest.

Everybody living in the Sun Valley area is rich, except for those working in the service industries; waiting tables, cleaning houses, janitorial work, gardening and such. They fill nearly all of these positions with ski bums who could not otherwise afford to ski unless they worked for one of the many ski lodges during the winter. One benefit of working for a ski lodge meant they could ski all day for free whenever duties allowed. They all took other summer jobs to support their life styles. Town merchants certainly knew of the ski-bum mentality and that the young dedicated skiers would work for peanuts just to ski, so wages barely met Federal minimum guidelines.

Rich people tire of their clothes, some are brand new or barely worn. They tire of ordinary household items and are constantly redecorating exchanging one set of pictures, chairs, lamps etc. for something new. Nearly everything in their lives, they don't want gets donated to The Gold Mine who sells these items for a fraction of their real value. For their patrons it is a gold mine. The workers at the Gold Mine are rich residents who donate their time for free. The city provides a comfortable cottage for free which houses The Gold Mine. They had practically no expenses and all profits from the business, which are substantial, get donated to the Library. This makes the Ketchum public library one of the most admired and envied libraries in America.

At the Gold Mine, I could buy everything needed to change my form. Getting there would not be a problem as The Village provided shuttles for residents and visitors to downtown Ketchum. However, getting to the shuttle might be a problem. The closest shuttle stop just happened to be right in front of the Lodge's door. The difficulty being I didn't know the shuttle schedule. I remembered passing these colorful shuttles while doing my morning run, and it seemed like one passed me about every fifteen minutes, which made some kind of sense. If so, I just had to stay situated and watch for the next shuttle. Between the buildings I could see a small part of the parking lot and the road that traversed it from where I sat. By the time I saw the shuttle, and it reached the Lodge unloading zone I would not have time to surreptitiously reach the same point. Running to catch the shuttle would point me out to everyone in the area. That must not happen. It seemed like I had barely formulated this plan than I saw the shuttle zip through my narrow observation window. Fortunately, the Village provided sky-blue courtesy vans with broad white brush strokes running down their sides outlining the Sawtooth Mountains. The vans markings made them easy to spot, and I looked at watch on my wrist. If my suppositions were correct, I had fifteen minutes to make it to the loading zone undetected. Getting there should not be a problem. After observing Critt and his team patrolling the grounds, I had a good idea about their schedule. All I had to do was time their movements and wait for an opening when they would all be out of visual contact with my path to the Lodge loading zone. Timed correctly, I could catch the shuttle and make the three-minute ride to downtown Ketchum undetected. This would give me fifteen minutes at the Gold Mine to make my transformation before catching the shuttle for a ride back to the Lodge. Altogether I would be out of their range for about twenty-one minutes. Critt and his team would not even know I had been missing.

The man who caught the Sun Valley shuttle at the corner of Sun Valley Road and Leadville Avenue heading towards the Lodge didn't look anything like The Reader. An old man stooped and bent with age who walked with a cane stood on the corner waiting for the shuttle. He was wearing black slacks cinched high above the waist as many old men wear their pants. Men with a pot belly for their waist find that pants ride better when worn higher than normal. A yellow and red long-sleeved plaid shirt tucked into his pants completed the picture of an old dodder who no longer cared for or had the energy to fulfill the image of a sartorial dresser. An ill-fitting green alpine hat tipped down over his forehead rode just above a pair of dark sunglasses with oversized lenses. The glasses looked like something Elton John might have worn back in his early years. Stumbling with his bent legs, the old man barely managed the small step that extended when the driver opened the van's door. Passengers on the shuttle saw a dark-skinned old man stumble to his seat. The dark skin was accomplished by mixing a woman's mascara with sun block. The Readers disguise had so effectively changed his appearance it was unlikely that even his old foster parents would recognize him. He had completely concealed his form.

The shuttle van stopped under the Sun Valley Lodge portico to discharge passengers and pick up a new load. A bent old man with a cane stumbled off the shuttle and took a seat vacated by a woman who had been waiting for the shuttle. Several knotty pine benches and chairs were tastefully arranged under the portico for waiting passengers. The Reader had to suppress a smile as he took the woman's chair. While riding in the shuttle he could not help but read the thoughts and feel the vibrations of his fellow passengers. Their thoughts ranged from pity to disgust and feelings of superiority. One passenger, a man nearing old age, prayed that whatever happened he would not end up looking so pitiful. He leaned back in his chair; eyes partially closed as though sleeping. The Reader keep an eye out for his killers. Every few minutes one would pass by barley paying attention to the old man waiting for a ride, or maybe just resting. After nearly an hour had passed, all four men congregated for a meeting under the portico close to the sleeping old man.

The killers were at a loss as for what to do next. Not one of them had seen anybody resembling The Reader. Critt hated to give up the search, but there were few options. Sitting quietly, The Reader had no problem listening to them discuss their plans. While he couldn't hear their voices clearly, he could read their thoughts and knew what they were saying. Critt decided they needed to split up and search independently.

He would leave Kyle Gunning here at The Lodge in case The Reader was still somewhere on the premises. They would drop Sergeant Julien off downtown Ketchum to patrol the streets. Critt would have Brian drop him off at the Sawtooth Lodge where he could watch Wyatt. There was the possibility that The Reader would show up there sometime during the day for his delayed meeting.

Brian was wrapped too tightly to do anything but sit in their van waiting for a call. Anyone spotting The Reader would call Brian to pick up the other team members. Having decided, Critt ordered Brian to go pick up their van which was parked on the other side of the parking lot. The black FBI van, bristling with antennas and dark windows, was too intimidating to park close to the Lodge entrance. Brian needed to visit the head before going to the van giving The Reader time to shuffle out of the entrance into the parking lot.

CHAPTER SIXTEEN
THE BATTLE

Sun Tzu teaches that the best wars are those that are never fought. The best Generals are those who win without fighting. However, he also recognizes that, at times, it is impossible to evade going to war. In which case, surprise is the strongest weapon to win the war swiftly.

The Sun Valley Lodge parking area is a five-acre oval with select areas reserved for buses and extra-large vehicles. Once out of sight of the killers' Reader hustled to the bus section and had no trouble identifying the black FBI van bristling with antennas. In one of the books he read, Reader understood that antennas of various lengths were designed for different frequencies. Being able to talk locally and great distances was a requirement for a variety of government agencies. In addition to their needs, the FBI stayed in touch with agents from the Department of Justice, their ultimate governing agency. The DOJ had its own radio frequencies.

Reader hid in the front of a tour bus parked parallel to the FBI van while waiting for Brian. It was only two long steps from the front of the bus Reader was hiding behind to the van's driver side door. While watching for the special forces agent to arrive, Reader cussed his luck at drawing the big beast as he called Brian instead of one of the smaller men. Krav Maga teaches many pressure points, some on the head, where it is possible to render a person unconscious immediately with one strike. The exact pressure point to hit, and with which part of the hand, depends upon the position of both men. Reader was well trained in these techniques, but had never been required to utilize them outside of the practice ring.

He had spent over three years honing his body and hands. Beating leather bags of sand and gravel daily with his hands had turned them into lethal weapons. It was the habit of many Dojo's to provide their audiences at major match tournaments with martial art exhibitions. Sage had performed at many of these exhibitions smashing stacks of cinder blocks or wood. He could punch holes in a cinderblock wall with his fists. His practices had covered his hands and fingers with callouses while making them hard as granite. These callouses were what Anita had noticed while giving him a massage, which she had not revealed to Critt during his interrogation.

While waiting for Brian, he found himself sweating and feeling nervous for the first time outside of a match. It was essential to knock Brian unconscious immediately without allowing him an opportunity to call his friends on the communications gear he was undoubtedly wearing. Sage was not concerned about his ability to knock the big man unconscious. Given Brian's size and training, Reader could not help but worry if he could accomplish his chosen task without killing him. He knew that he could kill the big man by driving his knuckles into his skull. His concern was hitting the man with enough force to render him unconscious immediately without crushing his skull. Fortunately, he didn't have to wait too long as Brian appeared headed for the van before Reader felt himself prepared. Ready or not, the moment of truth had arrived.

Brian stopped by the van's driver's side door with some keys in his hand, prepared to enter the vehicle. The van was equipped with remote door lock capabilities, which chirped when Brian pushed the remote-control button. Just as Brian reached for the door Reader tapped him on the shoulder and as Brian turned to see who had touched him Reader struck him in the temple just behind his right with eye with an extended middle knuckle on his right hand. Properly executed, the victim drops unconscious immediately. Reader's technique was flawless, and he caught the big man before he hit the ground.

The van was already unlocked, so Reader quickly opened a rear door and grabbing the unconscious killer under the shoulders dragged him into the back seat pulling the van door shut. He then found Brian's earpiece and a small microphone. Brian was a walking arsenal with a Beretta M9 in a belt holster behind his back, a Glock 19 strapped on his ankle, and a Benchmade 3300 Infidel knife in a custom holster hanging from his belt. Reader removed the earpiece and microphone, putting it in his own ear. With blacked-out windows, no one could see into the van, but anyone inside could see out. Reader quickly surveyed the surrounding area to see if his actions had been observed. The bus parking lot was usually not bustling with people and satisfied that no one had noticed what went on at the FBI van, Reader set out to quickly immobilize his giant adversary.

Looking in the Back of the vehicle, he saw a large storage cabinet with its drawers conveniently labeled. The drawer labeled restraints immediately caught his eyes and crawling over the seat helped himself to a handful of nylon tie wraps.

Crawling back over the seat, he rolled the heavy hit man onto the floor behind the front seats. He folded Brian's arms behind his back then secured them with the quick ties. Folding his legs back, he laced them together at the ankles then linked them to his hands, folding the man into U shape. Grabbing a big roll of cotton bandages, Sage stuffed them into Brian's mouth, securing it with still another tie wrap around his head.

Able now to hear what Brian's teammates might be saying and able to avoid any surprises, Reader climbed into the front seat of the van and got behind the wheel. Brian was supposed to pick up both Critt and Julien in front of the Lodge. There were usually several people assembled under the portico waiting for rides or just entering the Lodge, which made getting both men into the van without causing a scene impossible. No option seemed reasonable. He couldn't drop Brian off some place out-of-the-way and then go pick up his buddies because as soon as they opened the door to get in the van and didn't see Brian, they would react. Most definitely in a very unfriendly manner. He couldn't leave the unconscious Brian in the back seat for the same reason, although he could sense Brian starting to come around. If he called any of his teammates for help of some kind, it was likely to bring them all. He needed to find some way of separating the three men so he could handle them one at a time.

He sat in the driver's seat, thinking for a couple of minutes when he remembered seeing something in the back of the van while picking up the restraints. Leaving the driver's door open, he went to the back of the van. He opened the rear doors giving him access to the storage cabinet, and another drawer labeled 'Nite-Nite,' the drugs used to render an individual unconscious for extended periods. The bottles had long chemical names, which Sage ignored. Nite-Nite said all he needed to know. Inside the drawer were vials with three, six- and twelve-hour labels along with syringes. Just why the FBI needed such drugs was beyond his comprehension. Scanning the instructions, Sage pocketed four of the twelve-hour vials plus one syringe. Hell, if he couldn't use the same needle for all four men, that was their problem. Getting back into the rear seat with Brian, Reacher administered the first shot of Nite-Nite. This should keep the big killer out of commission for at least twelve hours if Reader understood the directions on the vials correctly.

Reader needed to get the three men left under the portico separated. Handling three highly qualified and trained specialists at the same time was beyond his capabilities without causing some noticeable commotion. He required the men to become separated. Another of Sun Tzu's saying from the Art of War:

'In battle, confrontation is done directly, victory is gained by surprise.'

Remembering this admonishment, Reader decided on a new strategy. Using the earpiece and microphone he had removed from Brian; he purposefully made his voice sound rough. Hopefully, his brief message would sound like the voice of Brian.

"Kyle. Can you come to the van and give me a hand? There's some gizmo that popped out of the comm unit in the van, and I can't figure out what it is supposed to do. I know you comm guys have all this special knowledge about communication equipment."

Reader listened carefully to the response to his request to see if his ploy was going to work. He didn't want all three guys coming at once, and since Kyle was the designated rover, it made sense that he would come alone. He heard Kyle's affirmative, "on the way" with no demurring response from Critt. Reader was banking on the team leader's confidence in his men to do their jobs while he could sit on the bench in the shade under the portico waiting for the van. The only question was if his voice sounded enough like Brian's to keep the rest of the team off-guard. He opened the read doors to the van and peeking through the window waited anxiously to see if his strategy was going to work.

In a couple of minutes, he could see the communications specialist shuffling across the parking lot coming towards the van. Hiding just inside the van, Reader waited for Kyle to poke his head into the van to see what was causing the problem. As Kyle ducked his head into the Van, Reader struck the top of his head hard with the toughened blade of his hand.

There is another place on the top of our heads taught by Krav Maga where the Sagittal suture meets with the Lambdoid seam creating a spot where the right blow will render the victim immediately unconscious. This intersection between the three plates of our skull is just behind our forehead. The plates are not joined at birth, so the baby's head can exit the mother's womb. The blow must also be struck with enough force to render its victim unconscious without continuing through the skull into the brain. Reader had busted hundreds of cinder blocks with the blade of his hand, and it would have been easy for him to crush Kyle's head.

In this instance, Kyle collapsed half into and half out of the van. Reader quickly pulled Kyle the rest of the way into the van removing the earpiece from his body. Closing the rear doors, Reader administered another shot of Nite-Nite without bothering with the restraints. He now had only two adversaries with which to deal.

Taking one of the two transmitters he had removed from his killers, Reader stomped on it, smashing it into small bits of plastic and metal. With Brian's earpiece, he could hear Critt and Peter almost simultaneously say, "what the fuck?" Critt went on to say, "it must be something with that communication problem Brian was talking about. Maybe we should go see what the problem is." Leaving their comfortable places in the shade under the portico, the pair started across the parking lot towards the FBI van. Reader had some of what he wanted. The team was now down to two men, although perhaps the two most dangerous. How was he going to handle both men when they arrived at the van?

Having lured Kyle to the van, Reader knew it would take about two minutes for Critt and Peter to make the same walk. That was how much time he had to figure out how he was going to take out both men without getting killed by one or the other. He needed Critt conscious and alive to find out who wanted him dead and buried out of sight. Remembering that Peter was the team medic gave Reader an idea. He opened both rear doors and pulled Kyle's body back out so that his feet were hanging out of the doors. Without much time remaining, he hurried back to the front of the van where he had left his cane. He quickly filled the syringe with Nite-Nite from another of the vials and put it in his pocket. Then he made his way around the big bus he had been hiding behind originally and hobbled into the path that Critt and Peter were taking towards the van.

"You men hear that loud pop?" he croaked with an excited voice while joining them in a limping, hobbling walk toward the van using the cane to make him appear handicapped. "I was just coming to see what caused the noise."

"It's no affair of yours pop," Critt said, dismissively trying to get the old geezer on his way.

By now they had reached the van and could see Kyle's legs sticking out of the back doors.

"Oh my God," Peter exclaimed, jumping into the van to check on his teammate. As Peter jumped into the van, Critt leaned in to see what had happened. As Critt ducked his head, Reader hit him in the temple on the pressure point with his knuckle knocking him instantly unconscious. Letting the body fall, Reader pulled the syringe from his pocket and jabbed it into Peter's leg. It took a minute for the drug to work its way into his system, but before Peter was able to react, he too fell unconscious.

Peter was out-of-the-way for twelve hours, along with Kyle and Brian. Using the FBI plastic ties he had appropriated earlier, Reader trussed-up Critt and hauled him into the van laying him on top of Kyle and Peter. Looking around to see if he had been observed and seeing nobody, Reader shut the van's rear doors and went to the driver's seat. He needed a quiet, out-of-the-way place where he could have his discussion with Critt. Fortunately, on his morning run, he had discovered just the place.

Sun Valley Village has an amphitheater on the backside away from the Lodge, where they provide summer concerts. No concerts were being held at this time since they were hosting the International ice-skating show. The parking lot for the amphitheater was off the main road and separated by a row of trees making it almost invisible. Reader drove the FBI van and its cargo of killers to this parking lot where he opened the read doors and pulled Critt back out, dropping him on the asphalt. Critt moaned and opened his eyes, seeing Reader for the first time.

"Yep. I'm the Reader, the guy you have been trying so hard to find and kill. Have to say, you guys gave me a real scare. By the way, your head will ache for about two hours, and then the pain will gradually go away." Reader was sitting on the rear bumper of the van sounding very casual, like discussing the weather with a buddy.

"What the hell did you do to me, asshole?" Critt snarled without the same casual tone in his voice.

"Just a little Krav Maga. I couldn't take on all four of you guys at the same time in a fair fight. Not that you guys would ever fight fair." Reader still had the same conversational tone to his voice.

"What happened to my team?" Critt sounded concerned but not particularly worried. His tone was demanding.

"It's called Nite-Nite. Something I found in this swell FBI van you guys have been using to tool in around town. It's got some fancy chemical name which I didn't bother learning. The shots I administered are supposed to work for twelve hours. Hopefully, I'll be long gone before any of you wake up."

"What do you mean any of us waking up? I'm awake now, ass wipe." Critt sounded angry and not the least bit intimidated.

"Yeah, temporarily. You're only awake now because I want to know who ordered you to kill me and dispose of my body. Did you have a spot already picked out, or were you going to wing it? Maybe find a place out in those lava fields between here and Twin Falls where you could dump my body in a crevasse.

Nobody in their right mind would ever traipse around out there. My body could lay there and never be found for a hundred years. Anyway, who did order you to kill me?"

"Go to hell, jerk-off," he sneered, squirming to get out of his restraints. "You ain't getting nothing out of me."

"My, my. What a vocabulary. A real potty mouth. Oh, I know you guys are all trained to resist torture. Anyway, too late now. It's your lucky day, well at least as far as the torture business. Fortunately, I don't have to bust your balls or threaten your wife and kids."

As soon as I asked the question, I got the answer. "You probably do know that I read minds, right? That little statement about your wife and kids. The two boys. That's known as a clue."

"You couldn't have got shit. I didn't think nothing." Critt sounded a bit defensive and stressed, as though he was hoping what he was saying was the truth, but was afraid otherwise. I think mentioning the wife and kids had him worried.

"Let's see. Secretary of Defense, Roger Horowitz. Sound familiar? That's the man giving the orders. Now the question is why? Why does he want me dead?"

Critt just laid where he was shaking his head. It was apparent that Critt had no Idea why he was tasked to kill Reader. The only answer I could read was 'threat to national security.' That's a catchall phrase that covers anything those in power can use to dispose of unwanted individuals, whether they are a threat to national security or simply pose a personal nuisance. I was one of those individuals representing a problem. Whether it had something to do with national security, which I highly doubted, or I was just a nuisance, didn't make any difference. Horowitz wanted me dead and gone.

Knowing that Critt didn't have any more useful information, Reader said, "I guess I'll have to go ask him. You wouldn't know where he is right now, would you Critt?"

It was evident to Reader while reading Critt's mind that he didn't know where the Secretary was, but there did flash into Critt's mind the image of his telephone.

Reader had searched each man relieving him of his hardware and personal items, including wallets, cell phones, and any papers they were carrying. He had dumped everything into a gym bag found in the van. He started searching the bag laying things out in the rear of the van as he emptied the bags contents.

"Good lord Critt. You guys planning on starting a war or something? There must be twenty-five or thirty pounds of guns and knives in here. You surely didn't think you were going to need all these weapons just for little ole me, did you.?"

"Fuck you, Reader." Critt was growling and writhing about on the ground, straining at his restraints.

"Oh, here it is. This pretty little pink telephone with the cute bunny rabbit on the case." Seeing that Critt was getting all worked up, Reader wanted to have a little fun. After all, these were killers sent to end his life. In reality Critt's telephone was a simple ugly black phone with no markings.

Critt knew what Reader was doing, but couldn't keep himself from tossing and squirming around on the ground like the trussed-up bully that he was.

Reader turned on Critt's phone, which thankfully didn't have any password protection. Not that this would have been a problem, but it saved time. "Let's see Critt, just which of these numbers is the one for the Secretary?"

It was more than likely the last number Critt had entered into his cell. Reader assumed that once Critt has completed his mission, he was to call the Secretary with the news. To be sure, he asked Critt, "which one of these numbers is for the Secretary?"

Critt was apparently out of witticisms as he kept his mouth shut; he even stopped thrashing around on the ground. His silence was welcomed but unnecessary. By merely asking, Reader read the answer in Critt's mind. To place a call to the Secretary, he would need to silence Critt, so Reader administered the last dose of Nite-Nite to the still struggling killer. Once Critt was unconscious, Reader hoisted him back into the rear of the van and shut the doors.

This group of killers was no longer a problem, and Reader now knew who wanted him dead. He did not know why the Secretary had placed a hit order on him and could think of no way to find out short of asking the man himself. To do that, he had to find out where the Secretary was located. Reader remembered Anita telling him that there was some big-government meeting going on in Sun Valley with a lot of government big-whigs as she had called them. Anita had also told him she would be hosting a number of their wives, giving them a tour of the Village and Ketchum. If he could find out where she was, perhaps the wives could tell him where the Secretary was staying.

There was no way Reader could know that this nightmare and long day were barely beginning.

CHAPTER SEVENTEEN
LOOKING FOR THE ANSWER

Using Critt's phone, Reader called the Secretary's number.

"Horowitz."

"Mister Secretary. My orders were to call this number when the mission had been accomplished. We have completed the mission." Reader was banking on the fact that Horowitz would not likely know who was calling him or if he knew the name would not understand what he sounded like on the telephone. The Secretary of Defense does not talk with the hired help.

"They will never find the body?"

"Correct."

"Good then. Thanks." The call ended with no further words.

Reader couldn't decide if he should be relieved or disgusted. That a human life could mean so little to such a man. He needed to discover just why the Secretary wanted him dead, and his body disposed of never to be found. Horowitz ended the phone call before Reader could read his mind and find out why.

Why did these people want him dead? It had to be something to do with his visit to Sun Valley. The only person Reader though who knew of his visit to Sun Valley was Wyatt West at the Sawtooth Ski Lodge. He did not think Wyatt had any reason to be responsible for the kill team. For that matter, how could a resort manager even have the connections to order suck a hit? When he observed Wyatt at the Sun Valley Lodge, there was no sign that Wyatt had any interest in seeing him dead. Just the opposite. Wyatt wanted Reader to help solve a problem. So, what brought the killers to Sun Valley, and how did they know where to find him?

Wyatt mentioned Jim Bledsoe at Quantum. Could Bledsoe be the reason someone sent a hit team to dispose of the Reader? That didn't seem likely. When he met Bledsoe and worked for him at Quantum, there were no negative vibrations from the man. It had to be somebody and something else. Thinking about it, Reader thought contact between Bledsoe and Wyatt highly unlikely. Wyatt got the Bledsoe information from someone else. Who? Someone who knew both Bledsoe and Wyatt. That was about as far as Sage could go with his present knowledge. Whoever that intermediary was must hold the key. It seemed the only way he would get the answer was to confront Secretary Horowitz directly, and to do that, he had to find out where the man had been staying.

Using Critt's phone, Reader called Anita. She had given him her phone number before Reader took off for his morning run.

"Hi, this is Anita. Who's calling, please?" She sounded very professional, not recognizing the telephone number displayed on her cell.

"Anita, thank God you are safe. This is Reader. Were you contacted by some men looking for me?

"Yes. They scared the hell out me. They knew I hosted you on the plane ride, but I divulged nothing else. I did not tell them where you were staying." In her voice you could hear the relief as she talked with Reader. "Are you all right?"

"Yes. Thanks for holding out. Those guys are a nasty business. I feared they might have been a little physical with you when I finally met them. They are hard men on a mission and would do almost anything to get their way."

"I too feared they might want to hurt me," she responded with what sounded like relief, "but we were in my boss's office with him and the secretary was just outside. They were menacing, but otherwise, they didn't threaten physical harm. They wanted to know what you looked like, so I gave them a generic description. Oh, and I didn't mention the callouses on your hands. It seemed like something you might not want the world to know about."

Sage didn't want to confirm her suspicion, but he thanked her anyway. "Anita, the reason I called is that you mentioned being hostess to the wives of a bunch of Washington big whigs I think you said. Are you still with them?

"Yes, we were discussing lunch plans before going to the ice-skating show. Why is that important?"

He didn't answer her question. "Would you ask the ladies if they would know where Secretary Horowitz is staying? It's crucial."

"Sure, give me a minute. She didn't cover up the speaker on her cell, and Sage could hear her talking with the ladies. It only took a minute before she came back on the phone, "they say he is staying at Senator Kim's ranch, which is up the valley a few miles."

"Senator Kim? Do you know where the ranch is.?"

"Not exactly. I know it is somewhere off Adam's Gulch Road. Adams Gulch road takes off highway 75 about ten miles north of Ketchum. I'm sorry, I can't be more specific."

"No, that's fine. You've been great. What is Senator Kim's full name? I'll Google his address and location."

"It's Christopher Kim. He's the senior senator from Hawaii."

"Okay, thanks a lot, Anita. You've been a big help. I probably won't be at the ice-skating show, but I will call you in a couple of days to see if you're free."

"Hey, you better. And watch out for yourself. Those guys I saw this morning are very scary."

"Ya, I know. I've seen them. I'll be careful. And thanks, Anita. Talk to you later."

While he had Critt's phone in his hands, he used it to Google Kim's location. Seeing the place displayed on Google Maps, he read that it was about a twenty-minute drive. If the Senator was hosting the Secretary of Defense, it meant he undoubtedly had excellent security. But Reader was driving a government vehicle with government license plates plus he had four sets of military identifications. If he was careful, Reader should be able to drive right up to the Senator's house. But first, he had to get rid of the four sleeping bodies in the back of the FBI van.

Still using Critt's phone, he searched for motels in and around Ketchum, Idaho. He wanted some place off the road with privacy where he could unload the bodies without being seen. A single stand-alone cottage would be convenient. It took two minutes, but just south of Ketchum right along the Big Wood River Reader found a motel that fit his requirements. Big Wood River Cabins sported ten individual cabins right on the river promising privacy, and it was only five minutes south of downtown Ketchum.

Big Wood River Cabins looked like it had been built forty or fifty years ago. The cabins reminded Sage of pictures he had seen of hunting lodges cheaply built by hunters used only during deer hunting season. Not the place where government dignitaries would stay. Sage went into the office, which the owner had tried to make modern with new sand-colored linoleum on the floor, polished knotty pine paneling, and a leather sofa to give the place a homey feeling. There were two racks of brochures advertising river rafting trips, bike riding trails, canoe rentals, hiking adventures, local restaurants and skiing lodges. This time of year, was the offseason, and Sage had no trouble renting the most remote cabin barely visible from the office. Sage would love to have used one of the hit team's identifications and charge cards for registration, but he was concerned that when the powers that be discovered that the hit team was missing, someone might check the local motels to see if the team was staying there. Instead, Reader used one of his fake ID's. As he was the only guest, there would be no problem with nosey neighbors.

Warped weathered pine board siding on the outside had seen several coasts of redwood stain. One sagging wooden step led to a faded green door. Inside, a rustic wood floor partially covered with a red and black braided rug held a double bed, two straight back wooden chairs with faded patterned cushions that looked like something from the 1940s. On one wall hung a terrible picture of mount Baldy. The image was of such poor quality; the owner was not concerned about guests walking off with the treasure. One small square window with four panes covered by checkerboard patterned curtains flanked the door. To make the room more inviting, the curtains matched the braided rug.

On each side of the bed stood a small ugly pine nightstand holding a cheap metal lamp with faded yellow shades. Completing the décor was a small Ben Franklin wood-burning stove with a metal ash bucket filled with kindling and two small pine logs. Sage didn't bother checking out the bathroom as he had no plans on visiting the facility, and the temporary guests wouldn't be complaining any too soon.

Backing the FBI van as close to the door as possible, Sage opened the rear door and checking that no one could observe his actions he began dragging the hit team into the dingy room. The bed would only hold two of the four, but as they had all been knocked out, it wouldn't matter to them whether they spent time on the floor or the bed. Since rank has its privileges, and because he was lighter than Brian, Sage dumped Critt on one side of the double bed. Kyle, being the smallest, got hauled in and laid next to Critt. I dumped Peter and Julian one on each side of the bed. Satisfied that the four men would remain undiscovered for a few hours, Sage left and locked the door, hanging a do not disturb sign on the outside knob.

My time had come to visit Kim's ranch and have a talk with the Secretary. There were undoubtedly security guards at the ranch, but no one there knew what The Reader looked like. Stopping by The Sun Valley Lodge to pick up my small gym bag and change into my own clothes, I set out for Adam's Gulch Road. It was there I hoped to learn why the Secretary wanted me dead.

CHAPTER EIGHTEEN
THE PARTY

Thank God for internet maps and phone GPS. It took me twenty-five minutes to reach the ranch. Secretary Kim had chosen well. The scene was very pastoral. Looking at the main buildings from across the Big Wood River, one got a sense of serenity. From Adam's Gulch Road, I could see two guards posted at the river bridge. On the seat beside me was the bag of guns, knives, wallets and phones liberated from the hit team. Going through the wallets, I decided Peter Julien's military I.D. looked enough like me to get past the guards if they should ask for identification. I was banking on the military appearing van bristling with antennas and equipped with government license plates to get me past the guards. With my car idling on the side of the road while preparing myself mentally, a limousine from one of the ski lodges passed me heading towards the ranch. Saying a silent prayer to whatever God's might be, I followed, driving slowly towards the bridge.

Both guards were big burly men with a no-nonsense attitude. When I approached the bridge, they both stood erect, showing off their six-foot heights and toned body's by wearing tight military-green tee shirts. Both had pistols strapped to their belts, and both carried fully automatic rifles held across their chests. The scene would have been intimidating except that even here, nearly two hundred yards from the house, I could feel the party vibrations. The air reeked of excitement. I have never been to a horse race, but I've watched the Kentucky Derby a few times, and the excitement is palpable, even though the TV. One time I went to a bar to watch the race, and the general enthusiasm and party atmosphere was the same kind of feeling I got at the guard station.

One of the drawers in the van held a folder with bright red borders. The folder contained warnings about the nite-nite drugs I used on the hit team. Holding up my folder showing the colorful red edges, I waved at the guards when I got to the bridge.

"Is this senator Kim's ranch?" I tried to sound like a typical government sycophant; it seems is always on the evening news whenever I bothered to watch.

One of the guards approached the driver's side window, and the other guard went back to leaning against the bridge supports.

"Yeah, what ya got?" His voice was not demanding, more curious, which made me feel a whole lot more at ease.

"I don't know. This folder for Secretary Horowitz was dropped off at the Lodge by mistake. They asked me to bring it out for him. I can give it to you if you want."

I counted on the guard being lazy, plus he probably was not supposed to leave his post. In any event, he waved me through with a salute. He probably assumed I belonged in the military given the van I was driving. I saluted him back and headed across the bridge, taking a big breath at the same time. Without realizing it, I had been holding my breath through most of the encounter.

A small rise between the river and the main house provided a decent view of the ranch layout. Senator Kim's house looked like it belonged in Arizona. It featured a prominent Spanish hacienda complete with a red-tiled roof and full wrap-around porch with graceful arches. Sandy colored clay pots full of red geraniums sat under each arch. The house had been constructed in a large U shape with a swimming pool in the center. The pool was open air, but it looked like it might have a retractable roof. I could see a lot of people walking around holding drinks. There were several smaller Spanish style houses scattered about between the Douglas-fir and Lodgepole pine trees behind the main house. Way off in the distances I could just catch the top of a gabled roof which looked like it might be a barn or stable. I suspected that the senator probably had horses for his guests. The house, yard and setting all said MONEY in capital letters.

There were expensive cars parked everywhere. You couldn't turn around without seeing a Lexus, Cadillac, and a Lincoln, and that's not counting all the limousines. I parked the van with the nose pointed out for a quick exit between a Lexus and a Subaru SUV. Even out here in the parking lot, I could hear the laughter and buzz of conversations. It sounded like everyone was having a grand old time.

It turned out the car that entered just ahead of me carried a senator from Oregon. I heard the security guys talking about the people who were here, and one of them mentioned the senator who had just arrived. I followed behind him a few yards as he circled the house, coming in from the backside, next to a large beautiful kidney shaped pool with a blue tile bottom. He had one of those braying voices that carried forever. He immediately went up to a colleague and asked, "is the party all set for tomorrow night?"

"No, haven't you heard? We moved it up to tonight. The fun should start around eight-thirty. Old Kim hired a band and everything."

"Tonight? The senator said, sounding surprised. "What about tomorrow night?"

"The President came back a day early so he'll be in the White House tonight. We moved it up to tonight because there's some asshole called The Reader running around. He reads minds, and Horowitz is afraid with all these congressmen and senators running around town, they might bump into this Reader fellow and have him discover out plans. So, to speak."

The man speaking to the Oregon senator gave me a quizzical look, so I hastily moved off as though looking for someone, holding my folder with the red border highly visible. I kept hoping that no one would ask what the folder contained as it was empty. My only fallback was that it contained classified information.

A bar had been set up under a big red canopy next to the house, and nearly everyone milling about held a cocktail, wine or beer. It seemed like an enjoyable gathering with those doing the milling exuding high spirits in every meaning of the word. I'm not big on politics and have no regard for politicians. Watching them strut around with their pompous attitudes was sickening, and then I saw one of the Supremes. I couldn't remember his name, but I had seen pictures of the Supreme Court justices from time to time, and I recognized one of the members here at Kim's ranch house. He and the Vice President of the United States were huddled in a confidential corner, sharing a laugh at something. I wasn't tuning into anyone in particular right then as I had to continually sweep the energy fields for some threat or a challenge to my presence. I knew this was a high-powered gathering, but I had no idea it includes men of such stature. Not that senators and members of Congress don't have stature, but not like the V.P. and a Supreme. Something big was happening, and I wanted to know what they were so afraid I would learn bumping into someone around town.

Not into politics, I had no idea the President had not been in Washington DC and was returning this evening. What that had to do with anything posed a mystery. I had to find out what was happening and was at a loss as to how to proceed. In reading the surrounding minds, all I could pick up were threads about how wonderful their lives would be tomorrow. It seemed like everyone was getting a promotion. In my imagination, I could associate their feelings with people working in a corporation where the CEO announced a big bonus and salary raise for all of his employees.

I was standing by the side of the pool trying to look frustrated; well okay, I was frustrated, when a girl in tight white shorts and a red tank top with no brassier and lots of cleavage came up and asked me if she could help me in some way. Perhaps get me a drink? She was pretty in a farm-girl kind of way with freckles and a warm smile.

Being unsophisticated in the male-female relationship business, I couldn't tell if her question implied something besides a drink. To play it safe, I pretended ignorance. Besides, with my folder surrounded by bright red borders and my general body physique, I was hoping she thought of me as being a military man.

"I'm supposed to drop this off with some big army general, but I don't see him anywhere." There were plenty of uniforms both inside and outside by the cars to make my statement believable.

Giving me a full wattage smile while making sure I had a good view of her ample bosom, she replied, "I think all the generals who were supposed to come are here already." I returned her smile with my own full wattage smile while acting like she was the hottest thing in Sun Valley, I asked in all innocence, "What's happening at 8:30?"

"Boy, you are out of it, aren't you? I thought everybody here knew already. It's supposed to be a secret, but with that being said, that's the only thing people are talking about, it's hard not to overhear. The President will drink his cocktail tonight at ten o'clock as usual; only tonight, it will have a little extra." (giggle, giggle) "Enough to put him into the ground for good." In saying this with a scowl, everything I previously saw as pretty about her vanished.

It was common knowledge that the President adhered to a strict routine. Every night at precisely ten o'clock, one of his secret service agents made him a Jack Daniel's cocktail, the Gentleman's Brew. With the Bitters and Ginger Beer, it was unlikely that he would notice a few drops of a special drug developed by the CIA, which mimicked a heart attack. After a couple of sips, it wouldn't matter, anyway. He'd be dead.

This whole gathering suddenly made sense; The V.P., a Supreme Court Justice, plus the giddy mood. Tonight, they were going to kill the President and swear in the V.P. as the new President. Ten o'clock in Washington, DC, was eight o'clock in Sun Valley. Give the President a few minutes to die and be declared dead before someone in Washington would call Sun Valley, and the party could begin. Those in attendance here were those promoting the President's death; they are the ones who would benefit from a regime change. That they were celebrating the death of their President was sickening.

What could I do?

Excusing myself from the suddenly ugly girl, I made my way as officiously as possible, waving the red-bordered folder as though it was a sword granting me special privileges. Once outside, I hurried to the FBI van and drove off, hoping no one would pay attention to my hasty exit. The guards didn't even move as I got to the bridge. They only worried about cars going the other way.

It was now nearly one o'clock in Sun Valley, making it three o'clock in Washington. In seven hours, the President was scheduled to be murdered. Was there any way I could stop this insanity?

Chapter Nineteen
Flying Blind

The only way I could think of to stop the assassination of the President was to tell him of the plan. But how? One did not just pick up the telephone and call the President of the United States. Especially someone named Sage with no real identification. Seven hours, and the clock just keeps on revolving. How in the hell could I stop this assassination?

Someone had to tell the President what was happening. But who? I didn't know anybody who could talk to the President. There was no one I could call. I knew that if I could somehow speak to the President, I could convince him of the truth. By reading his mind, I could tell him things about himself and his marriage that no one else knew. If I could gain his trust, I could get him to react. The proof would be when the Secret Service agent fixed his evening cocktail. After mixing the drink, the President would order the agent to drink it himself. But how do I get in to see the President? I sure couldn't do that in Sun Valley, Idaho.

Wyatt was still a little traumatized by the visit of Critt and his team. Sitting in his office, he was going over everything that had happened, and he was convinced that someone in his company was responsible for The Reader missing their appointment. The problem was, the only person who knew the Reader was coming to Sun Valley was Kurt Flanders, the partner at Samuel, Ratcliff and Hamilton responsible for overseeing Sawtooth Ski Resort. It was inconceivable that Kurt would be opposed to Reader's visit; after all, it was Kurt who was responsible for the Reader being here. Kurt did work in an office with several other managers plus the senior partners. It was possible that one or more of the firm's employees knew about the Reader's visit and pulled the alarm switch. But who could that be? And why? Mulling this information over in his mind, he was startled when his secretary informed him over the intercom that he had a call. He told her he wasn't taking any calls. She then told him it was The Reader who sounded desperate.

Picking up the receiver, he said, "hello, this is Wyatt." Even to himself, he sounded stressed. He was anxious that perhaps The Reader had connected the problems he faced to someone at Sawtooth, and that was the reason he called.

"Wyatt, this is The Reader. I'm sorry for ducking our meeting this morning. Hopefully, you got the message from Katrina."

"Was that her name? She didn't introduce herself, but yes, she did tell me you couldn't make our meeting. Is everything okay? I had a visit from four tough-looking men who were looking for you."

"Yes, I'm fine. Thank you. Wyatt, I stumbled onto something pretty serious, and I really, really need to use your airplane for the rest of the day. Would that be possible.? I will reimburse you for the expenses and whatever you might charge. I'll even throw in the free consultation we have been planning. Could I please borrow your plane and pilot?"

Wyatt felt a sense of relief. Reader wasn't calling about someone at Sawtooth, causing him grief. "My God Reader, where are you going? What's the big problem.?"

"Sorry, Wyatt, but I don't trust these telephones to be secure. I know how NSA and probably every other government agency with alphabet initials are probably monitoring every telephone conversation. I'm using a borrowed phone they would have no reason to be monitoring, but I'm not too sure about your phone."

"That's sounding serious, Reader." In his office, Wyatt was breaking out into a sweat. Would he be in trouble if he let Reader use the company plane? It probably would not be a secret for long.

"It is serious, Wyatt. I wish I could describe the circumstances, but it's best for both of us if I don't say anymore. Keywords trigger an automatic instant tap for any phone conversation. How about the plane? I promise to tell you everything when I return. And Wyatt, if you let me have your plane, I promise you, you will not regret it."

Wyatt was sweating freely now, wiping the sweat from his brow with the sleeve of his shirt. If the Reader was desperate enough to ask for his airplane, it must be dire. He didn't know much about the Reader; and letting a perfect stranger have the use of the company's sixty-five-million-dollar aircraft was not a rational decision. Still, his company was already in deep trouble, and unless his problems were solved shortly, letting the Reader use the plane would be the least of his worries. "Sure, okay, Reader. I'll have to call my pilot. It may take a half-hour or so for him to get to the airport and get the plane ready."

"That's okay. I'm a little out of town myself, and it will probably take me that long to get to the airport."

"Hey Reader," Wyatt sounded stressed, like he was about to undergo a colonoscopy, "what's your destination so I can tell the pilot. He has to make a flight plan."

Reader had to think for a minute. He didn't dare say Washington DC. Those words were likely trigger words in NSA search programs that would have the government examine their whole conversation. While he hadn't said too much regarding his problem, the fact that he was in Sun Valley heading to DC was probably all that would be needed to start a full-scale investigation. Better to keep it sterile for now.

"How about Miami, Florida?" With all of his reading and television watching, Reader was confident that once in the air, he could have the pilot reroute them to DC.

"Okay, I'll tell the pilot. Good luck on whatever it is you're doing."

Wyatt turned off his cell, thankful that the call had ended. Whatever the outcome, he was committed. Having delivered the company's sixty-five-million-dollar plane into the hands of a man he had never met was nerve-wracking. Not getting this stranger even to sign a rental or lease agreement was practically criminal. No deposit. No credit cards on file. Nothing. The tension in his body, coupled with the anxious feelings about his actions, had him in a real quandary. What would Kurt and the company do when they found out; and they were bound to find out sooner or later? His only solace, if you could call it that, was a rule he remembered reading from a poster by Bob Parsons he had hanging on the wall of his room at college. It was Parson's rules for success and part of Rule number four was a saying from Parson's father; 'Well Robert, if it doesn't work, they can't eat you.' For some crazy reason, that weird saying of Parson's dad brought a little smile to his lips, helping him relax a bit. They couldn't eat him.

Sage raced to the airport, anxious to get in the air. He had less than seven hours to figure out how to reach the President.

Chapter Twenty
Dialing for Help

By the time Sage reached the airport, the pilot already had Sawtooth's plane at the gate waiting for him. The pilot was standing by the stairs leading into the plane. Reader didn't recognize the pilot as he had never laid eyes on the man, but he would always remember that plane.

Heading to the stairway, Sage held out his hand to the pilot, telling him he was the passenger. Shaking hands, the pilot informed Sage that his name was Captain Fremont. Sage introduced himself as Sage, hoping that in whatever conversations the pilot might engage in with control towers along their route, the name Sage would not ring any bells. He was not sure whether the pilot had to inform the tower of his passenger's name, but it was better to be safe than worry about what the name Reader might provoke.

They entered the plane, and the pilot gestured towards the seats telling Sage to make himself comfortable. "We're heading to Miami, correct?"

"Once we are in the air, will you be able to change routes?" Sage tried to sound nonchalant, hoping the pilot would not detect the anxiety he was experiencing.

"Oh yes, it happens all the time. Want to tell me now or wait until we are in the air?" The pilot's voice had a dry soft, comforting tone suggesting that everything was just as it should be. The voice tone you hear from the pilots in the movie The Right Stuff.

"I'll tell you in the air if that's okay?" Sage responded, happy to know that so far, his plan was working. To say he had a plan would be stretching it, but getting a ride to DC was the first part. He could not talk to the President stuck here in Sun Valley. Now that Sage had a ride, he only needed to visit the President. How in the hell was he going to get in to see the President? He didn't know anyone in Washington, and there was no way he could walk up to the White House and ask to visit with the President. He knew he wouldn't get within a hundred yards of the White House, let alone the President. And who was he going to call? Anybody with that kind of access might be part of the conspiracy to kill the President.

Sage could experience the plane taking off, and once they had leveled off, he made his way into the cabin.

"Captain Fremont, I need to go to Washington, DC, and I need to land at National AirPort."

Regan National was the closest airport to Washington and the White House, but it was off-limits to most commercial and private planes. It had once been the main DC airport, but as the government grew, so did their need for airplane transportation. The traffic at National became more than the airport could handle, which led the government to build Dulles Airport. Dulles Airport was built in Loudoun and Fairfax Counties Virginia. It was convenient that Speaker John Foster Dulles happened to own several hundred acres of undeveloped land there which he was happy to sell to the government for a substantial amount of money.

"I don't know about National, Sage; it's off-limits for our kind of travel."

"I know that Captain, but this is truly an emergency." Sage figured that he needed to be as close to the White House as possible as every second counted, and he still had to make his way from the airport to the White House.

"I'll see what I can do, but no promises," the Captain responded. "What is the nature of the emergency?"

"Oh, God, Captain. I wish I could tell you, but if I told you, I'm sure you know the old saw about the need to kill you afterword. I know that is not exactly the quote from the old movie." He said this with a lop-sided smile, hoping the Captain had a sense of humor.

"I like those spooky stories the best," the Captain grinned back. But I need to have some reasonable explanations for landing at National.

"How about changing course and let me think about the reason for a bit? I cannot tell you the real reason without endangering your life. After tonight it won't make any difference. Does this plane have a transponder that tells the ground where we are and where we're heading?"

"Yes. That's an FAA regulation. The transponder does not give our final destination, but it tells the ground our position, heading, and speed. Why do you ask?"

"The people who pose a great danger to me, and so to you and this plane, would be a lot more than unhappy if they learned I was in the air heading for DC. If we're lucky, they may not know I'm missing, however, I've already had several surprises today, and a few more may be in store. It would be better for all if you could turn the transponder off before changing directions."

"That's definitely against regulations, but I guess we could have a malfunction. Happens regularly with some planes."

"Great, let's have a malfunction if that's okay with you. Then head for DC and National."

"Okay, you're the boss. Wyatt said to take you to where ever you wanted to go. I'll change course now and try to come up with some plausible explanation. You do the same."

"Sure thing, Captain. Talk to you later."

Sage went into the back towards the gallery. He hadn't eaten since breakfast, and although he only ate once or twice a day, all of this morning's adventures had built up an appetite. Rummaging around in the drawers and cabinets, Sage found the makings for a ham and cheese sandwich. Doing work in the kitchen, preparing food was meditation for Sage, and he used this time to figure out a way to reach the President. He didn't know anybody to call. Who could he call who would know somebody to call who had that kind of access? Thinking about that as he spread mayo and mustard on the artesian bread found in the cabinet, Sage remembered reading about some bloggers in the DC area who seemed to have a connection with one another. Maybe he could reach one of them.

Grabbing a can of Mountain Time Golden Ale from the refrigerator, a local Sawtooth brewery favorite, Sage headed further back to one of the big comfortable white leather chairs with a work table in front. Sitting down, he took a bite of his sandwich and started Googling bloggers in Washington, D.C. There were dozens of hits on Google, but most of them were duds. The bloggers only had a few dozen, or sometimes a few hundred followers which would not be the horse-power Sage needed. Taking a sip from his can of beer, Sage kept looking. By the time he was halfway through his sandwich and beer, he was getting discouraged when he came across a name, Herbert Riverton, known as Herbie. Perfect. Somehow it made cosmic sense that his blogger would also be called Herbie. He wondered if this Herbie had the same feelings about his nickname as Sage had felt about his. He figured probably not. It would be too easy to use some other handle if he found the name Herbie offensive. Herbie had over five thousand subscribers to his blog, PSITHURISM, plus another couple thousand who checked in from time to time to get his opinion on the news of the day. The blog name was perfect for Washington DC. The sound of wind rustling leaves in the trees.

Getting Herbie's phone number was easy, but Sage figured a blogger probably spent most of his time on the computer and might respond to an email request faster.

HERBIE, ARE YOU AVAILABLE FOR YOUR SHOT AT A PULITZER?

Sage had to wait for almost five agonizing minutes before getting a response. He was so nervous it was difficult to eat his sandwich. His mouth was so dry it required another beer from the refrigerator.

WHO IS THIS?

Holy shit, he answered. Sage almost spit out his last bite of sandwich.

MY NAME IS SAGE, AND I HAVE A PULITZER WINNING STORY FOR YOU.

I couldn't say The Reader as I had to assume that all of Herbie's communication lines were monitored. If there is a computer program in the NSA or CIA or FIB or somewhere with trigger words, the name Reader would probably be on that list. This time Herbie answered almost immediately.

BULLSHIT. I'VE NEVER HEARD OF YOU.

CAN I CALL YOU TO DISCUSS THE DETAILS?

Sage figured he would have him hooked if he could only get him on the phone.

OKAY. YOU GOT MY NUMBER?

YEP. RIGHT HERE. STAND BY.

Using Critt's cell phone, Sage dialed the number pulled from the blogger's website and waited for Herbie to answer.

"All right, hot-shot." Not a friendly salutation. He sounded pissed and disturbed, as though I had interrupted something great. "This better be good. I don't have time for your bull shit."

"Hi, Herbie. It's good to talk to you. Before we go any further, let me introduce myself. I can see you looking at porn while sitting in a dirty cream-colored lounger, downstairs, with a generic laptop covering your legs. You're wearing polka-dot shorts, which is the only clothing on your body. Look across the room, Herbie," – here Sage was directing the blogger to look so he could read his mind– "you have a picture of the Lincoln Memorial hanging next to one of the Jefferson Memorial. How am I doing?"

Herbie sounded disturbed but not yet a true believer. "Anybody could have walked in here and told you all that stuff."

"Yeah, Herbie, but no one walked in and told me that stuff or the fact that your mother is upstairs is right now fixing you a late afternoon snack of hot dogs and corn chips."

"So okay wise guy, (I knew I was getting close to setting the hook) what do you want?" Herbie sounded more inclined to listen, but I wasn't sure I had the hook set deep enough.

"Listen, Herbie. I need a small favor. But before we go any further, let me tell you I am sitting on the most explosive story of your lifetime. Hell, it's the most explosive story of the past hundred years. Unfortunately, this story has a very brief span before it hits the news big time. You have only a few minutes to get in front of this story and ride it to a Pulitzer, or it will be lost forever."

"Yeah, if you have that kind of story, why are you calling me?" He sounded peevish.

"I told you I needed a small favor. Well, here is the sixty-four-million-dollar question. This is the reason why I am calling you. Do you know someone in Washington DC with the stature to call and get a late evening meeting with the leader of the free world?" I couldn't say President as that name like Reader was probably on the trigger list.

"Are you shiten me? What the hell has that got to do with anything?"

"Listen, Herbie, if you ever thought about hitting the big time, now is your chance, but you have to pay attention. So I know I have your full attention, I won't tell anybody about the fact that you're fucking your mother."

"YOU TOTAL FUCK." He shouted over the phone in over-all shock. "What do you want?" Much more subdued. Now he sounded frightened.

"I need to get in to visit with our countries leader as soon as possible. The sooner, the better. It has to be tonight. Before the evening gets too late. I'm on my way to DC. I need someone who has the power to call this person and get in right away. Now, do you know anybody like that or not?"

"Why do you need to see the President? I can tell you there is no way you can smuggle a weapon into the White House."

I'm not sure where this weapon business came from. I suspect in my new friend Herbie's world, that would be the only reason someone wanted an evening pass to see the President.

"Herbie, I don't want to kill the man, and please refrain from using that word for him. It isn't safe. But I cannot say anymore on the telephone. My phone is probably safe, but I imagine every government agency in Washington is listening to your phone and tapping into your computer network, hoping to get a heads up on your next big scoop. Now, so you know now I am the real deal; your mother just entered the basement carrying your snack. She's wearing a blue halter-top and black stretch pants. She's pretty hot."

I lied. It was like I was in his body, watching his mother come down the stairs. No, not really, but his subconscious was sending out so many signals it was like I could see her in the flesh, so to speak. Pinched face with stringy blond hair in a ponytail and pendulous boobs. Through the phone, I could feel Herbie getting aroused just watching his mom enter the room with her swinging breasts.

"I can see why you like to get her into bed. Now, do you know anybody in Washington with the kind of power I am asking about?"

I could tell that Herbie was beside himself with run-a-muck emotions. He didn't know whether to shit-or-go-blind as my real dad would say.

"Well yeah. I might know somebody like that." He was not committing unless he knew more.

"Okay, look. A few hours ago, I stumbled on something that will probably blow this country apart. We have only a few hours in which to avoid a real, and I mean a genuine catastrophe. It is not possible to discuss this on the telephone without risking both of our lives, plus it might even trigger the very event I am trying to prevent. I may already have said too much. Please trust me. I could not know these things I said about you unless I had a special gift. Surely you can see that."

I think he was hooked, but I still needed a lot more from him. I needed somebody who would bust ass. The mention of his mother was the turning point. No one was ever supposed to know about that.

"What do you want?" Angry but ready to get on board.

"First, you need to find out if this person you know is in Washington. You may not know that several of the big wheels in Washington are out of town."

"Nothing is going on that I don't know about," he said rather bristly, like maybe I had insulted his power as a great blogger. "Let me check out my sources. I'll call my contact. You want me to call you back?"

"Yes, either way. Provided your source is in town, ask him or her if they know where the Vice President is at this very moment?" Should they don't know or think he is in town, we might go to the next step. If they know the VP is out of town, hang up immediately and hope like hell no one was monitoring your call. I should tell you, that if you cannot trust your source, your life might be in danger."

"Jesus, Sage. What are you getting me into?

"Hopefully, a Pulitzer. You know the old saying, you can't make, and omelet without...anyway make the damn call. We don't have a lot of time, and if you bomb out, I have to try somebody else."

"What if my source thinks the VP is in town?

"Then ask this person if they will meet me to discuss a very real, a severe national problem. All you need to do is get your contact to meet me. It's my job to convince the contact to make the call I asked about earlier. But your contact has to have the standing or be able to call and get into see our leader this evening. You can attend and get the scoop of your life. But we have to get in to see the man this evening – early. After that, disaster strikes, and there is no putting the genie back in this bottle."

"What do I tell my source to get them to call the leader you are talking about and set up a meeting?

"Good question, Herbie. You catch on quickly and don't tell your source a God dammed thing. You are not to convince the source to call the man. That is my job. Tell your source you know someone with confidential information for him, and him alone, that must be delivered in person tonight to avoid a major catastrophe. You can vouch for me now that you know my powers. Please do not mention any of this on the telephone with your source. Say that you have verified evidence that I am telling you the truth. No need to specify what that evidence is. Tell your source that once we meet, I will tell both of you all the facts concerning this catastrophe and can convince you of its authenticity before we meet with the man. If they or you are not completely blown away by my story, you can kick me out of the car and go your merry way. Please make the call now."

"Is that all?" Herbie was sounding a little excited but still lost in a daze.

"Yes, that's about it. Oh, and this is very important. If you get your source interested, please tell them not to make the call until we meet. We know for a fact that the person I am talking about will have telephones that are being monitored, and the wrong word on the phone could start the whole ugly chain of events. Your source must be able to convince the man to have this evening's meeting without being too specific. The reason for the meeting must have something to do with their position in the government. Not anything to do with a national emergency. Have you got that?"

We ended the conversation, and I waited with great anticipation for Herbie's return call. If this didn't work, I didn't know what to do. God, I hated to depend on a pervert named Herbie for all of what was to happen. My original mother always used to say, 'God works in mysterious ways.' I truly felt that this was a situation my mom would call mysterious, not to mention ridiculous.

I figured it would take Herbie a few minutes to make his call and find out if we had a rendezvous. In the meantime, I went forward to the cockpit and sat in the copilot's seat.

"What's the good word, Captain?"

To say I was starting to feel pushed would be an understatement. Somehow, someone found out I was meeting Wyatt and sent a hit team to dispose of my life and body. I discovered the reason for this action, but still did not understand who knew what, or who was pulling strings. If they found out I was still alive, and headed for Washington, DC.; I could expect someone to shoot me out of the sky. To save the President's life and prevent a catastrophe, I had to see the President in person before 10:00 pm, and all of my hopes were resting on some pervert blogger with my old hated nickname. I needed the Captain to give me some good news for a change.

"I've turned off the transponder and changed course for DC. Our current ground control tower is Omaha, and they keep asking for position and destination. I've lied about our position and told them we are still on course for Miami. Haven't gotten permission to land at National, but still working the problem. When asked for a reason for landing there, I told them I had a High government person on board with an emergency meeting at the Capitol. That's where we stand at the moment."

"What is our ETA for National at present?

"Flight time is a bit over four hours. More like four and a half because we spent some time heading towards Miami, but that's not too much of a deviation. We've been in the air a little over one hour, so our expected time to reach DC is 5:45, local time. We could pick up a little time from the jet stream, but I may have to deviate up ahead to miss a thunderstorm, although, at our height, it may not be necessary. If we have to change course, it could add about another ten minutes or more to the flight"

"Okay. That's great. I'll figure-ground time at six pm. Let me know when you find out about the airport. Getting in at six leaves me four hours to accomplish my task once I'm on the ground. I'll probably need every second, so landing at Dulles would be terrible. Especially with the traffic."

"I'll let you know as soon as I hear something."

The Captain looked over at me and smiled. There were multiple expressions on his face, and I could read his mind. He was nervous about our flight and concerned about the FAA and the transponder being turned off. That could cause him to lose his flight license, but unlikely. His smile was one of hope and best wishes. I could see and feel that he wished me well while being fidgety and starting to show a little forehead sweat.

As I was getting up to go back to the main cabin, I put my hand on his shoulder and gave it a small pat and returned his smile. "We'll make it work, Captain. By this time tomorrow, you could be a hero." ***Or possibly dead***, but I didn't say that.

Back in my seat, I picked up my unfinished drink and took a swallow. Waiting for Herbie's call was eating at my soul. If he failed, I didn't have a backup plan. I suppose I could try another blogger, but I didn't see anyone on my initial search with better credentials. And I didn't dare call up my California congressional representative. For all, I knew he would be part of the Cabal. I got up and paced up and down the aisle, trying to think of some other plan of action in case Herbie bombed out.

Six hours and losing time. In six hours, they will kill the President of the United States unless I can somehow reach him before he takes that fatal drink. Who am I? Sage is a made-up name with no history, no driver's license, no SS number, no address; in short, Sage is a man who doesn't exist. My fake alibi names are no better. The SS numbers are false, as is the address and everything else on my driver's license. My real name would mean no more since it also does not have an SS number, address, or any meaningful data.

How does a nobody reach the United States President in six hours with a message to save his life? My best hope is a sex addict fucking his mother. Heaven help us...I guess it's time to pray.

CHAPTER TWENTY-ONE
BAD NEWS

Menlo Park 2:00 p.m. local time

Honey was not accustomed to feelings of inferiority or anxiety either, but right now, she was feeling a little of both. "My good damn God,' she thought; 'my plane took that fucking Reader to Sun Valley, and he could wreck the whole thing.' While she was remonstrating with herself for something she might have done wrong, her very private cell phone rang.

"Honey."

"You say the sweetest things, darling. This is Ray." Under normal circumstances, Ray would not have been nearly this fresh with a customer, especially one with the stature of Honey Samuels. But Ray had been smoking grass and had a few too many Jack Daniels and coke which had him spinning somewhere in the clouds.

"This better be good, Rayess, and I sure ain't your darling." You could practically cut paper with her sharp reprimand. Using his full name was a signal that you better watch yourself.

"Sorry, Honey, that just sorta slipped out. Having a little too much fun here. Thought you'd like to know about your Reader feller."

She waited about five seconds before exploding. "We'll for fucksake, what is it?" Honey had been doing a little of her own imbibing, and although she rarely let it show, just now with a stoned drunk on the line, she wasn't that careful.

"Got a call from a buddy in Sun Valley. I had him keep watch on that plane you are interested in and told him to definitely watch out for that Reader feller. He told me the plane left Sun Valley at about one o'clock local time heading for Miami. The plane had one passenger. The flight plan did not list a name for the passenger, but people at the airport said the plane left with the same man who was on the plane last night. They say someone heard him referred to as The Reader."

"My God Ray, it's damned near two o'clock here, which means the fucking plane has been in the air for two hours, and I'm just now getting a call?" She was sobering up quickly.

"Sorry, Honey, but I just got the call myself. I was lucky even to catch this guy as he was preparing to take off for a few days. I don't know why the delay in reporting the plane's departure."

"Well," Honey relented a little as Ray usually did first-class work, and she valued his honesty, "thanks for the call Ray. It may not make any difference, but if anything else comes up, please let me know."

"Sure thing, Honey," but she had already killed the call.

Sun Valley Idaho 3:10 local time

Roger Horowitz, who usually never had more than a sip or two of hard liquor at any public function to never let himself be caught in an embarrassing verbal slip, had violated his strict behavior code on this celebratory occasion. They were mere hours away from celebrating a new President, who he had in his back pocket, along with the very drunk colleagues surrounding him, so he had given himself a small tap-out. As he walked around the pool, admiring the nearly naked girls that had shown up from somewhere his private cell phone range.

"Horowitz."

"Roger, it's Honey. I may have some unpleasant news. The Reader is on a plane headed for Miami."

"That's impossible, Honey. The Reader man just disappeared."

"Are you certain, Roger?" I just got a call from one of my detective friends who told me our plane left the Sun Valley Airport over two hours ago carrying The Reader as the only passenger."

"Well, hell, Honey. Anything's possible, but I got a call from the team leader over two hours ago who assured me that this Reader man just disappeared."

"I'm just passing the information on as I get it, Roger. If it's incorrect, then I'm sorry, but I can only report what I hear."

"Yeah, I'm sorry, Honey. Didn't mean to bark at you. I'll check back, but I sure the hell hope you're wrong."

Roger lost no time in finding a secluded place to call back the number on his phone left by Critt's phone call earlier.

Sage was startled to feel a buzzing in his shirt pocket; then, the phone started ringing. He picked it up before realizing that it was Critt's phone. Who would be calling Critt while he was supposed to be on a mission? Surely not his wife or friends. But what if it was some emergency? He had to answer to stall the beginning of a search party to find the missing hit team.

"Critt, here." At least that was how Sage imagined a tough special forces man would answer the phone.

"This is Secretary Horowitz. Captain, you reported the successful conclusion of your business a few hours ago. Did you not?"

"Yes, sir mister Secretary." Sage felt that the less said, the better. And what had prompted this call? A feeling of unease settled over Sage as he could feel the uncertainty and doubt in the Secretary's mind.

"How do I know I am talking to Captain Critt Rayess and not someone who has his telephone?"

Sage gasped and had to cover the mouthpiece quickly. The surprise phone call left him no time to think about the situation and have an answer. What was he supposed to say? How to respond to such a question? What would the real Captain Rayess say in response to such a problem?

Afraid his pause in responding might have already given him away; Sage plunged ahead before he chickened out entirely and ended the call. "Well, mister Secretary, what would make you think someone else has my private phone?"

"A phone call I just received suggested you might have failed in your mission. Where are you now, Captain?" The Secretary sounded like he knew he was being played.

"Well, Sir, we're just getting back from the desert. Had a little errand to run over to the lava flats for disposal action. Getting our gear sorted out now ready to return to base."

Sage hoped like hell what he was saying made sense, but he could feel that the Secretary was suspicious. All the vibrations showed Horowitz was having a problem believing this was Critt on the phone.

"And what military base would that be Captain?" Horowitz believed that if someone had confiscated the Captain's cell phone, he was unlikely to know the base where Critt was stationed.

Sage was momentarily stumped as he had not read the killers minds to know where they were stationed. At the time he confronted them, this was not an important issue. Surely somewhere in the mess of wallets, papers and equipment he had confiscated, there was a mention of the team's base. But that information was all back in Sun Valley. It took a moment for him to realize the answer was in the Secretary's mind.

"Why mister Secretary, all four of us are stationed at Mountain Home."

Sage was worried that his long pause was another tell. What triggered the Secretary to be suspicious in the first place? Someone may have seen the Reader after he was supposed to be dead, perhaps someone at Kim's ranch. But nobody there knew what the Reader looked like. Everybody in on the plot to kill the President must have been warned to watch out for some fellow who reads minds, but all they could have was a vague description. Sage had learned that even his killers did not have his picture. What did trigger the Secretary's suspicions? It was impossible for Sage to know what had caused Horowitz suspicions. Still, it was clear that the man had severe doubts about who he was talking with on the phone.

Horowitz realized that if there was even a remote chance he was talking with the Reader, everything in his head was an open book. Not wanting to take a chance that his mind was being read, and with no way of determining the truth by talking with the person on the phone, Horowitz ended the call with a terse, "thank you" speaking to the air while the phone was being put away. He was almost sure that the person he had been talking with was not Captain Rayess, but just in case, it was best to not disrespect the military, and a couple terse words spoken in the air would suffice.

Mountain Home Air Base

The secure red phone on Colonel Hill's desk rang again for the second time in two days. "Colonel Hill."

"Colonel, Secretary Horowitz. Have you heard from the team you sent to Sun Valley yesterday?"

"Well, no mister Secretary. We rarely keep tabs with a team in the field unless they need some specific information or directions."

"Could you get in touch with your team to verify their position? I have reason to suspect they may not have succeeded. Get back to me at once."

"Yes sir, mister Secretary. Right away." The call was ended.

Ten minutes later, the Secretary's phone buzzed. "Horowitz."

"I am afraid you are right in your fears, mister Secretary. I have been unable to make contact with any member of the team I sent to Sun Valley. What would you like me to do?"

"I don't mean to be shitty about this Colonel, but I was told you had the finest, toughest, best trained, and most experienced special forces personnel available."

"Yes sir, mister Secretary. I always thought so as well."

"Get the FBI to put out a trace on their van and have another team fly into Sun Valley and begin a search for the missing men. I can't believe some asswipe named The Reader could take out four such highly trained men, but the simplest answer is usually the right answer."

"I'll get on the van issue right away, mister Secretary, sir." But he was talking to a dead phone.

Sun Valley Idaho—Kim's ranch

Doctor Azem Dushaj is the Secretary of Transportation, which is responsible for the FAA. Secretary Dushaj was also a guest at Senator Kim's ranch and a vital member of the conspiracy ready to assassinate the President. Horowitz did a frantic search for his colleague before spotting him at the poolside, admiring the voluptuous view of a well-endowed young lady. Grabbing the Secretary's shoulder in a firm grip, Horowitz whispered in the doctor's ear, "come with me. We may have a problem."

After walking Azem to a more secluded spot, Horowitz laid out the problem. "It looks like that Reader asshole we've been trying to find is on a plane heading for Miami. I need you to contact your buddies in the FAA and find out where that airplane is at this moment. It's a G-650 owned by Sawtooth Business Resorts located in Sun Valley, Idaho. I have the plane's identification on this paper," which he handed to Azem. "Let's take a stroll while we wait for an answer."

The two secretaries walked towards the base of the hill near the stables while Azem called Katie Wilcockson, the Acting Administrator for the FAA, who in turn had to call the CEO of the Air Traffic Organization, the group responsible for the nation's air navigational srvices. Horowitz and Azem could do nothing but sweat and swear while waiting to hear back from the FAA. They were both startled when Azem's telephone started bleeping like a strangled dog. "Sorry about that," Azem said with a sheepish grin on his face as he answered the call. "I wanted a signal to get my attention. It looks like I succeeded."

For the impatient Secretary Horowitz, the call lasted far longer than should have been necessary until finally, Secretary Azem said into the receiver, "okay, hold on for a minute Katie." After making sure the cell phone's speaker was turned off, he turned to Horowitz, "I'm sorry, Roger, but the plane you were asking about took off from Sun Valley about two-and-a-half hours ago headed for Miami, Florida. After being in the air for about thirty minutes, the pilot radioed the control tower responsible for traffic in the region that the airplane was in at the moment announcing some troubling electrical disturbances, and he turned off his transponder. There has been no contact with the plane since that broadcast."

To say that Horowitz was upset would be a severe understatement. His face was beet red from pure anger with the blood vessels in his neck pulsing with every heartbeat. At issue was the fact that if the President were notified of the proposed coupe, his life as he knew it would be over. "We've got to find that bastard, wherever he is," he snarled in a voice and tone that would boil water. "I will assume that about the time he turned off the transponder was when they changed course for Washington, DC. Have the FAA see if they can pinpoint that spot and then start checking control towers between that location and DC. See if the pilot called in for a course change or for any information that would help us find out where that plane is now."

Azem stood in a daze looking at Horowitz until the Secretary barked, "anytime now, mister Secretary." Remembering the cell phone in his hand, Azem started barking orders to poor Katie, who did not understand what she had done wrong.

After Azem's call to Katie was terminated with further instructions, Horowitz, who, while fuming had turned away from the conversation, turned back around putting his arm around the shoulders of the smaller Azem. "We've got a problem, Azem. Stay in touch with the FAA in case they come up with something. I need to call someone in the Pentagon and get started tracking that plane. Our guys can estimate the speed of that plane and figure out where it should be in the sky. Hell, the CIA or the FCC can trace their cell phones and pinpoint their location. We'll have the bugger shot out of the sky before he even sees Chicago."

CHAPTER TWENTY-TWO
PLAN B

In the main cabin, Sage laid stretched out on one of the white couches breathing a relaxation exercise to control anxiety. The stress of waiting on Herbie was forcing him to utilize the mental discipline learned in martial arts when he heard an announcement from the pilot.

"Mister Reader, could you come up to the cockpit for a minute? Now! It's pretty important."

Sage had no idea what could be that important, and with all the angst that went with waiting for Herbie to call, he didn't need any more bad news. Time was flying fast, with the President scheduled to die in five and a half hours. And now something important from Fremont. "Shit," Sage was muttering to himself.

Taking a final deep breath and slowly letting it out while releasing the remaining tension in his body Sage stood up, making his way to the forward cabin.

"What is it, Captain?" Sage asked, sinking into the copilot's seat while hoping for something harmless, but expecting bad news.

"The FAA has been trying to contact me over the radio asking for our position. I've not responded, but I'm starting to worry about what they might do. I'm sure by now they are aware of our course change. What do you want me to do?"

It was clear that Captain Fremont was having second thoughts about the entire flight and especially turning off the Transponder. Sage sat in the copilot's seat and thought about their situation.

Somebody had been keeping close tabs on his location, even tracking him to Sun Valley. They knew about his plane ride, and by now, they probably knew he had commandeered the plane for another trip. If these were the people responsible for planning to kill the President, they would guess his destination was Washington DC. Since they knew next to nothing about Sage, they could not see if he had any connections in DC or not. They would have to assume that he did. Therefore, he could not be allowed to reach DC. Would they shoot down an unarmed civilian plane? Hell, yes. Given the alternative, hell, hell, yes. What to do?

Turning to face Captain Fremont Sage decided his only hope was to tell Fremont everything. If his reasoning was accurate, Fremont's life was also on the line.

"Captain Fremont. I'm sorry, but I believe our problems are much more severe than you realize. I did not think they would find out about this trip so quickly." With that said, Sage started by telling Fremont his name and describing his incredible talent and how that had led him to Sun Valley. He spoke of the attempts on his life this morning and how he had handled the situation. Then Sage explained his visit to Senator Kim's ranch, trying to find out who wanted him dead and why. When Sage got to the part where he overheard the plot to kill the President, he could tell the pilot was having second thoughts.

"Captain Fremont, would you like to see Mandy and Chuck grow up and become adults? Are you and Arlene happy in your married life together? And how about your two dogs, Quigley and Fletcher? I'm sure you have a lot to live for."

Sage could see the Captain starting to get upset. In a moment the Captain said, "what the hell? Who are you, and how do you know about my personal life?"

"I told you, captain. You know that I am called The Reader. I read people. I just read your mind. Now, do you believe me?"

Fremont had a lot to digest and, while intelligent, wasn't the fastest thinker on the planet. Sage could see the emotions play across his face as he processed the information just received. After giving the Captain a couple of minutes to consider what he had so recently heard, Sage asked, "Captain if what I told you is the truth, what do you suppose those people planning to kill the President will do, when they discover the location of this plane?"

If the situation weren't so dangerous and sick, the expressions now canvassing the Captain's face of utter confusion would be funny. He had to assume that Sage was not making up this unusual tale. In that case, he knew the answer.

"They are going to shoot us out of the air, aren't they?"

"Yes," Sage replied, with a sadness he did not understand, "I think so. And now, let's get all the cell phones turned off. We know they can track the damn things everywhere. Give me your cell, and I'll get mine. I may have a couple or three."

Fremont dug his cell out of his case on the floor, handing it to Sage. Sage returned to his seat and grabbing Critt's phone, and both of his, removed the batteries from each phone, then the sim cards. With this chore accomplished, he returned to the cockpit.

"Captain Fremont, is there any way we can avoid surveillance? I know they have spy satellites and ground radar stations all over America. And if we do succeed in avoiding detection, we sure can't land at National. They have probably already contacted National and know our ETA," estimated time of arrival.

"I'll have to hit the deck," Fremont observed as though talking to himself. If we fly close to the earth, ground-based radar stations will not be able to see the plane." No sooner had the words left his mouth when the plane went into a steep dive.

"Hold on, mister Sage," the Captain suggested unnecessarily. Sage would have been in ecstasy having such an exhilarating ride in a jet airplane if he wasn't so worried. He had practically forgotten all about Herbie when he remembered the blogger. My God. He had to get his phone and at least make the call to get a progress report. There was no way for Herbie to contact him if he did make a connection with someone who could get them in to see the President.

With air screaming past the plane, even in the ordinarily quiet G-650, conversation was difficult. Signaling the pilot with his finger that he would return soon, Sage left to contact Herbie.

The phone was picked up after just one ring. "The Sizzler." I should have guessed how he would answer.

"Herbie. What's the news?"

"Oh. It's you. I don't know yet, Reader. Just waiting for a call. I thought your call was the one I was waiting for."

"Okay, Herbie, there's been a change of plan. I can no longer land at Washington, where I had planned on landing." Herbie started talking. Interrupting Sage continued, "No, I didn't tell you I was on a plane or where we planned on landing. I only told you I was on my way to DC. I was going to get to our meeting place, that is, if we had a meeting. We've run into some difficulty, and it's going to be tough making our appointment, but it must take place or the world as we know it will surely end. That is not hyperbole."

"What's happening, Reader? You have me scared." Sage could feel the perverts fear over the cell.

"There are many powerful people who do not want me to reach DC with my message. Herbie, this is all part of the big Pulitzer story for you if we can pull it off." Sage was hoping that mentioning the Pulitzer would help calm Herbie's nerves. "Give me your impression about the chance your contact will come through?"

"I honestly don't know Reader." The Sizzler sounded a little more in control. "I believe we have a chance, but these people are sometimes hard to read. They always want to know what is in it for them. Ya know? I had to tell the Secretary a big fat lie about how you had some devastating information about her department that she and the President had to hear tonight."

Herbie was so upset that he didn't even realize he had used one of the words almost guaranteed to alert the wiretapping computers and therefore invite telephone surveillance. He had also just given Reader the name of his contact. There was only one cabinet-level position held by a woman: Sheila Garvey, the Secretary of Education. Recently confirmed by the Senate, it was unlikely that she would be part of a conspiracy that had been in the planning stage for months, if not years.

"That's okay, Herbie. You did really good. Thanks for trying and keep it up. Look, I'm in a bit of a jam and don't want the bad guys finding me so I have to keep my phone turned off. Keep putting the pressure on your secretary friend. I was hoping to be in DC by six, but it's looking like it'll be a little later. If you do get your contact to meet with us, I'll try to be there by seven and will have to give you a location at that time. If I can make something happen faster, I will, because our time is growing short."

"Well, Reader, I will say that you are making life interesting. I'll keep trying to set up a meeting."

"Okay, thanks. Promise your Secretary that she will not be sorry if we meet, but very sorry if we don't. That isn't a threat Herbie. It's a simple fact of life. I wish it were different. I'll try the call later before landing, if possible. Oh, Herbie, and this is the most important thing of all to remember. Under no circumstances mention my name or the title of the person we wish to meet over the phone line. That is sure to launch an attack on both of us. Talk to you later."

Without waiting to hear Herbie sign off, Sage terminated the call and took the phone apart for the second time before returning to the cockpit.

"I can go faster, but there's a risk of overheating the engines at this lower altitude. Also, we're making one hell of a racket, and some folks might get upset and call it into the police and the FAA. Probably not a big risk because by the time all of that shit happens, we'll be long gone."

Sage listened to Fremont's comment about the engines getting hot and couldn't help but make a statement of his own. "I don't know much about this surveillance business and tracking airplanes, but it just makes sense to me that the sooner we're on the ground, the better off we'll be."

"Oh, shit, Reader. That reminds me. I just remembered an Air Force buddy of mine stationed at Wright Patt in Ohio. We can be there in just a few minutes. If we land there, we can have him fly us on to DC."

"Isn't that a big Air Force base?"

"Yep, the biggest U.S. Air Force Base in the country." The pride just oozed out of Freemont as he talked about Wright Patterson Air Force Base.

"That might not be a good idea, Captain." Sage was struggling to find some solution, and the fight to survive seemed to be a losing cause. It was getting difficult to press forward and keep his spirit from sagging. "Secretary of Defense, Roger Horowitz is part of this conspiracy to murder the President. For all we know, he has a group of fighters out of Patterson Air Force Base already in the air looking to shoot us down. We don't know who on that base we could trust even if we could get there."

"Well, that might be true Reader, but I know my buddy, and he would not be part of any plot like you described. He lives on the base but has a little home in Clifton, where he stashed his parents. That's about ten miles from the Wright Patt. Clifton is only a couple of miles from the Springfield-Beckley Municipal Airport. This is a neat little regional airport that my buddy Jed bought into a few years ago for his retirement, along with my Air Force buddy. If we land there, he would almost certainly have a plane that could get us to DC."

Sage had to think this over for a couple of minutes. By now they were searing the ground they passed at about 600 miles an hour. Under any other circumstances, Sage would have been euphoric, but he was too focused on their problem to notice the treetops they barely skimmed. Fremont had earlier explained that the Satellites would have a harder time picking them out of the ground clutter this close to the deck. Sage wasn't buying it, but he was pretty sure that radar would pick them out of the sky if they were any higher.

"I have a cell phone that the authorities are not aware of is mine." Sage hated to disclose that he lived with several aliases. 'Let's see if we can get your friend on the phone."

Leaving the cockpit again, Sage went back to his seat, locating the phone he used for everyday business under one of his fake identities.

Settling into the copilot's seat once more, Sage asked Fremont for his friend's phone number. There was no way Sage was going to have the Captain try to make a call while flying 600 miles an hour at literally tree-top level.

After finding the number, Sage dialed and heard the answering voice, "Hello, Colonel Baka." The tone he used while answering the telephone sounded so military. Sage wondered if this manner of speaking was taught, or it just emerged over time, like their stiff posture and stilted walk.

Sage quickly muted his phone and talked to Fremont. "Your buddy is a Colonel?

"Well, yeah, didn't I say?"

"No, you didn't say. What is his job? Title? Status? Whatever the hell it's called. What if he's in charge of hunting us down and shooting our asses out of the sky?

"That could be. But once I explain our situation, he will help us out. I know he would."

"Jesus, Captain. If he is in the fricking military, he's gonna follow orders."

"Hello, is anybody there.?" The phone was talking as Sage had been ignoring the Colonel who was on hold with the phone muted. Sage unmuted the phone, speaking into the receiver, "yes, please hold a minute Colonel, we're having a little cockpit problem. Be back at you in a second." Placing the phone back on mute, Sage turned to Freemont. "Well, Captain. What in the hell do I say now?"

Waiting for the Captain to speak, Sage could think about only one thing. He had less than five hours to save the President and he was talking to one of the most powerful men in the military responsible for shooting them out of the sky.

CHAPTER TWENTY-THREE
PLAN C

Back in Menlo Park, after giving her secretary orders that she was not to be disturbed by anybody for any reason, Honey Samuels alternately paced her office then sat outside in her Zen garden, sipping green tea. It was moments like these that she wished she was still a smoker.

In Sun Valley, Secretary Horowitz was closeted in one of the Senator's three offices with Secretary Dushaj. Both men were on their secure satellite phones, giving orders, and receiving status reports. Both men were sweating streams under their arms and around their necks staining their shirts with wet blotches. The men's ties were loosened, the neck button was undone, and jackets were thrown over the back of a vacant chair. Horowitz, the military man still sat ramrod straight as if gravity and age did not affect his body. Dushaj was slumped down on a couch, looking like a beached baby whale when a sudden sharp outburst from Horowitz who was on the phone shook him out of his stupor.

"GODDAMMIT MAJOR, YOU'VE HAD NEARLY A HOUR TO FIND THOSE BASTARDS. WHAT KIND OF AMATEUR HORSESHIT RODEO ARE YOU RUNNING?"

The room fell silent as Dushaj could not hear what the dammed Major was saying back to Secretary Horowitz, but from the look on the Secretary's face, it wasn't pleasant news.

After terminating the call, Horowitz said to Dushaj in a more reasonable tone, "They have four God dammed shooters plus a Boeing E-4 AWACS for support flying over a five-hundred-mile square patch of dirt, and they can't find one damn white bird."

"Maybe they're looking at the wrong patch of dirt, Roger." Dushaj spoke in a quiet, timid voice, but you don't get to his station in life by being timid. It was more of a ploy to calm down the Secretary of Defense.

"Yeah, I think the dim shit Major figured that out. He just agreed to expand the search area." Horowitz seemed to have calmed down, but the fire still burned in his eyes, and his body remained rigid. It was only a matter of time before he would explode if the missing plane was not found soon.

•   •   •

In the Gulfstream, Sage unmuted the phone in his hand. "Hello, Colonel Baka. Please don't terminate this call until you have heard me out."

"Who is this, please?" The Colonel did not sound pleased.

"My name is Sage, and right now, I am on a plane with someone you might know. I call him Captain Fremont, but I suspect you know him as Colonel Fremont, retired." Sage looked at Fremont to make sure the Captain was on board with his conversation.

"Yes, I know Colonel Fremont. What is this about?"

"Colonel, I don't know your specific position at Wright Patt, but I'm guessing that you either run the whole show or at least one of the Air Force wings stationed there. Have you...." Colonel Baka interrupted Sage;

"if you are with Fremont, put him on the phone."

"I would love to do that, Colonel, but right now, Colonel Freemont is kinda busy trying to save our worthless lives."

"What's going on, Sage? What's this call all about?" Colonel Baka was getting impatient, snapping questions like a mule team driver with a twenty-foot bullwhip snapping at the rumps of mules that were not pulling their share of the load.

"Colonel, are you familiar with an order to find and shoot out of the sky a white Gulf G-650 heading towards Washington DC?"

"Sure. It's all over the base. Everyone from the FAA to the CIA, plus of course the Air Force, is looking for that bird."

"Colonel, your good friend Captain Fremont is flying that plane at about 525 knots at tree level heading for Clifton. We're hoping to make it there before being shot out of the sky. He is too busy dodging trees, cell phone towers, radio station antennas, and the like to talk on a cell. We cannot use the radio for obvious reasons."

"Why are you calling me? What does Miles want? And where is that Reader fellow?" Baka did not sound pleased. The tone in his voice had that police sound when they say, 'step out of the vehicle, sir.'

"Colonel Baka, I can only hope that you are someplace where no one else can hear this conversation. Your life, my life and Colonel Fremont's life all depend on this being private."

"I'm in my office, Sage. What's going on?" Where is this Reader? The Colonel was still shooting bullets. Short, concise statements. It sounded like barking.

"We need you to meet us at your Springfield airport where we will land if we don't get shot out of the sky first. Then we need to hide the plane immediately where we are not in the view from anyone in the sky, including satellites. Our ETA is 30 minutes. Can you meet us there? We will explain everything to you at that time, and you can meet The Reader. Please trust your friend Colonel Fremont."

"Hold the phone close to Miles, so I can hear him speak. I need to know this isn't some hoax." At least Baka was giving us a chance to hang ourselves.

"Hello, Edward." It was awkward for Fremont to speak sideways while keeping his full attention on flying the plane. "I,.. no... we need your help and discretion. Please talk to Sage." Fremont nodded his head, letting Sage know that he needed to pay attention to his flying.

"Okay, Colonel. That's about it for Fremont. He's too damn busy right now to talk. Will you help us? You cannot let anyone at Wright Patt know we are landing at Springfield."

"Miles may not have told you, but he was my CO for a few years. He's one of the best men alive. If he needs me, I'll be there. It'll take me about fifteen minutes to reach the airport."

"Thank you, Colonel. I hope we make it. I believe the only reason we are still in the air is because the pointy heads at the Pentagon who do all the calculations assumed a flight pattern from Sun Valley. We're coming in a little more from the south and a bit east of where they are looking. If they don't find us in the next thirty minutes, we'll see you at Springfield."

"Roger that Sage. Hope to see you soon." The call was terminated.

"Well, hell Miles," Sage had a smile in his voice as he used the Colonel's given name, "if you can get us to Clifton without getting us killed, we might have a shot at saving the President."

Chapter Twenty-Four
Colonel Baka

Secretary Horowitz, with a frown on his face, was sitting on one of Senator Kim's desk chairs looking out of a window facing the pool where nearly naked girls were bouncing around half-drunk men dancing to some music that mercifully did not penetrate the Senator's office. The search planes had been called back to their base. It was evident that The Reader's plane had managed to land and hide before being sighted by ground-based radar, satellites or aircraft.

Sitting across the desk from Horowitz was General James Selva, Chairman of the Joint Chiefs of Staff. Selva was the force behind the planned assassination of the President. A small bitter man with four stars on his jacket, he had spent the past two years planning the coup; coaxing, seducing, blackmailing, and charming co-conspirators into joining the grand plan. In a closed cabinet meeting two years ago, President Dunning had announced his intention to declassify and release to the public all of Nickols Tesla's papers confiscated by the CIA upon Tesla's death. Tesla's work included several large chests of documents, notes and books that had belonged to him. Among the many papers to be declassified were Tesla's notes, diagrams and plans for free energy. One of the most brilliant and gifted inventors of any age, Tesla's papers contained descriptions and ideas for a variety of sophisticated devices all appropriated by the military for military use. Selva was determined to prevent President Dunning from releasing this information to the public, where any foreign government could access the same technology enjoyed by the U.S. military in which they currently had a monopoly. Free energy, while a blessing for humanity, also has the potential for seriously lethal weapons, which the military-industrial complex had been exploiting for several decades. According to Selva, this technology should not be released under any circumstances, even if it meant killing the President.

"Well, General, we seem to have lost track of the plane and this Reader fellow." Horowitz, who rarely showed deference to anyone, respected the General treating him as a top dog. Selva had an imposing demeanor that demanded respect.

Being a small man at only five foot ten inches, he had a Napoleon complex reeking of power that was not to be denied. Horowitz continued, "at least we know he didn't make it to DC. It seems unlikely that he can make it to Washington before tonight, and his chance of seeing the President is pretty slim."

"Do we know if he has a contact in town?" Asked Selva. Like most of the beltway crowd, Selva used the standard synonym for DC. You were either in Town or on the Belt, distinguishing those in DC versus those outside of the district.

"The only thing we know about the bastard is that he can read minds," Horowitz answered with a sneer in his voice. "Apparently, very accurately," he continued.

"Should we pull the plug on the big show tonight?"

The General seemed deep in thought for a few minutes before replying. "No, let's let it play out for a while. We can cancel right up until ten o'clock. However, we need to get that crowd outside to slow down on the booze. After the President is down, we have to hold a big news announcement before several television networks and other news outlets. It would not be seemly to have a bunch of drunk congressmen running around with the newshounds." General Selva shook his head in disgust.

"I'll go have a talk with the Senator and get him to go slow with the free drinks." Horowitz stood to leave the room as he was speaking.

"Hold on a second, mister secretary." He said the word secretary with a small s rather than capital S just to let Horowitz know who was the top dog. "We need to have the FAA and DOT keep up the pressure. Homeland Security can help. They can contact all police agencies between say Indiana through Ohio and West Virginia to DC. If we knew what that bastard Reader looked like, we could have him shot on sight. And send in that buffoon of a VP. We've, (a euphemism for 'I've), got to cut his legs off a little. He's getting a little too high and mighty out there."

•   •   •

Springfield Municipal Airport has runways heading both north-east and north-west. The north-east runway was lined up almost perfectly with the Gulfstream's flight path allowing Captain Fremont the luxury of coming in hot before screeching to a halt. Looking out of the cockpit window as they were screaming down the runway at about a hundred miles an hour, Sage caught sight of a man over by a large hanger waving his hat in the air. "I think your Colonel friend is over by a hanger; we just flew past, signaling to us with his hat."

"Good eye's Sage." Fremont was getting a kick out of calling Sage by his real name rather than The Reader. "We'll catch him on the taxi runway after making our turn."

The Gulfstream came to a screeching halt almost at the very end of the runway. Showing absolutely no emotion as though this was an everyday occurrence, the Captain made the turn onto the taxi runway, then revving up the engines went screaming back towards the hanger where the man was still waving his hat. "I know we want to get under cover ASAP, but aren't you pushing it a little, Captain?" Sage was nervous as hell. He was sure they would careen past the end of the runway, and now Freemont was flying back down the taxi runway blurring past people and equipment off to the side.

"We're pushing our luck, Reader. If we can get out of here alive without getting the whole damn place blown up, I'll be tickled. This place represents Ed's retirement. Everything he owns is tied up here. I don't want him to lose it because we pulled our plane into his hanger." Just as he finished speaking, the Captain put the plane into a tight turn into a hanger his friend was signaling for him to take. No sooner was the aircraft inside, and even before Fremont could kill the engines, the hangar doors began closing.

Colonel Baka didn't look anything like the Base Commander of the largest airbase in America. Khaki shorts, with flip-flops on his feet and a blue flowered Hawaiian shirt, his buzz-cut black hair was topped with a gray Greek fisherman's hat. Ruddy complexion, the six-foot Colonel looked in peak condition. No sooner had Fremont stepped out of the plane and hit the concrete hanger floor when Baka scooped him into his arms for a big bear hug. "Okay, fly-boy, let's hear about this big emergency; if I'm about to get hit with a ton of ordnance out of the sky, I want to know why?"

Sage and Fremont took turns filling in the Colonel on everything that had transpired over the past two days. The briefing took less than five minutes when Baka finally said, "well shit. Let's look outside and see if we have a military caravan bearing down on our unlucky souls. If the flyboys or satellite caught a glimpse of you boys sneaking into my hanger, they wouldn't waste any time." Looking around outside and seeing nothing moving towards them, Baka continued, "we would have seen some action by now if they saw you, so I guess we're home free temporarily. What's next, Colonel?" Baka still referred to his former commander as Colonel.

It was Sage who responded. "Colonel, it's imperative that I reach Washington, DC, and the President within the next four hours. Is there any chance of renting a plane?"

"Holy hog wallow boy," Baka spoke with a slight hillbilly accent Sage had difficulty placing at first. "If the President is in the kind of danger you tell us he is in, you can have your pick of our inventory. We only own three of these planes outright, but have an interest in several others." Having said that, Baka spit a stream of tobacco into a Folger's coffee can conveniently located just inside of the hangar doors. Colonel Baka was a hillbilly cowboy from Tennessee, and while his intelligence and mental discipline were never in dispute, his language and habits still retained part of the hillbilly society of his youth.

"I saw a turboprop sitting over by another hanger as we taxied in and..." Fremont was saying.

"More like flew past," Sage interrupted.

"Yeah, well, is that SAAB 340 available?" Fremont finished.

"That's one of our newer partnership additions. It's a small business jet we lease or rent to companies, so far though the government is our biggest user. I own one-sixth interest along with five other guys. Our business manager handles leasing contracts.

"Is the plane available for a few hours?" Fremont wasn't sure he was qualified to fly that particular plane, but it didn't hurt to ask.

"Well, she's just sitting there, so I guess it's available." Baka seemed to be rooted in thought for a second, then added. "I'm not sure you're qualified on that plane though Colonel. It has some new instruments that are different. You know, like a compass and altitude meter." He couldn't help but jerk his old commanders' chain. "Are you up to date on turbos?"

"No, but I think it might be okay if you just ran me through the setup once. You know, show me where the pilot sits, which button starts the engines, and so forth." The Colonel had to get in his jibes. Fremont wanted to get in the air and was hoping his friend would help them get going without all the b s.

"Yeah, it'd be like showing a turkey how to fly, but I'm pretty you could do it, Colonel. However, I can fly you and save the paperwork grief."

"Hell Bock, (Fremont's name for his old buddy) that'll be great. Let's get started. Oh, by the way, do you have privileges at National? My friend would prefer to land there if possible."

"Does a calf know how to suck milk? Hell, yes, I can land at National. Do it all the time when I have one of them damn Pentagon meetings. Let me hit the office for the log and to file a flight plan. Just take a second."

Sage had watched this exchange listening to the two old comrades trade insults, and while the words and expressions sounded real, there was an undertone in Colonel Baka's demeanor that seemed just a little off. Sage kept trying to get into the Colonel's mind, but the only thing he could pick up were fragments of an old kid's poem; 'ladybug, ladybug, fly away home, your house is on fire....' The rest of the words were blurred, kind of how drunks slur their speech making it difficult to understand what is being said, or in this case what is being thought. It was almost like the Colonel didn't want Sage to know what he was thinking, so he kept his mind on something trivial to hide his real thoughts. All Sage could pick up were the words to some childhood ditty plus an old song. Outwardly the Colonel was all smiles and backslaps, just a good ole buddy, but something was off. Sage couldn't figure out what.

They all trooped over to the primary office building, where Colonel Baka arranged for them to get the SAAB. As they were waiting, Fremont said, "Colonel, let's leave the destination open for now. Just enter it as a qualification flight. No real destination."

"Oh yeah, good thinking. Let the bastards guess."

Sage excused himself and went looking for a landline. Surely a business would have a business line or two. Seeing a vacant office with a telephone sitting on a desk, he went in and immediately called Herbie.

"This is the Sizzler." Sage heard the answering voice and thought at least some things still seemed reasonable.

"Hi Herbie, this is The Reader. How's, it going? Do we have a date?"

"Hey man, I don't know what kind of shit you're into, but this is turning out to be a pot full of piss. My contact won't meet unless we tell her what the meeting is about."

"My, my Herbie. Such colorful language from a real honest to God wordsmith. Look, Herbie, I've said all I can on the phone. I am certain your line is not safe. Please stress the immediate danger to our way of life if this meeting does not take place. Convince her, Herbie. You must have some tricks up your sleeve to wrangle a meeting or comment from your sources. It's up to you to sell this meeting. You know I can convince her of my legitimacy once we're together. By the way, how's mother doing?"

"That's not necessary, Reader. I'll try once more, but she's being stubborn."

"Make it happen, Herbie. I'll call in an hour or so. Still making my way to sin city. And I don't mean Vegas."

"Okay, Reader, I'll try." Herbie didn't notice, but Sage had already terminated the call.

Going back up front where the Colonel and Fremont were waiting, Sage waved his finger in an air circle signaling, let's get the show on the road. He didn't know how much graver his day would become. The only thought in his mind as he walked over to the SAAB was less than four hours left.

CHAPTER TWENTY-FIVE
CHANGING PLANS

Menlo Park 3:00 p.m.

Sitting in her private Japanese Zen garden, Honey was getting sloshed. Very uncharacteristic and most unprofessional, but the only door to the garden was to her office, and her office door was closed and locked. She had also given her private secretary an order that she was not to be disturbed for any reason. Given the inadequate information she received regarding The Reader, she was becoming more and more concerned about a Casus belli. She didn't want to disturb Roger again, but the uncertainty and lack of information were driving her nuts.

The Dogwood, in full blossom behind her seat with its colorful streaks of red, did nothing to calm her nerves. This time tomorrow, her way of life as she knew it could be in the clouds or the dirt. She needed some answers.

"Horowitz."

"Roger, it's Honey." Concentrating on not slurring her words, she spoke slowly the way drunks talk when struggling to sound sober, thereby making her sound wasted. Horowitz didn't notice or didn't care or was unconcerned. She continued, "I was just wondering if there is any news about our wandering Reader?"

"Oh, hi, Honey. Our problems are over. We have an ally guaranteed to deal with the situation. You can stop worrying." He noticed the inebriated state of his California colleague, but didn't deem it necessary or proper to mention it over the phone. He had known Honey for over forty years and never once had to worry about her performance. She was gold. "I'm sorry I didn't call you right away, it's been a little tense here, but we squared away everything. We have resolved this troublesome problem."

"Thanks, Roger. I just felt a little guilty since it was our plane that hauled his ass to Sun Valley."

"Not your fault, Honey. Stop worrying. It will all work out."

Honey was trying to end the conversation without sounding drunk when the line went dead. Roger never said goodbye.

Betrayal

Sage felt chagrined and disappointed with himself. He attributed his poor memory performance to the mental and physical stress he had been undergoing. It should have been obvious at the very beginning. The duplicity Colonel Baka's had exhibited was back when they first met when the Colonel kept asking about the Reader. How would the Colonel even know that name unless someone hunting for The Reader told him?

Colonel Baka was in the pilot's seat with Captain Fremont riding shotgun. Sage was in the main cabin when he got a jolt, like a shock that went through his whole body. Never had anyone's thoughts had such an effect on him before, and at first, he was puzzled as to their origin. Then he calmed down and felt as much heard Colonel Baka's thoughts. Maybe because Sage was no longer in the cockpit cabin, the Colonel who was no longer guarding his thoughts, let it slip out he had no intention of helping Reader and Fremont. Perhaps he thought unless The Reader was in his actual presence, he couldn't read his mind. As Sage concentrated on the Colonel's thoughts, he discovered that Baka was not only aware of the search for the Reader, but was part of the planned Presidential coup. As CO for Wright Patterson Air Base, he was in a position of high power and responsibility. Sage couldn't pick up what was in it for the Colonel, what his reward for betraying the country would be, but as things now stood, the Colonel had already arranged for their immediate apprehension upon landing at National Airport. Once the Cabal became aware of Colonel Baka's timely appearance in their plans, it was decided to handle the elimination of Reader and his pilot in Washington on the ground rather than shoot the plane down, possibly injuring or killing civilians when the plane wreckage hit the earth. The jolt Sage experienced earlier was his body reacting to all the negativity jumping from his pilot's mind.

The question was, what to do about it? If he incapacitated the Colonel, could Captain Fremont pilot their aircraft? And where would they land? Surely this plane had a transponder giving their exact status. The hunters would know where their quarry was all the time.

Everyone in on the conspiracy knew Reader and Fremont were flying to Washington D.C. with the express intention of somehow warning the President. The conspirators had people monitoring all White House communications and were certain that so far, I had made no attempt to reach the President. How Sage planned on revealing their plot to the President was discussed by all the players assembled in Sun Valley, and the consensus was there was no way Sage could ever reach the President in the next four hours. Even if he avoided capture at Reagan National, and that was flat out impossible. Still, they wanted him dead for what he could reveal about their plans. The Reader might talk to someone who could cause them problems later. Their only safety was the immediate disposal of The Reader and his pilot.

Sage intuitively knew all of this, which only made him concentrate harder on some way to thwart their plans. He had to see the President personally before ten p.m.

Colonel Baka was enjoying himself flying one of his favorite planes. He had never liked his former commanding officer, although he had worked to hide those feelings. While his old buddy Fremont and that freak in the back were congratulating themselves on escaping the noose, he was the one tying the knot around their necks, and he loved every minute of it. There is such deliciousness in reveling over a situation in which you are in total control of your adversaries. Especially those who have no clue, or in any case, no power to change their destiny. That was until Sage quietly slipped up behind him and placing his powerful hands on the Colonel's head and neck applied pressure to the exact points necessary to induce instant sleep.

"Captain Fremont, take over this plane, right now, please!" Reader's voice had an urgency Fremont had never heard before.

The Captain had been listening to one of Baka's stories about mountain life when he heard Sage bark out his command. Glancing over at the now sleeping pilot shocked him, but to his credit he immediately assumed control of the plane.

"What the hell, Sage? What d'you do that for?" Fremont seemed confused and with good reason.

"Your ole buddy is in on the fix Captain. He stopped blocking his thoughts when he thought we were helpless and in his control. He is part of the coup to kill the President. I will pull him into the back cabin and fix it so he cannot do us any more damage. We have to figure out a place to land near D.C. Washington National is out of the question. Our old buddy here has the whole damn army ready to make us both disappear. The Colonel will be out for about five minutes, long enough for me to get him into restraints."

The Captain was angry and confused. He had known Colonel Baka for many years and could not believe his good old buddy was playing them. Was that why he had been enjoying himself so much? "Are you sure Reader?" he asked, reverting to the old name for the man now called Sage. That indicated his mental status. He was confused, worried, and alarmed at what they now faced.

"Yeah, Captain," Sage replied with weariness in his voice. "There wasn't any doubt or question."

"What did you do to him? I've seen no one go out like that so quickly and quietly. What did you do?"

"It's an old, old practice from the far east. I'll explain it sometime. Let me get this piece of shit out of here, and we can talk about our future. Whatever that might be."

CHAPTER TWENTY-SIX
PLAN D

Sage pulled the treacherous unconscious Colonel from the pilot's seat, dragging him into the rear cabin where he tore the blue Hawaiian shirt off his body then ripped the shirt to shreds. Using long strips from the shirt, Sage bound Baka's hands behind his back then his feet before bending his legs up behind his back, securing them to his hands. He was conscientious about leaving the ties tight with no wiggle room. He would periodically check to make sure that the Colonel was still securely restrained. Sage could not watch him full time as he still needed to work out their next moves with the Captain.

After finishing his work in the main cabin Sage returned to the flight deck to see that Fremont had moved over to the pilot's seat, leaving empty the copilot's slot.

"Well, Captain, do you have any thoughts?" Sage asked, slipping into the empty seat. To say his worries were multiplying by the second would be a gross misstatement. Every move they wanted to make was being blocked. "I'm sure," he continued, "they are watching us by every radar station and plane in the sky. They know where we are, our destination, and when to expect us to land. At this moment, I don't believe our chances of survival are any better than a bare candle burning in a heavy wind, to borrow one of your old buddy's mountain phrases."

"Well, you've got the ole buddy part down. He sure as hell isn't a current buddy. As for your question, I've been thinking. I'm sure Colonel dickhead Baka has everyone in Washington D.C. primed for our landing at National. We're less than an hour away. I suggest we maintain our present course until the last second. There's a small regional airport called College Park not too far away. It's the oldest continually operating airport in the World. Today the airport is primarily used by business planes and small commercial aircraft. They won't be expecting us there."

Fremont paused as though thinking. "At National Airport, they don't know that Baka is no longer flying the plane and the tower there will not know my voice from his. I'll go into the D.C. area low, like we'll be landing at National, then make a last-second flight adjustment for College Park flying as low and fast as possible. That won't hide our plane, but it will take them a few minutes to figure out what happened and where we're going. Hopefully, they won't have time to assemble a reception committee to meet us in College Park if we land fast and skedaddle. Sorry, sometimes my ole buddy's mountain verbiage slips in. Can you arrange for someone we can trust to meet us with a vehicle? Preferably something the authorities will not immediately detect?"

"I don't know, Captain. Let me get to work on that. I've been trying to set something up to meet with the President, but haven't been having a lot of success. I've got a few minutes, so let me get busy. I need to turn on some noise back in the main cabin, so our friend won't hear us making plans. Be right back."

Sage went back to the main cabin to check on the Colonel. He had regained consciousness and was squirming against his bonds, trying to free himself.

Seeing his enemy return, the Colonel spits out, "That was a thousand dollar Dolce and Gabbana shirt you destroyed asshole."

"Wow. At least you're tied up with quality rags," Sage couldn't help but smile. "Let's see how well they're working." With that, Sage rolled the Colonel back onto his stomach so he could check the bindings. Satisfied that nothing seemed to be coming loose, he found the entertainment system which included a collection of Country and hillbilly music. Naturally. A lot of Dotti Jones and Winston O'Neal, Jimmy Haynie, and Charlie Stewart plus a little Elvis. To be mean, Sage loaded in several songs starting with "Don't Be Cruel" by Presley. Turning up the volume, so the whole cabin was vibrating Sage went back up front to make some calls.

CHAPTER TWENTY-SEVEN
THE BEST-LAID PLANS

Back in the copilot's seat, Sage called Herbie using his burner. He figured that the government was probably on to his use of the phones borrowed from his would-be killers back in Sun Valley.

"This is the Sizzler."

"Herbie, this is The Reader. Give me some good news."

"Sorry, Reader. My contact won't budge without more information."

He really sounded sorry, but now was not the time to let up. "Goddammit Herbie, we're running out of time. You need to be more persuasive. I know for a fact that the story you'll be telling is worthy of a Pulitzer. I cannot guarantee that you have the talent to win the prize, but after reading some of your posts, I'm impressed with your ability. The minute I explain anything more over the phone, our lives become forfeit. Believe what you want, Herbie, but that is God's own truth. Now convince that witch we need her. I need you both to help me with the project. Can't say names anymore. Can you try again?"

"I can try Reader. But the Secretary is getting pissed off. I have explained how you can read minds and that your information is of vital importance to save the world as we know it, but so far, she hasn't budged. What is the big crisis?

Herbie sounded frustrated and weary and a little whiney. Threats would be of no value, and I couldn't tell the truth over the phone. "Okay, Herbie, give it another shot. You can tell the Secretary that unless she meets with me, tomorrow she will be out of a job. Just ask her to check around town and see how many high-ranking officials are not to be found. If she makes any calls, she has got to be very cautious. Her calls must not sound like an emergency. She is just checking to see if this or that person has a few minutes to see her tomorrow. Nothing serious. You got that, Herbie?"

"Okay, Reader, I'll give it another shot." He didn't sound very optimistic, and I was losing faith that he would succeed. Time to come up with another plan.

Captain Fremont was on the radio and checking coordinates for our flight plan, so I went back to check on our duplicitous Colonel. I could tell by the sweat on his face he had been straining at his bindings.

"You son-of-bitch," he yelled at me when I came back to check on him. "You're a dead man. You're both dead men. Both you and that traitor upfront." In his anger and frustration, the Colonel was frothing at the mouth. After turning down the volume on the King singing "Jail House Rock," I couldn't keep myself from rubbing it in a little.

"Gee, Colonel. I sure feel alive for being so dead. And your old commander upfront is looking pretty good for a dead man as well. Maybe you should think about your own future. As for this traitor business, we both know who that is just as we know that treason is punishable by death."

I flipped him back over on his face to check that his restraints were still secure. Satisfied that his efforts to free himself were not relaxing his bonds, I returned to the forward cabin after turning Elvis back to full volume.

After killing the microphone, Fremont said, "I think we're good for College Park. I've been monitoring their control tower radio traffic, and so far, there has been no notice for them to watch out for our plane. I'm pretty sure Colonel Baka has Washington National convinced that he has everything under control and plans on landing there. We're probably good to land at College Park, but as soon as it becomes obvious that our plans have changed, you know they'll pick us up heading for the Park in no time flat. I've been doing some math in my head and believe we'll have about three to five minutes after landing before the angry Fed's show up in force. And knowing how pissed they're gonna be, we can bet the force they show up with will be substantial."

I thought about what he said for a minute before replying. "I guess that lets out any kind of airport transportation like a shuttle, I added a bit facetiously to lighten up the mood a little. What if I try to book an UBER?"

"That might work if the car meets our plane as soon as we reach the front apron. Before the alarm sounds, we should be out of the airport. The car must be in the exact location. If we have to hoof it any distance or wait for any length of time, we'll be sitting ducks. There won't be any place to hide."

"Is there a map of the airport in that pilot kit by the seat?"

"I don't know, here...check it out," he replied, handing me a briefcase full of aeronautical flight information. There were all kinds of maps, tables of radio frequencies for various airports, and control towers plus other technical stuff I could not identify without studying. Looking over the maps, I found College Park Airport. It had only one main runway with a lot of apron parking. There was a pilot's lounge just back of a big apron. The pilot's lounge did not look very big, and there was a car parking lot on the other side of the lounge. If an UBER was waiting just outside of the pilot's lounge, and we taxied right up to the door, we should be able to deplane and by running through the room be in the Uber in less than a minute. It looked perfect.

If I could get an UBER. And if he would wait where I wanted.

I placed the map in front of Captain Fremont, pointing out the pilot's lounge and parking lot. There was no way to tell if the apron would be free of planes, but we should be able to get close enough for our purposes unless there was some kind of damn pilot's convention.

Fremont said it looked good, so using the burner, I called Uber in College Park. After explaining my needs, Uber hooked me up with a local driver with whom I went over my needs once more. I described an emergency meeting in downtown Washington D.C. and the need for the driver to be at the airport waiting by the pilot's lounge when we arrived. The driver, a foreign Indian sounding individual, named Jawaharlal Ramnarace, assured me he would be there waiting. Just to make sure he was there; I volunteered a hundred-dollar tip if he was there and waiting. I explained that we were having some airplane difficulties and would land anytime between thirty to sixty minutes from now. The tip was to ensure that he would be there when we arrived. I was sure that our lives depended on his being there.

After ending my call, I looked at Fremont for confirmation. He just nodded, concentrating on our approach to Washington National.

Time was disappearing at a rapid clip, and I still did not have a way to visit the President. With just over two hours to save his life, my usual optimism was getting one hell of a workout. Pessimism and discouragement were sapping my strength and hopes. What if my pervert blogger failed to secure an appointment with the Secretary? I didn't have a backup plan. There was no use in asking Captain Fremont for help at the moment as he was busy on the radio. God, I never felt like I wanted or needed a drink, but this was an exception, and I didn't dare take a drop.

CHAPTER TWENTY-EIGHT
RECEPTION

Ronald Reagan Washington National Airport has one main long north-south runway and two shorter runways, one running northeast-southwest and the other northwest-southeast. Captain Fremont posing as Colonel Baka was talking to the tower requesting the northeast-southwest runway as we were coming in from the southwest. This runway pointed almost directly towards College Park, giving a straight shot to our preferred destination once we passed Washington National. The airport is covered like candy pieces on a child's birthday cake with hangers, aprons, maintenance sheds, security buildings, airport lounges for congressmen, and many unidentified buildings. Across the Potomac River from DC, it sits less than a mile to the Pentagon with a convenient light-rail connection. Since we were number-one enemy of the State, we could expect a full complement of Pentagon personnel for our reception committee. This did not even count a full complement of representatives from Joint Base Andrews, just a few klicks away in Maryland.

There was no way we could know how much of the military and Pentagon establishment were signed on to the assignation plot. Still, with the Chairman of the JCS and the Secretary of Defense as two of the ringleaders, it's a fair bet that the number was not small. A lot of heads would roll into the Potomac from the banks on both sides of the river if we thwarted their plans.

The Captain and I did not understand what manner of reception we could expect at National, but we knew it wouldn't be pretty. The question was, once we pushed the throttles forward feeding gas to the engines as we sped down the runway, how long would it take them to mount an air posse to come after us? Could we make College Park ten miles away and land before they caught up with us? There was no doubt in either of our minds they would not hesitate to shoot us out of the air, whether or not we were over a populated area.

At the speed we could keep-up over that whole ten miles, it would take us between three and four minutes to reach College Park. Say another minute to land and park if Captain Fremont did another hot landing and taxi job. Hopefully,

Fremont's skill would keep our landing from being as dramatic as the landing at Springfield Municipal Airport, where I thought he would kill us both. Of course, at Springfield, the Captain was flying his own plane. How would the SAAB respond given the same treatment? I wouldn't ask Fremont, even if he wasn't busy trying to save our lives. Hell, the chances of us living another hour weren't that great, anyway.

It was nearing Eight o'clock in the evening as we approached Washington National, and with the setting sun at our backs, the view was spectacular. Captain Fremont had decreased our altitude as we approached the airport and cut the speed corresponding to a safe landing. The airport landing lights were blazing into the sky like an illuminated cross. I hoped that didn't mean we were about to be crucified. The river was shimmering with a golden sunset turning it into a portrait of glistening liquid gold. We skimmed over Alexandra and kept dropping towards the airport.

It surprised me when Fremont said, "I will not drop the landing gear. By the time those on the ground or tower notice, we should be hitting the throttle. The landing gear will only slow us down."

I'm not sure if he was talking to himself or me, but it made sense. I could clearly view the runway, and other than going much faster than a normal person would consider reasonable, we were practically skimming the river as the runway came up quickly. Just as we approached the south end, Captain Fremont pushed the throttles full-on racing us past the tower in seconds. The radio started squawking, so Fremont turned it off. He had no intention of calling College Park, letting the tower or anyone else know our destination.

As we sped by the north end of the runway, it was possible to observe a large convoy of cars and military-looking trucks parked along the edges. There was a significant gathering of men in camouflage clothing carrying rifles standing in a line next to the vehicles. I would have smiled and cracked a joke with the Captain, except the situation was too dangerous. We sure as hell weren't home yet. Sitting in the copilot's seat wearing headphones to hear and talk with the Captain, it surprised me when he said, "Sage, glance up on the ceiling for a switch that says Transponder and flip it off."

It seemed like there were a hundred switches up above our heads, and it overwhelmed me looking for one in the jungle of switches, and we didn't have a lot of time. Fremont didn't want to telegraph our heading with any more accuracy than they could pick up from the ground radar. The switches were arranged in 4 x 4 grids and bunched according to function, lights-interior and exterior, airflow, and purposes I couldn't decipher. I was about to give up when the communication grid of switches caught my eye, and sure enough, right there in the top row was a switch labeled Transponder. I switched it off just as we passed over the Washington Mall and the U.S. Capitol.

I was too busy looking for the Transponder switch to catch the shadows chasing away the sunlight crawling up the Washington Monument on our left side. As the sparkling city sped past below, I couldn't help but marvel at the beautiful lighted jewel that is our nation's Capital. The scene reminded me of a day many years ago when I was standing at the top of Gun Barrel looking down at the sparkling diamond run. Now, as then, I felt overwhelmed with anticipation and fear. I hoped for a different outcome this time, but the odds didn't seem great for that happening, and this time, there would be no waking up, ever.

Fremont had the plane screeching along at full speed just above the rooftops. Over on our left, flying by quickly was the Basilica of the National Shrine of the Immaculate Conception. Its spires seemed to be higher than our plane, which had me worrying about some other structures that might be in our path. The Washington Monument was the tallest structure in D.C., but did that include College Park? We were going too fast to maneuver around anything. While the city and surrounding buildings sped past at a blazing speed, it seemed like time dragged on and on, each passing second seemingly slower and slower.

As each second passed, I half expected a missile to blow our plane out of the sky. After what seemed an eternity, Fremont was changing course lining us up for the College Park runway. We were committed to landing there regardless of air traffic. Unwilling to talk with their control tower arranging for a clear runway we could only hope and pray there were no planes practicing touch and goes. Landing back at Ronald Reagan Airport would have definitely meant our death. By going on to College Park, we had the possibility of staying alive. Taking a chance that the runway at College Park would be clear of traffic was our only and best hope. If the runway was occupied, we would just have to try to land on the grass between the runway and trees on the right or the taxi road to the left. At the speed we were traveling, it was questionable whether our landing gear would handle a soft-landing surface. While we were risking our own lives, there was no reason to risk the lives of others.

Fremont dropped our wheels and headed for the runway at full speed. As we got a good look at the landing surface, we noticed a Beechcraft hurtling down the runway coming directly towards our plane. Being the ace pilot that he is, Fremont skimmed over the top of the Beechcraft and hit the runway at nearly full speed.

The College Park runway is a 2600-foot-long splash of asphalt 60 feet wide. Flying over the Beechcraft cost us about 600 feet of runway surface, leaving us 2000 feet, a little less than half a mile to stop our plane, which was traveling at almost 200 miles an hour. Throttles pulled back to full stop Fremont hit the brakes hard. Fortunately, we landed in an almost perfectly straight line, so our braking action didn't tend to pull us off the runway. The SAAB has great brakes that Fremont used to full advantage. The brakes began smoking about five seconds after Fremont hit them with all the strength in his legs. The airport buildings were all on our left side as we sped down the runway. We passed them in a flash, going about a hundred miles an hour.

The end of the runway was rushing towards us at breakneck speed and I was positive we were not going to stop in time. I should have had more faith in the Captain. About a hundred yards from the end of the runway, Fremont pulled a maneuver I've never seen before in an airplane. Hitting the left brake while releasing the right brake and using the wing flaps, ailerons, and tail Rudder in perfect symmetry, the Captain put our plane into a 90-degree turn while still on the runway. We went skidding sideways down the remaining runway, stopping five feet from the edge of the asphalt.

Revving up the engine's immediately, Fremont had us on the taxiway, leaving a trail of smoke from our overheated brakes heading for the pilot's lounge about a thousand feet away. I'm sure that if we had the radio on, we would have been getting an earful from the tower and other planes in the area. I would love to have listened to what was said about our landing.

To our delight, there was no reception committee, and we immediately looked up in the sky to see if an air posse in was on tail. Fremont wasted no time getting us to the pilot's lounge and killing the engines before we were stopped entirely. I unlatched the door and jumped on the wing before hitting the ground with Fremont right on my heels. We entered the building looking for the front door which fortunately was directly ahead. Blasting through the room, ignoring the startled commands, and yells from those already inside, we hit the front door. Still riding our lucky streak, the Uber, a Red Mercedes Bens E-Class sedan, was waiting with open rear doors. We both jumped in, pulling the doors shut and told our driver to hit the road heading south on highway one immediately. Turning around in the seat looking out the rear window, I was able to see a couple of people come running outside who had been inside the lounge as we sped through. Whether they got our license number, I didn't know, but they sure as hell got a good look at our ride. Damn, we couldn't have been in a more conspicuous car.

To stay alive, we would have to ditch our ride in very short order, hopefully, somewhere safe where we could continue on into the city without being observed. At least we were getting close. I had about an hour and thirty minutes max before seeing the President. How to get there from here was the problem. Our enemies would know we had landed and would be heading towards the White House. They couldn't say for sure whether I had secured a way to see the big man, but we could count on their efforts to make sure that didn't happen.

Within a couple of minutes, the treacherous Colonel Baka would be found and released. He knew what clothes we were wearing and could guess at our final destination. The odds of getting to the President in time were long and getting longer. As soon as we ditched the Uber driver and could get a little privacy, I would contact Herbie again. Still, that avenue seemed less and less likely to be successful.

For the first time since our skidding landing, I took a good look at Captain Fremont. Sensing my gaze, he looked at me with a weary smile. It appeared as though he had aged several years since we left Sun Valley. Was that just this afternoon? It seemed to me like we left ages ago. Without a mirror handy, I wondered if I looked several years older as well. It certainly felt like I had aged a few years, maybe more.

"Well, Captain, thanks for getting us here. I guess," I said, giving him the best smile, I could manage at the time. "That was one hell of a landing. I hope they'll be able to clean my pants."

After a weak, pathetic obligatory chuckle, but still probably more than the line deserved, he responded, "I saw an air force buddy pull a landing like that many years ago. Wasn't sure the landing carriage on the SAAB would hold up, but I couldn't see another choice."

I'm certainly happy he didn't tell me that before starting the skid. Speaking to our driver, I asked him to drop us off at a bar in Hyattsville just down the road a couple of miles. He was quick to remind me of my promise for a big tip.

"Hey, you promised me a big bonus if I was there waiting for you at the airport."

"You bet, and you've earned it. Just drop us off at any convenient bar."

"Okay, you got it," he responded. It only took him a second before continuing, "Franklins is right on the road just ahead, barely inside city limits. Have you there in one minute." He didn't ask about our important meeting downtown, for which I was grateful. I had been telling, so many lies for so long it was starting to feel natural, and I appreciated an opportunity to avoid more lying.

Sure enough, in just about a minute, we pulled up to this funky looking building that advertised themselves as a Brew-Pub and quirky gift shop. Franklins is a two-story building that sets catty wampus to the road. Large solar panels tilted up on the roof made the building seem unbalanced. The quirky part was visible. While I could certainly use a drink, and I'm sure Fremont could as well, we couldn't afford the time to stop here. Fortunately, I had a lot of cash to take care of my driver, sending him away happy.

Standing outside of Franklins, we looked around, trying to decide on our next move. Gallatin Street intersected highway one right in front of Franklins, and two hundred feet straight ahead was the Vigilante Coffee shop. The view from there was very advantageous because we would be able to see the bad guys before they saw us. Of course, that would only happen if our Uber driver was found and gave us away as being at Franklins. The way our luck had been running the chance of the Red Mercedes being found was a lock. Just getting out of the main target area for a few minutes would give us a little time to plan our next move. Hoofing it over to Vigilante's, we ordered a cup of coffee and grabbed a table by the window where we could see down the street to Franklins Brew Pub.

We had ninety minutes to save the President of the United States and prevent a coup that could potentially turn the country into a dictatorship.

CHAPTER TWENTY-NINE
DISASTER

Sitting at our table in the Vigilante coffee shop, I called Herbie.

"Sizzler."

His salutations were growing shorter again. I interpreted this to mean his frustration exceeded his abilities and he did not have a clue as to what to do next.

"Herbie, we're running out of time. Are you able to help me or not?"

"I'm sorry, Reader. I can't persuade the Secretary to help unless I can provide more information."

He sounded sad and depressed. I believe he bought the Pulitzer angle. Whether his disappointment came from missing out on a big story or failing to get an appointment with the Secretary, maybe both, I couldn't tell. His reputation as a go-getter, the guy who could approach anyone in D.C., was in jeopardy. It was time for me to try something else. But...... what?

"Okay, Herbie. Thanks for trying. There isn't much time left, but if you determine of a way to persuade her to call me, give it an opportunity." My next statement would sound mean, and perhaps I meant it too, at least a little, but a final prompt couldn't help. "I would love to help you get that Pulitzer. It seems a shame that such a perfect opportunity, a once in a lifetime chance at fame, goes by the wayside. Perhaps we'll cross paths again someday. Goodbye, Herbie." I disconnected before getting his response. It would not be seemly to have him witness my own fears and frustrations.

Blowing on his coffee to cool it down, Fremont observed, "it doesn't sound very positive, Sage. Do you have any other ideas about contacting the President?"

It would be so great if I could just plug in a number, call the White House and ask to speak with the President. I, being a nobody with no proper identification, well hell, even with improper identification, there was no chance my call would go through. I couldn't think of a way to get past the White House gatekeepers.

Answering Fremont, I said, "I'm thinking about calling the Secretary myself. The pervert slipped up in one of our phone calls giving me just enough information to figure out who he was calling. Sheila Garvey, Secretary of Education. Maybe if I talk to her in person, we could get a meeting. The problem is getting her to take my call. Especially now after all the calls from Herbie. She doesn't know me or anything about me unless Herbie told her I read minds. That may or may not help me. I guess there's no time like the present to see what happens."

I powered up Critt's phone and scrolled through his apps, seeking for information on the Secretary of Education. Her website had a politician's scattering of pretty words and optimistic promises. There was information about all the positive actions the Secretary was taking, but no way to access the Secretary except through her gatekeepers. I was just about to start the process when Captain Fremont got my attention.

"Sage, we might have a serious dilemma. Look down the avenue."

Ten big black vans and SUV's were crowding the road in front of Franklin's Brew Pub. I suppose the government gets a discount if they buy all-black vehicles. As the cars screeched to a stop, men in suits jumped out of doors, with many rushing into the pub and others scanning the streets looking for witnesses. My guess was they had found the red Mercedes.

"Oh shit!" I whispered just in case somebody near might hear my unusual question. "Was there anybody on the streets when we took off for the Vigilante?

"I don't know," he murmured back. "Don't remember seeing anybody, but we were in such a hurry to leave Franklins I wasn't concentrating on the roads as often as searching for a place to hide."

"Yeah, me too. I don't suppose it will be long before the gang starts a door-to-door search. There are several businesses in the area. Looking at a map of Hyattsville on the phone I saw a police station about a block away and a small park a few blocks in the other direction bordering the street."

Not familiar with the protocol governments and police practiced while searching, our next move was problematic. There were enough fellows in and around Franklin's to cover a wide area quickly. It wouldn't matter if anyone saw us leaving Franklin's heading up to Vigilante. With the number of men they had available, we could expect at least two or more heading our way checking places out. We had maybe four or five minutes to get lost.

Two serious looking men started walking up Gallatin Street towards our location. Two doors away down Highway One was Chez Diors, a café featuring West African fare. There were a pair of searchers walking down the sidewalk on both sides of the highway. I didn't care about Chez Diors, but there was a parking lot behind the restaurant, and from our window I could see several parked cars.

"Come on, Captain. Let's see if we can steal a car. It might be our only way out of this mess."

We were both moving out Vigilante's back door as I was speaking. Fortunately, this put us in a parking lot shielded from the view of searchers on both Gallatin Street and the highway. Unless someone were careless leaving a key in their ride, we would have to break in and hot-wire an older car if there was one in the lot. Any late model car defeats my carjacking skills. There was no lighting in the parking lot, only street lights, making it hard to see the makes of vehicles in the dark. Hurrying through the lot crammed with many kinds of new cars, we came across a 1956 Ford Mustang. Not a new car. Just the kind of car I needed.

One of my all-time favorite models. I never owned one, but one of my sparing mates from the gym had this model, and he drove me home one time. This was a car I could hot-wire in less than two minutes. Fortunately, the car was unlocked, but there was no key in the ignition, and I couldn't find one hidden under the floor mat or behind the sunshade. Within two minutes, I had the car running, and we pulled out of the parking lot onto a nameless service road running behind the establishments fronting the highway.

One block away was Farragut Street, where we took a right going away from the highway. I didn't turn on the car lights until we had traveled a couple of blocks. There was no way of knowing how long we had before the owner went looking for his car and then notifying the police that someone had stolen his vehicle. We perhaps, hopefully, had a few minutes to dump this ride and discover other transportation that would not be on anybody's search list.

I had Fremont pull up a map of the locality so he could navigate us to somewhere safe, if such a place existed. Highway one turns into Rhode Island Avenue, which dead-ends at Connecticut Avenue five blocks from the White House. The traffic was stop and go, which would make our trip into downtown D.C. about twenty minutes. After discussing it for a couple of minutes, we decided we had to lose the Mustang sooner rather than later. Coming up on our left was a Dunkin Donut shop with a large parking lot. I pulled in slotting the Mustang between a large new red Cadillac Escalade and a black Jeep Grand Cherokee. The Mustang had a much lower roofline than either vehicle, making it almost invisible from the highway.

We didn't have that much further to go, but with no way to contact the President, the best we could do at the moment was leave the Mustang and find some place to hole up where we could relax for a few moments.

My time to interfere with the plan to kill the President was down to just over 60 minutes. Two miles and a lifetime away sat a man about to experience a heart attack that would end his life.

By now, our pursuers knew we would travel on Highway 1. It was a fair bet that between our location and the Whitehouse, there would be a checkpoint with officers scrutinizing every vehicle and every person. Even if I could get into see the President, getting there required us to pass through the gauntlet.

It wasn't looking very promising, and my spirits were lagging even worse than before. Generally optimistic, I was finding it tougher and tougher to stay focused and believing in myself. Captain Fremont was excellent company, helping me feel less lonely and helpless, but he was no help otherwise.

With time running out, the situation was looking grim. From here, we could call a cab or Uber, but getting through the checkpoints would be nearly impossible. And I still had no way of even getting in to see the man, even if I could make it to the Whitehouse.

Pulling up my screen for Secretary Garvey, I accessed her website to see if there was any way of making contact. Important people, such as the Secretary of Education, and those who only think they are important such as their gatekeepers, make it challenging to have direct contact. You are invited to leave messages with the promise that every message is read and responded to at their earliest convenience. That could mean tomorrow or a week from now. But no way to access them. I had forgotten about Herbie until Fremont asked, "didn't that blogger have the Secretaries number?"

"Oh my God," I shouted. Here I had been wasting time trying to make contact when my pervert buddy already has the number. I was so tired and stressed out from what had already been a very long day that I was not thinking clearly. A day that started out with people trying to kill me. It was time to shake off the wearies and focus. I hadn't been training in the martial arts just for the physical. The mental training was equally important. I knew I could do better.

Herbie answered after the first ring. No greeting this time, just "I was wondering when you would call again."

"Herbie, I need Secretary Garvey's phone number right now."

"I never told you it was Secretary Garvey." He sounded petulant like I was stealing something from him.

"No, but it wasn't difficult to figure out who it was with all the hints you dropped. Come on, Herbie, let me give it a shot."

"What about my Pulitzer? If you can get her to meet with you, I might get left out."

I did not have the time or patience to argue with the man. "Herbie, do you know where the Dunkin Donut store is on Rhode Island Avenue? It's next to the interchange with Florida Avenue."

"Is that the one close to the Chicken Place?" Could have a guessed that was coming if I was thinking straight.

"If you mean KoChix, then yeah, Herbie. That's the one. How far from there do you live?

"About ten minutes. I live in Pleasant Plains. Why?"

My God. Time's flying away, and suddenly, Herbie is acting like he doesn't have a brain in his head.

"Do you have a car?" Talk about no brains. I should have asked him that to begin with. I was having trouble thinking clearly.

"I got a VW bus. I usually take a cab when I have to go someplace. Parking downtown is brutal unless you're a congressman or somebody important."

"Ok, never mind that. Please come here as fast as possible. We are about out of time. Come down Florida Avenue and we'll look for your bus. You'll see me waving on the sidewalk. Okay?"

"Sure thing, Reader. I'm on my way. Over and out." Good Lord. What in the hell does that idiot think this is? Some cops and robber video game? Over and out.

"Aargh!" If only I had a beer I could cry into.

Turning back to Captain Fremont, I said, "I guess you realize what's happening?" I could see frustration, worry and hope all conflicting with each other in the contours of his face. Mine probably looked the same as I continued with my thoughts, "It's possibly better this way if that pervert can get his shit together. We need new wheels anyway. I'm praying his line isn't tapped by any of the bad guys. Herbie mentioned the word President once, or maybe twice. Let's wait for him on the other side of Rhode Island Avenue. I'll watch for Herbie. You keep an eye out the other direction. If his call was monitored and the bad guys are on to us, they might come from any direction."

"Well, Sage. We have just about an hour. Let's hope we can stay alive a little longer. If we spot someone coming or someone tailing Herbie, what do we do?"

"Looking at the map on my phone, I saw we would have to go up to the Post Office to get out of the traffic. Depending on which way the posse is coming from, we have to believe we can locate some car we can steal or carjack before they catch us. I guess it's time to pray."

"Hell Sage. I've been praying for hours."

CHAPTER THIRTY
SECRETARY GARVEY

Near the crosswalk next to the post office a bus stop appeared with a couple of benches. Behind the benches grew a few shade trees and a small green hedge. The spot offered some concealment allowing us to watch for a vehicle speeding towards us while remaining somewhat hidden. Our anxious waiting was taking a toll on us both. Our nerves were continually on edge, never knowing from one moment to the next if we were about to be caught and killed. The chilling evening air had the scent of traffic exhaust, and neither of us had a jacket. Either our words spoken on Herbie's phone did not trigger an alert, or they were slow to get the word out to the bad guys, about where we were going to be for the next few minutes since no one appeared.

Much to our relief, an old orange 1980s VW bus come rattling and smoking down the street with no one following that I could see. It was dark, but the street lighting allowed visibility for at least a whole block, and even before I saw Herbie's van, I could make out the thing rattling along about a full block away. As I stepped out to flag Herbie down, I was praying that he had left his mother home. Given the nature of their relationship, it would not have surprised me to see her riding shotgun. Still, as the van drew to a stop by the sidewalk, it was evident that Herbie was alone.

I had already signaled Fremont, and without wasting any time, we bundled ourselves into the van; me in the front telling Herbie to move it. Without my asking, he turned down Rhode Island Ave towards downtown D.C. Looking at my map; I had him turn off onto an unnamed side street just before the Olde City Farm and Garden. Turning to Herbie, I said, "Okay, give me the number."

He didn't have to ask whose. He gave me the full ten digits from memory.

I immediately called Secretary Garvey on my Burner; afraid she might not answer if I called on the phone Herbie had been using all evening.

The phone rang several times, and I was afraid she wouldn't answer, or the call would go to voice mail when two of the words I most wanted to hear in all the world were in my ear,

"Secretary Garvey." Her voice was a little raspy, sounded like a smoker. She sounded tired and irritated.

"Madam Secretary, you don't know me, but please listen for a moment. I would hate for the gin in that cut crystal Waterford cocktail glass you or holding in your left hand to be wasted."

"Who in the hell are you? And how do you know I'm drinking gin with my left hand?" I could just see her scanning the room for a hidden camera or some peeping Tom standing outside the room by the glass doors on the balcony.

"Professionally, I'm known as The Reader. My recent acquaintance who goes by Sizzler has mentioned me to you this evening, and before you hang up, please know that your husband sitting across the room from you in his red velvet evening smoking jacket will be looking for a new place to live in the near future unless I can convince you to do us all a huge favor."

I was just rattling along, trying to throw in enough of my 'reading stuff' to get her attention.

"And don't try to find some hidden camera in your room, or a peeping Tom outside of your cozy little book-lined den. I don't need tricks or gadgets to know what you are thinking or seeing. I just read your mind. That is who I am. I am The Reader."

"Okay, mister Reader. You have my attention. Make it quick." You could practically hear the venom in the way she said mist-er Read-er. This was not going to be easy.

"Madam Secretary, I am certain your private telephone is monitored by powers within the government. They are probably not listening to our conversation. Still, every word is recorded: and if certain keywords are spoken, it triggers an alarm in real-time. At that point, they will begin listening to every word they hear; at which point your life, my life, and several other lives will be quietly disposed of, and we will never be seen again. Believe me, this is not an alarmist nutcase speaking. My day began with a chosen hit team of U.S. special forces personnel trying to kill me. That I am even able to speak to you now is both an act of divine providence and excellent luck."

"Whoever you are, what are you trying to do?" She sounded worried and tense. I was starting to sweat in Herbie's chilly Van. So much depended on getting her to help. I was terrified at the prospect that I might fail.

"Well, mam, I'm trying to save a life and our country. That probably sounds delusional, like a load of crap, but let me tell you your exact thought right this second: 'I should call the police and have this guy arrested.' If you do that, you will be out of a job tomorrow."

"Why are you trying to scare the crap out of me? What made you choose me? How come I deserve your attention?" Firing off question after question without even waiting for an answer. She was starting to sound a bit hysterical.

"The reason I am calling you is that I have been told you can call the leader of our country at this time of night and ask for an emergency meeting."

I was pleading with everything I could think of that sounded convincing.

"Madam Secretary, we are about out of time. If you would please meet with me for two minutes, I can prove that everything I just said about an emergency is true. Bring your security, have them check me out, and if you are not convinced about my story after two minutes, you can have them kick me out of your car on the street or have me arrested. Just please, give me two minutes. And it has to be within the next few minutes, we're running short of time. If you are not totally convinced about my story, you can go back home and probably be there before the Ice melts in the single malt scotch drink your husband just poured."

"Okay, mister Reader. I'm convinced." Her reluctance was palpable even over the phone. I could also hear the weariness and resignation in her voice. "Where are you?"

She sounded like someone who was not sure, but thought in case there was any truth to my worlds, it should be checked out. If there was even one chance in a million, I was right, she could not afford to take that chance. Kind of like when you are in bed at night and hear an unusual sound. You are not sure what caused the disturbance, and you don't want to be bothered; but just in case it is something important, you reluctantly drag yourself out of bed to go see what caused the sound.

"That isn't important." My own impatience was edging up towards panics-Ville. "How soon can you meet me at Lafayette Square? Please be quick."

"I can be at the square in roughly twenty minutes. Where will I meet you?"

"I'll be standing at the corner of Pennsylvania Ave by the Rochambeau Statue. Behind me will be an old orange VW bus. Please, just stop and pick me up. You can have one of your secret agents be in the back seat to check me out for weapons. By the time you pick me up, we will have just about fifteen minutes to save our country. Please, please be on time."

"All right, dammit Reader, I'll be there. If this is some kind of hoax, you can kiss your miserable annoying ass goodbye."

The line went dead, so no friendly goodbye. Boy, she sounded pissed. Still, I guess anyone at this time of night, relaxing at home with a cocktail would be unhappy about being disturbed.

"Okay, Herbie. You heard me talking to the Secretary. Get us to Pennsylvania Ave. If this works out, I promise to give you an exclusive story that will blow through this city like a hurricane."

Herbie started driving on Rhode Island Ave towards Logan Circle in his rattling old bus. We had about thirty-five minutes to save the President's life. Hopefully, Secretary Garvey would be able to arrange for a meeting. All we had to do now was have the Secretary arrange for a meeting, after which I needed to convince the President to gamble on my story about the plans to take his life.

We exited Rhode Island Ave. at 17ST NW headed towards Lafayette Square. At this point, we were roughly six blocks from the White House, and I was expecting a roadblock somewhere close to the President's house, perhaps one or two blocks away in each direction. This would put a roadblock somewhere at the beginning or middle of Lafayette Square, between us and our meeting place with the Secretary. Sure enough, there they were. The street we were on turned into Connecticut Ave just before it reached K ST NW. The checkpoint was visible one block ahead on HST NW. The east side of Connecticut Ave contains The Bombay Club and The Hay Adams Hotel. Sandwiched in between was the US Chamber of Commerce Building. Thank God for Google.

There are several large parking lots for these establishments that exited off from Connecticut Ave. Although the time was late, there were still a few vehicles entering and leaving the lots. Washington bureaucrats never sleep, it seems. I had Herbie exit the highway into the parking lot and stop to let me out. There was no way we could pass through the gauntlet in Herbie's bus. Wishing my associates good luck, I jumped out, hoping I could find some way past the checkpoint on foot. If only I had agreed to meet the Secretary outside of the blocked area. She could drive through with no problem. It was too late to try to arrange for another meeting spot, and we were running out of time.

Washington, D.C. is chilly this time of year, and of course, I didn't think to ask Herbie for his jacket. The cool evening was made even cooler by a slight breeze carrying a faint whiff of the Potomac River. I remembered seeing it as Fremont sent us cruising by at about 200 miles an hour. It didn't seem to be this close as we went by.

I live in the San Francisco Bay Area and spend several days a year next to the ocean. I never get tired of smelling the fresh tangy salt air, and although this river had a musky scent, it still reminded me of home.

Connecticut Ave led directly to Lafayette Square and the White House. The parking lots were well lit and shadows hard to come by as I went slipping through cars towards Lafayette Square, trying to appear like any other dignitary going into the Hotel. I reached the Hay Adams located across the street from the center of Lafayette Square. Once again, luck was on my side. Several people were crossing H Street towards the square, and I just joined in like part of the gang. There didn't seem to be any surveillance within the park.

I had worked up a little sweat Hustling along; that plus, my tattered nerves were on edge, no doubt adding to the salty spill down my cheeks. At any second, I was expecting someone in a suit with a phone plugged into his ear to jump out of the shadows and call me to halt. I managed to reach Pennsylvania Ave without incident and cross it to the south side, the side where I was to meet with the Secretary.

The Rochambeau Statue is within Lafayette Square, although the park isn't square, (what would you expect in Washington D.C.?) more of a rectangle, with the statue located in the southwest corner. Trees dot the south side of Pennsylvania Avenue, providing a lot of cover as I skulked my way along watching for someone who appeared threatening. I reached the corner of Pennsylvania Ave and Jackson without being noticed. At least I thought I was unobserved. Now, all I had to do was cross Jackson and wait for the Secretary who was due to arrive in about three minutes. There were still a few tourists walking down Pennsylvania gawking at the White House, so my presence didn't trigger any alarms. I suspect the surveillance was still focused on vehicles trying to reach the White House.

The next three minutes seemed to drag on for an eternity, and I suddenly started shivering. The sweat was drying, and in the cold air, this California boy felt like he was freezing to death. I didn't dare stand too close to the street in case they were watching. I wondered what happened to Captain Fremont and Herbie. I prayed that they were safe somewhere out of the danger zone.

As I stood contemplating all the day's events that brought me to this chilly corner of the universe, I saw a limousine come cruising down Pennsylvania. If it was the Secretary, she was looking for an orange VW bus which was not here. With no other choice, I jumped into the middle of the street, waving for the driver to stop. If this corner of the park was under surveillance, we were all dead.

There were two men in the front seat of the limo, and I could see a woman's head sitting in the back. At that point, I was pretty sure the limo contained the Secretary. What were the chances that a limousine would be here at this time of night with some other woman in the back seat?

I immediately started asking the universe for guidance. She had to listen and act. At this point, it was up to the Gods of fate.

CHAPTER THIRTY-ONE
THE GODS OF FATE

The Secretary was sitting in the back-bench seat, on my side of the limousine, with both bodyguards in the front, which surprised me. I hopped in the back forcing the Secretary to slide over to the other side of the car. She is a trim, petite lady of about fifty who didn't hide the gray hair sprinkled through her light brown hair. Kind of like the color often seen on an oak leaf in the fall. She had on dark pants with a white turtle-neck sweater covered by a dark, well-cut cotton and leather evening jacket, possibly a Loewe. A cigarette hanging from her fingers with smoke curling upwards confirmed my thoughts about her smoking and she didn't waste any time with a greeting.

"Okay, Reader. This better be dammed good, or you're toast."

I didn't bother with a greeting either. "Madam Secretary, could you please instruct your driver to park someplace very close. We're going to the White House, and we're in a hurry."

The driver heard my request and having hauled the Secretary to this place many times knew just the spot.

As we began moving, I wasted no time.

"My name is Sage, although my business associates only know me as The Reader. My day began in Sun Valley Idaho, where I had a nine o'clock business appointment. As I sat in the lounge of the Sun Valley Lodge, a man entered the front door with the specific intent of taking me outside where his three comrades were waiting to make me disappear, permanently. My ability to read minds gave me this information, which I verified during the next hour as they entered a massive search to find me. I subdued them one at a time and confirmed their intentions. I had several questions; the first two were who called for me to be dead, and why?"

I could see that I had the Secretaries attention.

"I can be very persuasive when the situation demands, and this one certainly qualified. In questioning their leader, the man I initially noticed, he could only tell me the name of the man who gave the order to make me disappear permanently, the Secretary of Defense, Roger Horowitz. My would-be killer could not tell me the reason. My killer's personal phone displayed one call received within the past several hours. Taking a chance, I called this number, which was answered by Horowitz. Pretending to be my killer, I assured him that the job had been completed. I still did not know why he wanted me dead, and the only way to find out was to ask him face to face, where he could not feign ignorance without my knowing."

Knowing that I had the Secretaries interest I continued, "Earlier I had learned that Senator Christopher Kim from Hawaii owns a ranch in the Sun Valley area where he hosted a large gathering of important Washington dignitaries. Assuming that this was where I would find Secretary Horowitz, I learned its location and sneaked into ranch headquarters. I could hear the party from a half-mile away. I didn't need to find the Secretary because I listened to some other guests talking about the big event this evening. James Selva, Chairman of the JCS, has been planning a coup against the current President for several months. Unhappy with the President's plan to release all of Tesla's papers to the public, he has convinced many high-profile Washington dignitaries to join him in a plot to kill the President tonight at ten p.m., roughly twenty minutes from now. Attending the party at Senator Kim's compound are the Vice President, at least one member of the Supreme Court, several senators, congressmen, many Generals, and Admirals plus several cabinet members and their staff. I saw all of this. Also included were several other wealthy essential members of the financial and technical industries, although I don't know their names. That is why I had to be so careful with you on the phone. I was not sure we could trust you."

My story was long, I know, but the Secretary was following along, if not actually fascinated.

"Since that time, I caught a ride on a private jet which was forced down near Wright Patt, stole a prop jet which was forced to land at College Park, and stole a car, all the while trying to avoid being captured.

"You may or may not know that about ten o'clock each evening, the President has one of his Secret Service agents prepare him an evening, end-of-the-day, cocktail. Only tonight, the agent will add in a few drops of a special liquid provided by the CIA that will simulate a heart attack. The revelers in Sun Valley are just waiting for the telephone call to announce the President's death, when a Supreme Court Justice will swear in the Vice President as the New President. The only way

I know how to convince the President that this story is real and to stop this assignation is to persuade the President to let the drink be prepared. After the cocktail is ready, the President is to order the Secret Service agent to drink the cocktail himself. To convince the President to try this gambit, I need to talk with him. That is why you are here. I need you to call the President immediately and beg for an immediate meeting, pleading some kind of desperate emergency that cannot wait until tomorrow."

I stopped talking and looked closely at the Secretary. She was on the edge of her seat staring at me with open mouth and a glazed look in her eyes. I wasn't sure whether she was in shock or disbelief.

Shaking off whatever she had been experiencing, she picked up her cell phone lying on the seat between us and started dialing. My God, I hoped and prayed she was trying to get us in to see the President and not have me arrested. My heart was pounding like a timpani drum at a rock concert. That she had not asked me any questions was kind of unnerving.

"This is Secretary Garvey. I need to talk with the President. Immediately."

I felt like my heart would explode. My God! She actually made the call.

She glanced over at me, and with a bold eye wink, while holding her hand over the speaker said, "White House switchboard. Real tough gatekeepers."

"Mister President. I'm so very sorry to be calling you at this late hour. A bit of an emergency just arose having to deal with that terrible school shooting in New Mexico last week. I need just a few minutes of your time to get your take on a situation that has come up, so I know how to handle it properly."

There was a pause while I assume the President was talking. Secretary Garvey appeared strained, like a marathon runner during the last mile.

"Yes, mister President. I mean tonight. Right now, if possible. I'm outside, just off Pennsylvania. I can be there in five minutes. I promise. It won't take over ten minutes."

A look of relief soothed the sharp ridges of her jaw and lips.

"Thank you, mister President. We'll be right there. Oh, I'm bringing one of my assistants who just brought me the news. He isn't dressed properly. I hope that's all right.... Bye now."

"Well, Reader, or I guess I should say, Sage, you've got your meeting with the President. I sure in hell hope you know what you're doing because I don't. I fear it will not go well for either of us if you cannot back up your claims."

"Madam Secretary, I read a saying once, I'm not sure where it comes from:

'he who has no hope, never has a fear.'"

"I sure as hell have the fear Reader." You could hear it in her voice, all strained and tight. Along with the rough cigarette voice, it didn't sound pleasant.

We now had twelve minutes. I wasn't sure how much time it would take us to get in to see the President. Hopefully, it would be before he had his cocktail.

Chapter Thirty-Two
Through the Gauntlet

We turned on 17 TH ST and went down about three or four hundred yards before turning left onto an access road of some sort. I could see the Eisenhower Executive Office Building off on my left. The Google map I had studied earlier didn't take me any further, and I couldn't make out whether the street had a name. I didn't ask the Secretary as she seemed uptight and nervous. Hell, I couldn't blame her, I was sweating bullets. Our driver stopped at the end of the street where there was an entrance to the South Lawn Drive. There were two guards stationed by the entrance, both holding rifles across their chests.

The driver lowered his window as one guard approached the limousine. He was a muscular, six-foot man in green fatigues wearing a helmet and what looked like a wide belt with a holstered handgun and a lot of external leather pouches. When he got to the car, we saw that his stern face was almost square with what looked like dark brown eyes, although he was standing with the light at his back-casting shadows on his face, so it was hard to tell. There was no smile or compromise in his demeanor when he said, "You cannot go any further, turn around and go back."

No, I'm sorry or please; just orders given in a rough voice used to giving orders and expecting immediate obedience. He sounded like one of the MP police guards you hear in war movies.

Our driver said, "I have Secretary Garvey in the back who has an appointment with the President."

"MY ORDERS ARE TO STOP EVERYONE FROM PROCEEDING BEYOND THIS POINT."

His voice had risen in volume and what had initially been staunch resistance had turned into a full-blown command of restraint.

Secretary Garvey suddenly lost her nervousness. She practically hurled herself out of the car demanding in her own stern voice;

"WHO IN THE HELL GAVE YOU THAT ORDER, BECAUSE IT WASN'T THE PRESIDENT. I JUST TALKED WITH HIM ON THE PHONE."

This was a lady who knew her place in Washington and the place of Palace guards, of every stripe.

"My commander, Madam Secretary. Commander Hawkins." He answered, and while his tone was commanding and gruff, it was at least lowered to a reasonable level as he was showing her respect.

Not to be easily dismissed, Garvey asked, "and what has his position got to do with White House Security?

For the first time, a crack appeared in the guard's stance, "I don't know Madam Secretary, I am only following commander Hawkins orders."

"Get your commander on the phone immediately. I want to get this resolved right now. I am here to see the President with his approval. He is expecting me. Now get on the phone, soldier."

I'm wasn't sure the guards were real military personnel. I don't know what made Garvey think they were, or if she merely said soldier because the guard was acting like one — just following orders. They were not military police; they didn't have the MP letters on their helmets.

The guard stepped away from the vehicle while slinging the rifle over his shoulder so he could hold it in one hand, then reached into a pocket of his vest retrieving a radio unit. It reminded me of one of those old Motorola Talk About walkie talkies; only this was all black. Pushing a button to speak, he turned to the side but we could hear him say, "Sir, It's Secretary Garvey, and she says she has an appointment with the President."

Looking back at the car he asked, "Who do you have in the car with you, Madam Secretary?

A very agitated Sheila Garvey responded in a curt, cutting voice. "What in the hell has that got to do with anything soldier? It isn't any of your God Dammed business, but just for the record, I have my driver, bodyguard and personal aide. Now get out of our way."

There was a brief pause as the guard looked at the Secretary, then the car, while muttering on the phone. It was clear that commander Hawkins, whoever he was, had heard the Secretaries response over the radio. After a slight hesitation, we could listen to the guard, responding, "Yes, sir. I'll let her pass."

Turning back to face the Secretary, our guard motioned us forward, saying, "it's okay, Madam Secretary. Just a little misunderstanding." To the other guard, he said, "okay, let them through."

Our driver started down the drive along the White House South Lawn, going straight for a while, then turning to the left, making a big sweeping turn stopping in front of the south side White House entrance. There were guards also posted here, but they looked like the regular White House guards you see all the time on tv when the President is coming or going. At least they didn't have the same appearance as those guards out by the street.

There was a long-covered walkway to the door flanked by a guard on each side. These guards were not carrying rifles, but they wore pistols and stood with their hand clasped in front of their belt buckles. They also wore identical stern faces with a look that said, 'don't fuck with me.'

I got out of the limousine first, holding out a hand for the Secretary. Garvey ignored my hand, helping herself out before addressing the guard on the left side.

"I am Secretary Garvey, and the President is expecting me." Her voice had some steel in it, authoritative, kind of menacing. It was the sound you hear from someone who has had a long, tough day and was not about to put up with a load of crap from anyone.

The guard replied, "yes, Madam Secretary. The President's switchboard just called and said to let you go through. I'll open the door for you where you will find a secret service agent waiting to escort you and your guest in to see the President."

"Thank you, sir." Secretary Garvey responded, brisk and terse.

The guard turned around, heading towards a dark wood door with Garvey right behind. I followed along, not sure what they expected me to do. This meeting was such a gratefully unexpected end to what had been a terrifying day. My clothes were rumpled, sweat-stained, and undoubtedly odor stained completing the picture of a bum with no call to be visiting the President. Certainly not appropriate dress for meeting the most powerful man on earth. The secret service man had a look on his face suggesting that I looked like one of those presents your cat leaves on the steps just outside of the front door. The air felt chilly, and I broke out in goosebumps the size of raisins. There were certainly a lot of nerves responsible for those goosebumps besides the cold air. Despite the tension I was feeling at the prospect of what might happen in the next few minutes, I still smelled the river. We must be much closer than when I last got a whiff of the musky odor as the scent seemed much stronger. For some inexplainable reason, this homey watery smell helped relax me.

The guard opened the door, and we could see a secret service agent just inside wearing a black suit, white shirt and blue tie. He smiled at the Secretary and frowned at me. "Is that all you have to wear?" The same look as the man outside by the door.

"Well,,,, ah, yes. I'm sorry, but I am from out of town and was not expecting to see the President today. When this all happened, there was no time for me to go shopping for other clothes. I'm sure the President has seen rumpled street clothes before." The story sounded lame, even to my own ears. How can anyone who looked like he had been hog tied and dragged behind a car expect to see the most important man in the world? If I was feeling stressed, inadequate and out of place before, the frowning guard only amplified my worst fears.

Still frowning, he said, "very well, just follow me." He took off, walking down a long hallway staying as far ahead of me as possible. Hell, I didn't mind. I was too tired, too anxious, and way too stressed to take much notice of the beautiful floor and grand assortment of pictures, let alone some secret service agent who might be offended by a little body odor. Several turns and hallways later, we came to another dark wood door with another secret service agent standing just outside. As we got closer, he knocked on the door, and a moment later opened with him motioning with his hands for us to go through. I'm not sure if the President spoke something we couldn't hear, or the agent just knocked out of courtesy before letting us in.

I was about to meet the leader of the free world. Suddenly my mouth was so dry it felt like I had been in Death Valley for a week with no water. I was shaking with frayed nerves and felt so out of place in my ordinary smelly soiled clothes. Thank the good Lord I was at least able to get out of those hideous clothes I purchased at the Gold Mine.

There was so much to take in. The Oval Office. The President. My God. I had read about this place a thousand times, and here I was. Gawking like a starstruck teenager meeting Brad Pitt, I barely heard the Secretary introduce me as the one who could describe the emergency. Suddenly I was on center stage with the full spotlight shining in my eyes. My varied reading program provided me with a phrase used by big game hunters describing a situation in which presented with an opportunity for a kill shot, the shooter freezes. They call it buck fever. I think this is what I experienced now that my big moment had arrived. I couldn't speak. My brain froze. All of my feelings of inadequacy, insecurity, and helplessness held me in some kind of trance. The Secretary looked at me with a question,

'well, what are you waiting for? I got you here.'

It was seeing the hope, fear, and anxiousness in her look that shook me out of my trance. Just like that, my paralysis disappeared. I had risked my life to be here at this moment, to see this man, to save his life. After what I had gone through, I was not about to let my stinking rumpled clothes and body odor intimidate me any longer. "Mr. President, I would like to tell you a story."

CHAPTER THIRTY-THREE
THE PRESIDENT

The President was wearing a tailored blue suit with gray piping and a red and blue striped necktie. His black hair was smoothed loosely against his skull with just a hint dropping down over his forehead, giving him a Robin Williams look. With barely a wrinkle in his attire, he still appeared rumpled, probably as a result of a trying day. His blue eyes could and probably would look friendly most of the time, but in this case, they cast a chill down my spine. I'm sure he didn't want this late-night interruption, and by an underdressed smelly civilian who looked like someone's idea of a California surf bum. Not only that, but I stood in his office gawking like a twelve-year-old boy watching a forbidden sex film; then, I started stuttering like one of those zombies you see mumbling down Dumaine street in the New Orleans French Quarter. And if all of that was not enough, I started out speaking stupidly using the word story. The President of the United States, at nearly ten o'clock in the evening, was not interested in any f-ing story. As scowls go, the President's was world-class; score it a ten.

I hadn't risked my life practically all day long to let a scowl intimidate me, even if it was a world-class scowl by our President, leader of the free world, the most powerful man on earth.

"My name is Sage. No middle name, no last name. Only Sage. Professionally I am known as The Reader because I can read people's minds. Not just their thoughts, but everything in their brains. All the information stored throughout their lives. For instance, right now," I paused listening to the President's mind; 'I gave up my evening for this, to listen to a smelly, poorly dressed, fucking storyteller who reads minds' "You were just thinking 'I gave up my evening for this, to listen to a smelly, poorly dressed, fucking storyteller who reads minds.' Those are your exact thoughts."

The President sat up a little straighter as though I might have slapped him on the cheek.

My story continued. "I could describe for you the morning you had in Miami, where your meeting with representatives from the Cuban expatriates went badly, which is why you returned to Washington a day earlier than planned. That's the main reason I am here tonight, because you came home a day earlier."

No one was supposed to know about the President's meeting with the Cubans, and certainly, no one knew that his meeting went off the rails almost as soon as it began. I now had his full attention.

"No one told me about your meeting. I just read your mind to prove my Bonafede's. My day began in Sun Valley, Idaho, where I was supposed to meet with a client at nine o'clock. Our meeting was to be at the registration desk of the Sun Valley Lodge. After my morning run and workout, I had a light breakfast, after which I sat down in the Lobby where I could watch the front desk for my contact. We had never met and didn't know what each other looked like, hence the arranged meeting place. I saw a tall, nice-looking man enter the front door and approach the registration desk, so I began standing to see if this was my contact when I received a very sharp mental image of danger. Looking around, I saw a second man standing just inside the doorway watching the registration desk, and reading his mind; I found that he was looking for me. He didn't know what I looked like, other than a vague general description, so he had been following my contact to see who he was meeting. As soon as I appeared, the man standing in the doorway planned on getting me outside somehow. If talking didn't work, he was prepared to knock me out and carry me outside where his three buddies were waiting. My initial thought was that these guys were all military, which later proved to be the case. They were special forces personnel with just a few weeks of active service duty left before retirement. They planned to incapacitate me, throw me into a waiting van, and ultimately make me disappear, more than likely in one of the lava fields in the surrounding area. Naturally, I was opposed to their plan. In order to save my skin, I needed information. Who sent them, and why?"

I now had the President's full attention. I think he was getting into my story. Glancing at the Secretary, I could sense her nervousness. She kept glancing between the President and me to see how well my story was playing.

"With a lot of luck, I was able to get the men separated and ultimately subdued. With a little persuasion, I discovered that the man responsible for the disposal order was someone you know very well, your Secretary of Defense, Roger Horowitz."

The President shook his head from side to side like what I had said could not possibly be true.

"My would-be killers only knew this much. They didn't know why? To find the answer to this question, I had to locate Secretary Horowitz."

I could see that the name of Secretary Horowitz rocked the President. He kept shaking his head in a negative sign of disbelief.

"I found the Secretary at the home of someone else I have reason to believe you know intimately, Senator Kim from Hawaii. Senator Kim's Sun Valley home looks like a smaller version of Windsor Castle set on a sprawling ranch outside of Ketchum. His ranch features many outbuildings plus a large barn which I believe is the stables. His home proper is across the Big Wood River, and I could hear a party in progress from there, a quarter of a mile away. I bluffed my way past the two guards at the river gate and drove into the main yard. The lot was full of Mercedes, Lincolns, Cadillacs, Lexus's, and Jeep Grand Cherokees. The first person I saw was the Vice President, along with several U.S. Senators, including Senator Kim. Nearly everyone was holding a cocktail glass or a beer bottle. A band was playing in the background, and you could hear the scantily clad girls laughing like it was the grandest ole party in the world. When I found one of the slightly drunk girls alone, I asked her what the celebration was for, and she looked at me like I was somebody's idiot stepchild. 'Why honey Chile, didn't you know, tonight we're getting a new President?' Suddenly it all kind of made sense. I remember seeing one of the Supreme Court Justices earlier, although I didn't know his name, just recognized him from a picture. Eavesdropping on other conversations, I heard one of the senators explain that tonight at ten o'clock, when your Secret Service agent prepares your evening cocktail, there will be a little something extra in it to simulate a heart attack. You are to die rather quickly. Your Secret Service agent will then call James Selva, Chairman of the JCS. It turns out that General Selva is responsible for planning and organizing this attempted coup. After Selva receives the call, they will swear the Vice President in as the New President, and the real party will begin. It will then only be about eight-thirty in Sun Valley."

I could see that the President was full of questions. Still, I wanted to finish before he could interrupt, so I hurriedly finished telling my story.

"I could not think of any way to warn you from Sun Valley. There was no one I knew here I could talk with, no one here at the White House would take my call. Who was I? Sage doesn't exist in any database in the world. There are no fingerprints available, no address, no telephone numbers. No family or friends. Nothing. He is a blank. Merely a cipher. I had to get here and see you personally to give you a warning. My first plane luckily happened to be a private jet that circumstances forced to land. The military had an order to shoot down our plane. I stole another plane only to have that one forced down just outside of Washington. I stole a car and with a lot of luck, and Secretary Garvey here, (waving a hand in her direction,) made it to the oval office before your ten o'clock cocktail. And that mister President is my story and why I had Secretary Garvey insist on meeting with you tonight. She was the only one in town I could find that was not in on the planned coup."

When I finished talking, the room was very still. It was so quiet I could hear my heartbeat. The President looked like he was in shock. I couldn't tell if he was angry, disappointed, frightened, disgusted, or simply too weary to feel anything. Secretary Garvey looked intimated, afraid to say anything, and I was through for the time being. The President could order me held on many different charges, and I would be lucky to see another sunrise.

The President sat for a few more seconds in what appeared to be deep thought before reaching for the black telephone on his desk. He had three different phones, red, white, and black. I didn't know what the colors signified except that I could guess the Red one was for emergencies. When he reached for the black phone, I thought, 'this is it. He's calling security to have me arrested.' Instead, it was to his secretary in an outer office. "Grace, get me the Vice President."

There was a slight delay where we all looked at each other for a minute. I wasn't sure where this was going, but at least the President wasn't calling security, yet.

"Hello Arnold, yes, I can hear the party. Sorry to bother you at this late hour, but Secretary Garvey just came to see me with some rather distressing information. Could you pop over here for a couple of minutes to talk with her? It won't take over five minutes; then you can get back to your party."

We couldn't hear what was said on the other end of the line, but we could read the President's face; the determination and guts it takes to run for the Presidency and succeed were clearly visible. His face revealed the anger he must have felt, but his voice sounded normal.

"Yes, yes. I see. I didn't realize you were out of town. Oh well, we'll handle it from here. Go on back to your party." The President dropped the telephone back into its cradle. No goodbye or so long, just clunk.

"Well, mister Sage. You may be on to something. There might be something to your name, after all. (a slight smile) The Vice President is indeed out of town, and I was unaware. He was supposed to be here filling in for me until I returned tomorrow. You seem to be on a roll, Sage. I'm sure you must have some plan worked out after going to all that trouble you went through getting here. Let's hear your thoughts."

For the first time all day, I could almost relax. I certainly had some thoughts on how we might proceed. Hell, I had to think about something today, or I would have gone crazy. Like everything else in my life, when I thought about doing something difficult, I just went ahead and did it. Worrying and hoping was for amateurs. Not that I was any kind of professional. Well, I do read minds rather professionally.

"Sure, mister President, I might have a plan. I'll tell you what I've been thinking."

Looking over at Secretary Garvey, I wasn't so sure she wanted me to proceed with my thoughts. That I had the President's attention was fine, but in her view maybe it would be better to let the President handle it from here.

No way. There was still a big chance to muck it all up, and I wasn't willing to take that chance. Sun Tzu would say that the battle is not over until the enemy has surrendered or been defeated. We were still in the catch-up and final steps mode. Until the threat had been eliminated, and we could start proving who all the perpetrators are and have them arrested, the battle was not won.

CHAPTER THIRTY-FOUR
THE PLAN

With what I would call a battle-weary face, the President leaned forward in his chair to hear my grand plan. I was as nervous as a high school boy about to ask his favorite cheerleader for a prom date. What if my big idea was a bust? How would we proceed otherwise? We couldn't let these bastards get away with what they were planning, yet if we acted precipitously, they might just call the whole thing off, and we would have no proof that they had ever planned anything. I was afraid to look at Secretary Garvey when I said:

"let the evening go ahead as planned."

The President looked at me like I was the mad hatter; "why would I let anyone poison me?"

"We won't give him get a chance to poison you mister President. Have Secretary Garvey escorted back to her car while I remain seated here in the background. I promise you the Secret Service man you call in to fix your evening cocktail will never know I am here. I am exceptionally good at disappearing. Almost as good as I am at reading minds." I gave the President a tired smile which he didn't acknowledge.

"Even if he spots me, you can just say that I will be spending the night here in the White House as your guest."

Secretary Garvey did not like leaving, with me left behind, one little bit. She also wanted in on the action, but I wanted the Secret Service detail to think that with the Secretary going, all would be clear. The President sat as before, leaning forward with his elbows on the desk, looking like he couldn't believe in this whole insane idea.

"Mister President, you might recall that earlier, I said I had subdued four highly trained special forces personnel. I believe I can handle one of your special agents. Once Secretary Garvey has left the room, call the agent in to fix your evening cocktail. Once your agent has the cocktail prepared, and he brings it to your desk, instruct him to drink it himself."

The President liked the idea. I could see a smile trying to break through his stern countenance. He wasn't sure what was coming next, but I could also read anticipation in his steely blue eyes.

"When the agent approaches your desk, I will move in just behind him in case he tries something violent. In that case, I will put him to sleep. One of the tricks I've learned in martial arts."

The President and Secretary Garvey both had this look of disbelief on their faces. How could this bedraggled rumpled stranger, who looked and smelled like a refugee from the homeless streets where beggars hang out, possible handle one of the President's professional bodyguards? The agent was certainly armed with a gun and highly trained. If all of my suppositions were true, and granted they had to be risking a lot to make that assumption; all the agent would have to do after the President ordered him to drink the cocktail himself would be able pull a gun quickly and shoot the President and me. The conspirators would then spin a story about how I had come in to kill the President myself. I could see and imagine the workings of just these thoughts in their minds.

"Mister President. I don't want their plans to succeed, nor do I want to see them get away if their plan fails. It would be all too easy for them to go back into the woodwork like the insects they are, where we could never identify all of those in on the plot. We need your agent to prepare the deadly cocktail to get proof of their plans. Then, we will have the evidence to unravel their whole operation. We can then identify and punish those involved. Please let the agent prepare your cocktail."

I could see the President wavering, yet as the various alternative ideas crossed his mind, he wrote them off one by one. Without proof, they could write the whole planned coup off as just a wild fantasy of mine. After all, who was I? The answer, nobody. Yet, if I was right, the President could not afford to make a mistake. He would be risking his life at the word of a stranger.

Looking me straight in the eyes, he asked, "did you find out why they wanted me out of the way?"

"Yes, mister President, I did. They believe you have plans to release all of Nikola Tesla's private papers to the public. General Selva is opposed to this because these papers contain many secrets the military has been mining for several years. Much of our militaries advanced weapons has come from these papers, and the General does not want the public, or our enemies, to have access to this information."

"Ah, yes. It all makes sense now." The President was scolding himself for overlooking such a harsh response from our military leaders. "Okay, mister Sage, I guess we'll go ahead with your plan. Are you genuinely, absolutely positive that you can control my agent if things go badly?" I couldn't blame the President for showing some nervousness. It isn't every day you let someone try and kill you with poison.

"Yes, mister President. Don't forget that I can read minds. If your special Secret Service agent even thinks about taking some hostile action, I will put him down in a nanosecond like he was a rabid dog. I promise."

"Well, you certainly showed not only a strong determination to get here, but a great deal of ingenuity and talent. I believe I can trust you to do as you say."

The President once again picked up the black telephone. "Grace, have the Secret Service come escort Secretary Garvey back to her car."

While this was happening, I thanked the Secretary for her very timely help while giving her a big hug, with my bad smell and all. There was no way I could have reached the President without her. I moved towards the rear of the room away from the President's desk.

The oval office has doors on both sides of the room away from his desk, plus one in the wall opposite his desk where visitors are escorted in to see the President. There are bookshelves on both sides of this door and large overstuffed soft beige leather chairs beside each bookshelf. I gratefully sunk down in the chair to the right side of the large dark cherry wood door as the agent called to escort the Secretary came into the room. I not only sunk into the chair, but I also disappeared into myself, withdrawing all of my energy and closing my eyes to the barest slit possible. Defocusing my vision, I was able to perceive the entire room as though I was looking through the bottom of a water glass. For all practical purposes, I was not present in the room.

Playing her part in front of the agent who came to escort her out of the building, although unhappy with the idea of leaving the center of action, the Secretary murmured, "thank you mister President. You have been most helpful as always."

"Goodbye, or I guess it's goodnight Sheila, thanks for bringing this to my attention and all you have done. I am very grateful. We'll be in touch soon. I promise."

"Goodnight, mister President. Have a wonderful rest of the evening."

Secretary Garvey left the room with the Secret Service agent, and the President sat back in his chair as though he didn't have a care in the world. I've often thought, as I watched various Presidents in news clips over the past few years, that they were all great actors who could have made a living in Hollywood. This President was no exception. Sitting relaxed in his chair, you would never know that he knew of the plan to end his life in a few minutes.

Picking up the black telephone, he barely glanced in my direction as he said, "Grace, send in agent Collier. It's time for my evening cocktail."

CHAPTER THIRTY-FIVE
CONFRONTATION

I waited and watched as an agent I had never seen before entered the room. Dressed as the other Secret Service agents, I had noticed he wore a familiar look. Yet, this man had a different feel about him from the others I had observed while going into the White House and, the Oval office. He had a stocky build with massive shoulders that barely fit through the wide office door. While his waist was thick, his large shoulders made his waist seem small, giving him a trim appearance often associated with those old lumberjacks from a long-forgotten past. He had a fresh farm boy look, all innocence, and curiosity, with just a hint of wonder and by-golly that he could ever be in such a place, and I could see why the President trusted him to fix his evening cocktail. Despite his innocent face, I detected an underlying anxiety and feelings of stress with the barest hint of fear. This was all I needed to confirm my worst suspicions. I guess I had been hoping that this whole episode was a hoax, even after all the attempts at my life.

The agent went into an alcove to the left of the President's desk with no greeting or waiting for instructions. As he opened the door, I could see a mini bar set up with a few different kinds of alcohol and a small countertop for preparing drinks. The agent never looked in my direction or seemed to be aware of my presence. There was a small refrigerator with ice, and a shelf above the whiskey bottles held a few cocktail glasses. Taking off the shelf what looked like a cut crystal glass, the agent began preparing the President's cocktail. Being a scotch drinker with nothing added but ice and water, I am not privy to the various cocktail mixes. I had no idea what constituted the President's cocktail other than some expensive bourbon, and I couldn't see what else the agent was pouring into the President's glass. The agent was also entirely out of view from where the President was sitting. It would be all too easy to add a few extra drops of some exotic poison without being observed. His back was to me, shielding me as well from viewing what he was adding to the cocktail beside the regular mixes. When he finished with the preparations, the agent restored the bar to its original condition before leaving the alcove and shutting the door. Unless you were paying close attention, you would have missed seeing him slip a little something into the left-hand pocket of his suit coat. Turning to the President, he walked over to his desk, holding out the cocktail glass like it was a precious jewel.

"Here's your cocktail mister President," he said with a forced smile holding out the glass, "I sure hope it's the way you like it." It was almost possible to smell his fear.

While the agent had been preparing the President's drink, my thoughts kept returning to Sun Tzu and The Art of War. The book has a chapter on Emptiness and Fullness, which fueled much of my work on learning to be invisible. In one passage Sun Tzu states,

Be extremely subtle, even to the point of formlessness. Be extremely mysterious, even to the point of soundlessness.'

Several famous Chinese scholars and generals over the millennia have added their own comments to Sun's dictums, and for this quote, I liked what Mei Yaochen added,

'Soundlessness means being so mysteriously swift that no one notices you.'

As the agent approached the President's desk, being mysteriously swift per Yaochen's instructions, I was right behind him although I'm positive he was unaware of my presence. As the agent entered and began preparing the President's evening cocktail, I swear the President himself had lost track of my existence. In reading his mind, I could find no hint of my presence there.

The President glance up at the agent holding his drink and stretching out his arms and back; the President rolled his head and neck a second before speaking. "You know Phil, I'm exhausted tonight, and my stomach is a little upset. I had an unpleasant experience down in Florida, and it's left a bad taste in my mouth. Why don't you sit down in this chair here," he waved his hand at one of the chairs facing his desk, "drink that swell drink yourself and tell me about your family."

I'm guessing the agent's name was Phil said, "oh, I couldn't take your drink mister President, why don't I just sit it here on your desk." If his fear had a distinct and terrible odor before, it was reeking at this point. "You might want it a little later on, or if it gets stale, I'll make you a new one."

"No, no, Phil, I insist. Sit down and have a drink with me. I'll sip on my water, and you can enjoy my cocktail and tell me about your family. I know you like bourbon, and this is an excellent brand."

I could feel the fear build in the agent and read the thoughts racing through his mind. 'Is this some kind of trick? Does the President know about the drops? What the fuck am I supposed to do?' Meanwhile, the President seemed to be enjoying himself, observing the agent squirm.

The agent seemed lost in thought, like he was frozen in place. It seemed like an eternity. Still, only a few seconds had elapsed when, in a lightning-fast move, the agent dropped the drink towards the floor reaching for the gun under his coat intending to end the President's life. He mentally telegraphed his move just microseconds before reaching for his gun. Before the President's drink even hit the floor, I had the agents head in firm arm hold while applying my middle knuckle to one of the head spots guaranteed to put him to sleep. He never even knew I was there until it was way too late.

The President blinked at me in surprise as though he had forgotten I was there. "My G..G... God Sage, he stuttered uncharacteristically, "was he going to shoot me? And where in the hell did you come from? I never even saw you come in."

It seemed the President had a slight case of amnesia, not remembering that I had never left the room. But I guess having stared death in the face they could forgive you for having a slight memory lapse. After all, I had become invisible.

Bending over the agent, I relieved him of his gun, then released his belt buckle, and removing his belt used it to secured his wrists. While doing this, I answered the President. "I never left the room mister President. And yes, he intended to shoot you rather than drinking the poison himself. He was unaware that I was in the room."

The President looked at a clock on the wall in the back of the room, "what time is it in Sun Valley Sage?" Having lived with a clock in my head nearly all day, I didn't need to glance at the watch on my wrist to answer. "It's ten after eight o'clock in Sun Valley. They will expect a call in fifteen or twenty minutes from their agent, or perhaps someone else here in the White House, to give them the sad news about your apparent heart attack and death."

"The BASTARDS!" The President shouted the word bastards. "We can't let them get away with this Sage." I was busy tying agent Collier's hands behind his back, then tying his shoelaces together in case he got cute and tried running, before looking back up at the President.

I was surprised and delighted that the President said We. For the time being, at least I was on the A-team.

"Mister President, the people in Sun Valley will not panic for at least thirty to forty-five minutes. That gives you time to have the Sawtooth Sherriff's department and local Ketchum police block the exit from Senator Kim's driveway, preventing their escape. I'm sure there are Secret Service agents inside of Senator Kim's home and on the grounds accompanying other members of your cabinet and high-ranking government officials. Besides, I'm sure there are many private bodyguards also armed. We cannot be certain that those responsible for this monstrous act will not behave precipitously ordering their hired guns to shoot it out with the local cops, although I hope that is not the case. I also suggest getting a military component there as rapidly as possible to arrest and detain everyone at the ranch. I'm not at all privy to the makeup of our military personnel and various functioning operational units, so I am at a loss as whom to suggest. Most, if not all, of those people at Senator Kim's ranch, have to know of the plot to have you murdered. There may be Secret Service agents there who are unaware, but that is questionable. These people need to be held accountable for their actions, and to do that, we must identify them. I can barely verify the presence of half of those at the ranch."

"Okay, hold it there, Sage. Let me get the ball rolling before deciding what to do with this piece of shit on the floor. And dammit, I miss my drink."

"Grace, get me the Sherriff's department in Sawtooth County Idaho and the chief of police for Ketchum Idaho. Then get General McTavish on the phone."

Within seconds it seemed like the President started issuing commands and requests. Meanwhile, I searched agent Collier's body for the object I saw him slip into his pocket after finishing the President's drink. Sure enough, I found a clear slim little bottle barely half an inch in length and smaller in diameter than a pencil. It had a convenient pop-up lid you could open with the thumb of one hand while pouring the contents out of the bottle. The President was watching as I sat the bottle on his desk. I was not about to open the bottle to sniff its content's. That it was nasty stuff, I had no doubt and was not sure just what the fumes might do to me, if anything.

Checking his other pockets, I found a phone number scribbled on a small white card with an Idaho 208 prefix. Not conclusive, but I would bet my delayed date with the world's ice-skating champion that the number was to somebody at Senator Kim's party. My guess would be General James Selva, Chairman of the JCS. Also, in his inside breast pocket, I found a first-class plane ticket to Rome from Dulles leaving at 12:30 a.m.

Finished with his call, the President sat back in his chair looking ten or fifteen years older than when I had first entered his office- what, barely thirty minutes ago. "Sage," he began in a quiet, almost solemn tone, "I don't know, if it is even possible to thank you. I know, being a politician who makes his living with words, you would think that they came easy. Still, in this case, I can think of no expression to adequately convey my gratitude. After listening to your harrowing experiences, over the past twelve hours, I'm not sure our country can ever repay the debt owed you."

"Mister President, seeing you alive behind that desk is all the thanks I'll ever need."

Shaking his head, whether, in fatigue or disbelief, I'm not sure, he said, "I don't know where to go from here? Who can I trust? How many of my precious, (here the venom came out on the word precious) cabinet members were in on the plot? How many generals, members of congress? God, what a mess."

"Well, mister President, here's the good news. If you would have my services for a few days, I'll be able to tell you exactly who was in on the plot and those left completely out of all plans and discussions. I don't even need to talk with them or spend much time in their presence. If you had them come into the room or I just passed them in the hallway, I will be able to tell you exactly who knew what, and when they became complicit in the coup attempt. That is what I do for my corporate clients. For them it's just somebody stealing corporate secrets, manipulating the books, etc. Helping you find the traitors and identifying your friends would be easy and a pleasure."

Before the President could respond, sleeping beauty began stirring. It was only a matter of a few seconds before he would regain full consciousness. I helped him sit up then pulled him up into the chair the President had tried to get him to sit in earlier.

The President was angry, you could see it in his eyes, yet at the same time, there was a sadness. "Phil, what on earth made you do it?"

Phil had trouble focusing for a minute. Even when able to see, he avoided looking at the President, instead kept his head hanging down, looking at the hand-woven Persian carpet under his feet. "I'm sorry mister President."

Waving the ticket to Rome under his face, I said, "maybe this has something to do with your decision."

With no additional prompting, he just blurted out, "twenty million dollars, a villa in Italy and a new identity."

The poor fool. There had to be several people who knew he was supposed to be the President's killer, and probably more than a few of them knew his new identity. I wondered how long it would be before someone gave him up? That is if they even allowed him get on the plane. The men behind this planned coup did not take prisoners or leave loose ends lying around. And this mercenary piece of shit sitting here with hands tied behind his back with his belt was most certainly a loose end. It would not surprise me one bit to find another hit team waiting just outside of the White House grounds to grab the traitor when he left the grounds to catch his plane to Rome.

With a wry sad grin, the President remarked, "well, it's nice to know how much my life is worth."

Mister President, "Have some of your other Secret Service agents come into the office. I can tell you if they were part of the plan to replace you, or if they are entirely innocent. We need to have somebody put this man in a jail someplace safe from any would-be assassin. Then I could vet the rest of your White House staff to weed out any other conspirators if there are any."

Without saying a word to me, the President picked up the black telephone and started speaking, "Grace, send in the other agents outside in the hall. In five minutes, I want all the rest of the White House staff to meet me in the East Room."

CHAPTER THIRTY-SIX
THE FALLOUT

The good news was that Phil Collier, the doomed Secret Service agent who poured the President's cocktail, was the only member of the President's security detail, and the only person in the White House, enlisted in the campaign to kill the President. Two clean Secret Service agents escorted Phil out of the White House, and I never saw him again. I never thought to ask whatever happened to him. After the East Room meeting was over, the President walked me back to the Oval Office.

"Sage, where are you staying? I'll have my driver drop you off at your hotel, but I would like to see you first thing in the morning."

"Golly, Mister President," (once the drama was over, I reverted to this shy, bashful boy of eight,) "when I finally got here to Washington D.C., there wasn't time to book a hotel, or find appropriate clothes for our meeting. If a car could drop me off at the nearest hotel, I would be very grateful."

"Nonsense, son." The President seemed to pick up on my adolescent behavior. "We have plenty of rooms here. You'll stay here tonight and first thing tomorrow I'll have a tailor in here to fit you with more appropriate clothes. I'm eternally grateful you didn't take the time to get all gussied up tonight. If there is anything, and I mean anything I can do for you; please let me know."

"Well, mister President, there are a couple of things. I started earlier today in Sun Valley with a borrowed private jet which was forced to land just outside of Wright Patt. The pilot of this jet, Captain Fremont, helped me escape two different times. Together we stole another plane which we had to land in College Park. A blogger named Herbert Riverton has a D.C. blog called Psithurism. He uses the blogger name Sizzler when you call him on the phone and is the one who put me in touch with Secretary Garvey. Captain Fremont helped me steal a car here in D.C. before being picked up by Herbert in his old beat-up V W van. Your opposition had the streets surrounding the White House blocked off, so I had them drop me off outside of the cordoned off zone. I had to sneak past the guards at the roadblock. Anyway, I'm worried that my friends are okay, and I need to take care of the plane and car we stole, plus I need to return the plane I started for here back to the owners in Sun Valley. There may be some damage to both of the planes and the car I stole. I'll gladly to pay for any damage, but first I would like to check on my friends."

"Oh, Sage, I'm sorry about all of your troubles. I had forgotten just what a terrifying day you had. Would you like to make some phone calls about your friends, or would you prefer I start the search?"

"Let me start by making a couple of phone calls. If I run into some problems, perhaps you can use your awesome power of the Presidency to help me out." I said this with a grin, trying to lighten up the mood, but I don't think the President was in the mood to be humored. "Also, I left the four men assigned to kill me tied up in a motel room in Ketchum. They didn't know the reason for the assignment, and I'm sure they had nothing to do with the plans to have you assassinated. They were trained to follow orders and believing that I was a national security risk attempted to complete the mission. I'm not at all sure we should punish them, but that isn't my call. However, they should be released pretty quickly. I imagine by now they are smelling rather ripe. Maybe a lot like me," I added, trying again in vain for a Presidential smile.

"Okay," the President started, "there is an office and phone just outside of this room. Just give me the name of the motel in Idaho where you left the men tied up, and I'll see that we care for them."

The President ushered me into an adjoining office with instructions on how to dial outside of the White House. He was about to leave me and take care of his own business when I remembered the small bottle; I had removed from Phil's pocket.

"Oh, mister President, your drink and the bottle I sat on your desk needs to be checked for poison. I'm not sure how long it remains potent, so it should be checked, sooner rather than later."

The President nodded his understanding as he left the room, no doubt wishing for an evening cocktail without the added ingredient.

The next five days were a blur of activity. True to his word, they outfitted me with several sets of new clothes and made the Lincoln Bedroom my home and office for the time being. I called Wyatt at Sawtooth Business Resorts in Sun Valley to explain my sudden departure. He assured me that all was well, and they had returned his plane undamaged. Since I promised to return and fulfill our contract as soon as the President was through with my services, he would not charge me for using his plane. Captain Fremont was hanging around town, waiting for me to have the time for an after-the-combat tour debriefing. We both had several stories to tell. I talked with Herbie and agreed to sit down with him soon to unload the full story, at least as much as the President would allow me to tell.

Only four cabinet members were in on the plot to assassinate the President along with eight senators, twenty-three members of Congress, and two members of the JCS, including General Selva. Three Generals and several colonels, captains, and lessor members of the armed forces took part of the plot to kill the President. Unfortunately, there were three helicopters at Senator Kim's ranch when the Sawtooth County Sheriff's department blocked the Wood River bridge. As the deputy sheriff watched, they took off carrying General Selva, Roger Horowitz, and Supreme Court Justice Woodrow Etheridge. Roger Horowitz and Justice Etheridge were later apprehended trying to flee the country. Selva disappeared and has not surfaced on anybody's radar. As the leader of the coup attempt, Selva is being hunted by every police and law enforcement agency in America and much of the civilized world. No one in or out of the press speculated about whether Selva had any foreign governments supporting a change in Presidents. I do not doubt that he or his body will turn up one day. I'm just not sure where.

On the fifth day, I satisfied the President that we had vetted everyone who worked at the highest levels in Washington, D.C., and identified the wealthy conspirators scattered around the rest of America's. They rounded up most of those wealthy individuals who helped finance and plan the coup, excluding Honey Samuels. The wealthy socialite under high stress decided on a gentler way out; she committed suicide. Several other wealthy shakers and movers disappeared and are still being hunted. Being uninterested in politics and politicians, I never found out what the punishment was for those individuals responsible. Catching brief snippets of the news from time to time, I heard words like treason and the death penalty bandied about, but I didn't listen to see or care who they were talking about. From my naïve understanding of the law, I thought they were all guilty of treason and deserved the death penalty, but that is just my thought. I am more than satisfied just being Sage and doing my martial arts.

Summoning me to his office on my last day, the President insisted that I sit down and have a drink with him. I suppose a little gallows humor was inevitable as it turned out to be the same cocktail that the President was supposed to drink and end his life. "To life without poison," he said, tilting his glass in my direction. "Hear, hear," I said, tilting my glass back at him.

"Sage, I, and this country owe you more than can ever be repaid. Please let me give you something as a memento of your timely, (here the President could not help but give me a wry smile) and much-appreciated service."

"Gosh, mister President." (Still the small-town bashful boy. I couldn't help but be myself.) "By now I'm sure you know that I don't have a political bone in my body. I did what I did because I didn't want my America to go through another assassination. From all my reading, I believe such an event is unhealthy for our country. I did not do it for a reward or gain. I did not know who you were when this whole episode began. After meeting you, I am thrilled that you are still alive. If I could get a ride back to Sun Valley and thank the owner of the Gulf Stream I borrowed, and complete the assignment he had for me, I would be most grateful."

"My God, Sage. You do take the cake. Sorry for such a poor cliché, but you do. You only want a ride to Sun Valley. I'm sure like in those old western movies you mentioned liking, you want a ride going west in a cowboy hat riding your horse just as the sun is setting." The President now sported a big grin on his face as he concluded, "I'm only sorry I can't offer you a horse."

The President chuckled at his attempt at humor. "I have been in touch with this mister Wyatt West and he told me about your love affair with his airplane." With a smile to make the Gods jealous, the President handed me a key and an envelope stuffed full of papers. "This is the title to a brand-new Gulf Stream G650ER. The plane comes with a lifetime warranty for all expenses, including all the fuel you could ever use. Besides, your grateful President on behalf of a very grateful country have authorized an operating budget of an additional five million tax-free dollars every year for the rest of your life to pay for your pilot and, ah...other personnel."

I was struck dumb. With a total loss of words. My very own G650, plus a pilot, and whatever. Or whomever? I felt myself sway like I was about to faint. No way was I prepared for such extravagance. I had hoped for a ride back to Sun Valley, but this? Oh, lordy lord. I had to gasp to get my breath back.

"Mister President. I do not know what to say. THANK YOU, will have to do. I am thrilled we could save your life and this country the agony of another Presidential assassination. With this lump in my throat, I think I better leave before I start bawling here in your office."

"You wouldn't be the first person to cry in this holy place. It would surprise you at the number of people who have used this office as their personal grief chamber." The President called for an escort to walk me out to a waiting limousine. As I was leaving his office, he said almost as a throwaway line, "oh Sage, your plane is at Reagan National along with Captain Fremont, and crew. Happy trails, as Roy Rogers might say. Or is it, sunny skies?" He said this with a broad smile and a big wink.

Ya know, politics be dammed, I might just get to like this President after all.

"Oh, and Sage," he called just as I was about out the door, "you may get a call from one or two from other heads of state. I'm not the only one in the world with loyalty problems."

Just what I needed. A reference from the President of the United States with more business. During the past few days, I must have told the President how people got in touch with me. I was not planning on answering that phone anymore. I guess I could only hope my phone never rang.

CHAPTER THIRTY-SEVEN
THE RIDE HOME

The President's limousine was nothing like the one used by Secretary Garvey. It had a full bar, the most relaxing soft leather seats imaginable, a complete entertainment system including a large thirty-six-inch flat screen. Then there was the scent. I'm not sure when this fetish developed. Still, I seem to be highly sensitive to odors, and this car came as close as I could ever imagine smelling like heaven. Not just the new car smell with fresh conditioned leather and luxurious carpets two inches thick, but I guess the best way to describe the scent is to say it smelled like success. This was what I wanted my whole life to feel like. I'm not sure what kind of atavistic mechanism in our DNA makes us respond to certain stimuli. Still, this scent of success included more than just succeeding in life. It had the scent of having arrived. The feel of catching the wave. When we surf through our lives, it seems like a constant battle to catch the wave at just the right moment. The scent in this limousine was that scent. We have arrived. We caught the wave at the perfect time.

I was so caught up with the car and its delightful surprises that I missed our short drive across the river. There was no time to drink one of the expensive liquors or play with the state-of-the-art entertainment system. With the car windows up, I missed the river scent, and the next thing I knew, the limousine was pulling up to the most beautiful white Gulfstream in the world. And parked right beside the plane was Herbie's old VW with Herbie and Captain Fremont both standing outside in the sun grinning like they just won the Miss America contest. Reluctant to leave such a plush interior yet eager to see my new plane, I took my exit thanking the driver for such a great ride. With a big smile of his own, he turned his head around, saying, "anytime, mister Sage. Anytime."

Hugging my two companions, I suggested we enter the plane and have a drink while discussing Herbie's Pulitzer. Both men were still grinning like they were in on some private joke, and I was the idiot stepchild who didn't get it. Frustrated yet happy to see that the bad guys had not apprehended or killed them, I let them lead me into the airplane.

The steps were already down, and Fremont led the way with Herbie right behind. I trailed along last, savoring every second of every glance along the sleek lines of my beautiful new plane. I was barely in the door when I finally understood the President's stuttering comment about other ah,,, personnel, and the grins on the faces of my two companions. Right inside, wearing her sleek white jumpsuit showing every fantastic curve of her gorgeous sculptured body stood Anita. With a cry of pleasure, she rushed to me with open arms giving me the warmest welcome I ever received.

"Anita, my love." I nearly screamed. "What, how, are you here?" I felt tongue-tied and nervous as hell. I sure was not expecting this. With Anita there, I scarcely noticed the inside of my spanking new plane. It was Fremont who finally broke into our kiss, saying, "Anita was Wyatt's idea. Once he found out why you so desperately needed his plane, he was beside himself with guilt. I guess it was one of his investors who figured out who you were and was responsible for nearly getting you killed. Anyway, he bought out Anita's contract with Sun Valley Lodge, and she comes with the plane as long as you want, or she wants, or whatever. My God, Sage, say something. I'm making a complete fool of myself."

"Oh, I wouldn't say complete, Fremont, you've got a way to go, but thanks anyway," I responded with a big grin of my own while extricating myself from Anita's warm embrace. Overwhelmed with emotions barely under control, I managed to ask, "what does a fellow have to do to get a scotch and water in this joint?

Anita gave me a playful jab in the side, and then in an I Dream of Jeannie voice, "coming right up master," she said with her beguiling smile. "Have a seat and take off your shoes. I don't want dirt on my pretty new carpet."

The three of us men went to the main cabin where a table had been arranged with four seats. Fremont, Herbie and I barely managed to sit down when Anita returned with drinks for all four of us then sat in a chair by my side.

"I am so thrilled to see all three of you guys." I managed to say this without choking up, then taking a swallow of my drink added, "when this whole thing came crashing down on our heads, I wasn't sure who would be left standing, if anybody. It isn't an exaggeration to say that each one of you is responsible for saving my life and the life of our President. Like I said to the President just a few moments ago (a little name dropping; I couldn't resist. How many times in one's life does one ever get to use that line?) I don't have the proper words to express my gratitude. I can only say thank you all from the bottom of my heart."

Anita pulled my head over and gave me another deep kiss. "Oh, Sage," she said. "You made it work for all of us."

I didn't know what to say, so I just shook my head and took another sip of my drink. I didn't recognize the scotch, but it was dammed good. "Okay, I need to give Herbie here," I said, patting him on the arm, "a story I promised several days ago. You all know most of the story by now anyway, so there are no secrets. I'll start with my second day in Sun Valley last week when four men set out to kill me."

It seemed like the events took forever when they were happening. Still, as I told the story to Herbie, skipping only those parts the President wanted me to exclude, it seemed to go by in a flash. I had barely started talking when I concluded with the arrest of everybody, except a few low-level people yet unidentified and of course, General Selva, and Honey, along with a few others who took the quick way out.

"What do you think happened to Selva?" Herbie asked.

"I expect that he had a hidey-hole already planned for and waiting in case things didn't work out. Probably in some country friendly to his desired goal. He would know that the death penalty was waiting if things went sour, so he probably had his escape already arranged." I waited a minute, and when nobody said anything, I continued, "it is challenging to hide anywhere these days. With social media everywhere, the world is a small place. He undoubtedly has false papers, a new name, maybe even new looks, but there will be one hell-of-an-effort to find him, wherever he is hiding. It will be something like the search for bin Laden. Somebody, somewhere knows where he is, and I expect we'll be hearing about the General one of these days. Maybe a few years, but ultimately. At least I hope so."

"Hear, hear," Fremont added.

As Herbie stood up to leave, he said, "we'll, I suppose I should go get busy writing up my Pulitzer story. Thanks, Sage, even if you scared the shit out of me."

"Thank you, Herbie," I said, standing up and giving him a warm hug and handshake. "Without your help, this would have never happened." I tried to stop myself, but before I even knew what I was saying, I added, "Say hi to your mother for us."

Without even breaking stride or turning around, Herbie extended his arm backward, giving me the middle finger salute."

"What's that about his mother?" Anita asked. She looked at me, then at Fremont. Neither one of us said anything. She was getting upset, so I quickly answered, "We just had a little difficulty extracting him from his mother's tender love. Nobody wants to leave their warm comfy home late at night to go banging around the city in a beat-up old VW without a heater."

She looked at me funny like she didn't believe my story, but gratefully she let it drop.

"Well, Captain," I said, looking at Fremont. "Are we going to sit here on the Tarmac all day, or are you going to fly us to Sun Valley? You do know how to fly this plane, don't you?"

"You know Sage, I was just starting to like you," he responded, but he wore a broad smile showing he wasn't serious.

"My, but you are quite handsome in your new suit, dear," Anita observed with a big grin. "A present from our President?"

"Probably, or maybe it's a present from the American people. At any rate, the clothes I arrived in had to be incinerated. I can still smell their stink on me nearly a week later. My God, but that was one hell of a day. I sure hope I never have another." With that said I took a large swallow of my scotch. "What is this scotch, Anita? I've never tasted it before."

"That, my dear, is a gift from your President. When he found out that you were a scotch drinker, he asked some experts to find him the world's best scotch for a valuable new friend. I can't pronounce the name, but it's a single malt from somewhere in Scotland."

"My, my, and here I thought the President was occupied full time just trying to find all the conspirators. I wouldn't have thought he had the time for all the extra stuff like this plane and having you here. I'm delighted and grateful beyond words that you came, but I barely left his side the past few days. Ya know, I'm getting to like this politics' stuff."

"For a smart man Sage, you sometimes seem so dumb. No, don't frown. The President of the United States has a gazillion people working for him night and day. He has but to say a word, and the whole town bows to his wishes. And don't you dare go all politics on me."

"You're right; I am kinda dumb. It's just that I've been so close to him the past few days I forgot that he is the most powerful man on earth."

"Do you think he will still release Tesla's papers?" She asked me the question, and for a minute, I forgot that this was what started the whole assassination scheme.

"You know, I never asked the President. It never even occurred to me. I don't know."

"Well, I think he should," she said with a serious look on her pretty face. "Don't you?"

Picking up my scotch, I stood pulling her up with me. "I don't know; I think we should go find a nice comfortable bed someplace and relax. And talk about it."

"Oh, relaxing, is it? Funny, but I always thought of it as an exercise in excitement, and don't you even think about talking politics."

"Oh, shut up and help me out of this blasted suit."

CHAPTER THIRTY-EIGHT
EPILOGUE

To say that the ride back to Sun Valley was fantastic, magnificent, beautiful, splendid, and terrific would not do it justice. My very own G650, my private pilot, and Anita. My God, Anita. Such a beautiful, skillful, and accomplished lover. She got me over my shyness with women quickly. It was almost worth the angst of the past week.

Almost.

When we landed at the Sun Valley airport and Captain Fremont had taxied us to a parking spot, the three of us had a little meeting in the back of our plane to discuss our relationships and future together. Fremont gratefully consented to continue as my pilot, but only if we didn't have to save the world anymore. He said his heart couldn't take another trip like our last outing to DC. I'm not so sure mine could either. We agreed that he would get a hanger for our plane and make sure it was always stocked and fueled, ready to take off at an instants notice. He had a house nearby and rarely drank, so he was prepared to leave at any time.

Anita loved flying and my company, but wanted to finish her degree in history. She had started college a long time ago, but was unwilling to go deep into debt for a degree. The hostess job with the Sun Valley Resort paid very well, and she had been saving money to finish her last two years at Idaho State University in Pocatello. She had played a role in our little adventure to save the world as we knew it and deserved a bonus that would cover the costs of her education. Sun Valley and Pocatello are only three hours apart, and we agreed to see each other frequently over the next two years. But before she enrolled back in school, there was that little issue of buying a spectacular piece of property along the Wood River, which I accomplished with her help.

I got the property and arranged for an architect to design and build me a modest lodge type house with a large fireplace and library/office besides a full-sized workout gym. I was looking forward to the time I could lose myself in my new home where I did not have to block out other people's thoughts in my head every second.

The problem Wyatt had at the Sawtooth Business Resorts turned out to be one of the junior partners at Samuels, Ratcliff and Hamilton Inc. After Honey took her own life, the investment firm was in shambles for a few weeks as the partners flailed away at each other, jockeying for position in the reorganized company.

During this fight, they ignored the problems at Sawtooth except for a woman, Sofia Alonzo, friendly with Kurt Flinders, the senior partner responsible for overseeing Sawtooth. Kurt knew he should not be having an affair with anyone in the company. Still, he was so smitten with the sexy Italian he let his little head rule his emotions. Sofia knew from Kurt's bragging how well Sawtooth Business Resorts was doing financially. Using passwords stolen from her lover, she accessed the company records setting up a dead drop overseas where she funneled money.

She started asking too many questions regarding Sawtooth after the company shakeup. She was afraid Kurt would lose the account, and she would lose out on her ability to skim off the profits. When I could find nothing amiss with the people at Sawtooth, Wyatt arranged for me to visit the primary investment firm in Palo Alto. As soon as I discovered the guilty individual, Kurt was dismissed from the company along with his lover. I recovered most of the stolen money, and Wyatt's company was once again making record profits.

I devoted myself to building my new home and visiting the Sun Valley dojo, where I worked out with Asahi Saito, ignoring pleas from companies and individuals who felt they were being wronged.

The Reader was semi-retired until the President of the United States called one day. His friend, the Prime Minister of Israel, was having problems with members of his own party trying to undermine his authority. The President wanted permission to volunteer my services to help his friend. Of course, I agreed, and the next day I was in the air with Captain Fremont. No hostess.

While in Israel, I saw a poster advertising an ice-skating show featuring the beautiful world champion, Katrina Novalotski. With working on the house, and getting my life back in order, I had completely forgotten my promise to the girl who had helped save my life. I owed her at least the dinner promised at our last meeting. Funny, but I could still feel the kiss I planted on her cheek back in the Sun Valley Lodge, at least in my mind.

I discovered where she was staying and made my way to her hotel, the Waldorf Astoria, in downtown Jerusalem. Luxury, thy name is Waldorf. My oh my. I thought the Sun Valley Lodge was luxurious, and it is, but not in the same league as the Waldorf. Here you can even rent a Mazzarri to tool around in if that is your thing. Otherwise, prepare to be pampered. I'm not sure how an ice-skating team can afford such luxury, but then I don't know much about ice-skating finances.

I spent my days with the Prime Minister and my late evenings with Katrina. She has a pleasing sense of humor and a fantastic mind, not to mention her incredible body and beautiful looks. Dedicated to her current profession, she is none-the-less interested in developing her mind and learning about the world. I spent three evenings helping her learn to be invisible. The lady has such a fabulous presence that it was difficult for her to rein it in and hold her energy in a tight shell. I was rewarded with a fantastic night that we both knew was our last time together, at least for now. Katrina promised that when her ice-skating career ended, she would come back to Sun Valley for a visit and to see where we both were in our lives at that time. I have a great attraction for both ladies in my life. I can barely wait to see how it turns out.

Sage is still unlisted with no address, no phone, no fingerprints and no social security number. My new best friend is an old man with a young smile, Asahi Saito. I still have my burner, but I changed the number to one I gave to only one person — the President. Otherwise, The Reader is retired.

About the Author

Clark Viehweg is a former CIA contractor with experience at every level of top-secret programs. He is the bestselling author of *Hokee Wolf*, and his books utilize real-world characters in explosive situations. Using Metaphysics, magick and the paranormal, Clark explores the reaches of human consciousness. After traveling the world for government programs across Asia and Europe, Clark now lives in Utah with his wife and two dogs.

He loves hearing from his readers at clarkviehweg07@gmail.com.

NOTE FROM THE AUTHOR

Word-of-mouth is crucial for any author to succeed. If you enjoyed *Sage*, please leave a review online—anywhere you are able. Even if it's just a sentence or two. It would make all the difference and would be very much appreciated.

Thanks!
Clark

Thank you so much for reading one of **Clark Viehweg's** novels.
If you enjoyed the experience, please check out our recommended
title for your next great read!

Hokee Wolf by Clark Viehweg

HumanMade Top 105 Best Suspense, Thriller, and Mysteries of All Time

View other Black Rose Writing titles at
www.blackrosewriting.com/books and use promo code
PRINT to receive a **20% discount** when purchasing.

www.ingramcontent.com/pod-product-compliance
Lightning Source LLC
Chambersburg PA
CBHW011136100726
47898CB00009B/2997